THE
LIVE RINGER

by

MARY BAKER

Copyright © Mary Baker 2011

The Live Ringer

The right of Mary Baker to be identified as the author of this work has been asserted by her in accordance with the Copyright, Designs and Patents Act 1988.

All rights reserved.

No part of this publication may be reproduced, stored in a retrieval system, or transmitted in any form or by any means, without the prior permission in writing of the publisher, nor be otherwise circulated in any form of binding or cover other than that in which it is published and without a similar condition, including this condition, being imposed on the subsequent purchaser.

A CIP catalogue record of this book can be obtained from the British Library.

Published in Great Britain by
Cam Publications
76 Commercial Road
Hayle
TR27 4DH

Cover design by Felicity Jane Laws

To George Ragless

1906—1993

once of

Bonnets Farm

Capel

Sussex

Also by Mary Baker

Light Airs
The Dummy Run
A Purposed Overthrow
The Purpose Of Playing
Seventh Child

1

Nathan Wyatt, who prided himself on never being late, arrived in a flurry of breathless apologies, just as Hannah Thirlbeck was about to give up hope, and assume that he had forgotten her existence. But he was there at last, and the windy street became less drab, the evening once again auspicious.

"I only got here myself a few minutes ago," lied Hannah. At twenty-three, independent and supposedly adult, she should have known better than to try so uninspired a pretence when shivering with cold, but Hannah had previously regarded Nathan as unattainably in a different league, and she was flustered to be out with him, because fair haired, thirty-year-old Nathan had the handsome face once classed as matinée-idol, and a neat build that made the tall and sturdy Hannah look clumsy in comparison; but it was a feeling she knew well, as she resembled her mother's family, and they blundered through life with the heavy tread of carthorses. There was nothing neat about Hannah or her relatives, since all had functional rather than decorative figures, and thick brown hair that vanquished any lotion or potion designed to tame it.

"My father telephoned," explained Nathan, recovering his breath. "He hasn't rung in months, yet chose to contact me the very second I was half-way out the door. I started to explain, but he never hears anybody's voice except his own. An added complication was that I went straight into a childish sulk, and brooded on how he'd ruined my entire existence. A bit of an exaggeration, I suppose, but that's the effect he has on me. It's the only inheritance I got from my mother."

"Sounds like normal family life," commented Hannah, too glad at leaving the chilly street to pay much attention to what Nathan had said. The pub was not particularly attractive, with harsh lighting and irritatingly loud music, but even the regulars at the bar, who looked around in resentment at the entrance of unknown intruders, were more welcoming than the cold of the February night outside.

"My father would be highly affronted to hear himself described as normal. He's one of the more spectacular examples of mankind — according to him, at any rate."

The father could well have been right, in Hannah's opinion, because his son was very spectacular indeed. Nathan, like Hannah, worked for the Farrenton Film Company, but she was a mere production assistant, while Nathan rejoiced in the far grander title of associate producer, although accountant would have been more accurate, as he dealt with the raising and managing of finance. His main qualification for the job seemed to centre on having been at school with Romney Farrenton's only son, another associate producer, whose rôle consisted primarily of agreeing with his father: an instructive example of filial devotion that Nathan was apparently determined not to emulate.

"I'll be the macho male, and take it for granted that the complexities of ordering a drink are too much for your delicate feminine brain to cope with," said Nathan, heading towards the bar. "I'm prepared to delegate lesser tasks though, so you're permitted to choose which table we sit at."

"The responsibility's overwhelming." Conscious of the other customers' hostility, Hannah retreated to a corner, wishing she had the courage to tell Nathan that she hated everything about alcohol. The smell of the most feeble wine was enough to bring back childhood memories that she would prefer to forget, yet admitting to such an unsophisticated outlook might cause Nathan to dismiss her as a hopeless provincial. Glancing around for a solution to the dilemma, Hannah spotted a wastepaper bin beside one of the tables, and recognized her salvation.

"I've been summoned to the presence, so a referee is essential," said Nathan, putting a glass of wine down in front of Hannah.

"You'll have to translate."

"After having ignored his son practically from birth, my father has commanded me to visit him tomorrow for some unknown reason. You'll have to come too, Hannah, because my father and I can only meet when there's a peacekeeper present, and I want one who'll be on my side."

Quite definitely that was family life as Hannah knew it. The official surname to which she answered might be Thirlbeck, but her mother had been born a Chisholm, and the Chisholms claimed as their own all children produced by any family member, while the non-Chisholm parent remained an insignificant outsider. Despite such clannishness, no Christmas gathering ever passed without one Chisholm getting into an argument with another, the ramifications of which could linger until Easter. There were many quarrels because there were many Chisholms, but sheer force of numbers usually ensured that a majority managed to stay on speaking terms, if only to sneer at absent relatives, and a clique of Chisholms would decide that they did not like Nathan Wyatt, without the bother of actually meeting him.

"I'm not enthusiastic about family get-togethers," said Hannah.

"My father's hardly family. There was a divorce shortly after my second birthday, and he whizzed off to have more kids with an adolescent airhead. Then she was dumped for an even younger bimbo, and so on, and so on, until a sweet and guileless innocent managed to prise a wedding ring out of him last year. But, of course, some women are attracted to much older men, especially if those men have money that isn't ageing along with them."

"My father flitted off with a girl, and he never has a penny."

"Then he must have irresistible charm, in distinct contrast to my father, a bully who shouts and throws a tantrum if he doesn't get his own way. But to resume the saga of Owen Wyatt; it finally dawned on him that ingénue Flora is a calculating gold-digger, because he told me that he's kicking her out, and when my father kicks somebody out, they don't half get clobbered. Even at my advanced age, the thought of tomorrow's encounter is rapidly sending me into a deep depression." Nathan sounded rueful rather than troubled, but he started drinking and continued to drink: excessively, in Hannah's view, because she had a father whose dependence on alcohol made her regard anybody downing more than one glass of wine as a potential lush.

"So, why are you slaving in the British film industry's worst paid job?" asked Nathan, to fill the conversational gap.

"I'm learning the ropes." Hannah forced herself to look away from Nathan's rapidly emptying wineglass, and adopted a casual tone, although having a job with a film company still seemed something of a miracle, no matter how undistinguished Farrenton productions were. She hoped to be a director one day, and her films would have insight and passion, in which problems intrigued rather than depressed, because those films were destined to become classics, of course, more alive than reality. "All I've got to do now is work my way to the top."

"Well, while you're *en route* I trust you realize that I'm the most important person in the Farrenton Company. If I don't get my hands on some money, the greatest screenplay remains nothing more than a pile of paper. I hope you're taking note of these words of wisdom."

"Absolutely. The only bit I don't understand is how on earth you persuade backers to part with the loot."

"Then I'll explain." Nathan took another swig of wine, pleased to have a chance to boast, and Hannah seized the opportunity to tip the contents of her glass into the wastepaper bin. Nathan seemed so much less attractive when associated with alcohol, but Hannah continued to mime sipping a drink to stay in his good books. "First, think of a film star, one who happens to be flavour of that particular month. Then select whichever sucker you hope to relieve of the burden of riches, and, in the star's name, invite him to be wined and dined at the poshest of posh hotels. When he shows up, tell him that the star's devastated not to be there to meet him in person but, alas, Hollywood called."

"No one's fool enough to swallow that," protested Hannah.

"You've yet to discover just how conceited the mega-rich are," said Nathan, with the supercilious disdain of a conman for his victim. "Anyway, the next thing is to inform Mr Moneybags that the Farrenton Company has the elusive star under contract for the prospective film, and add that, if Mr Moneybags will condescend to become an executive producer, he'll have the chore of constantly mixing with glamorous stars, and those selfless endeavours are the reason why an executive producer's screen credit is invariably the most conspicuous."

"If he's that stupid, how did Mr Moneybags get rich in the first place?"

"One of life's mysteries," replied Nathan, sighing with theatrical self-pity. "Here I am, talented and industrious, yet wealth doesn't want to know me. Of course, I didn't help matters by choosing to work in the British film industry, so I suppose I've no right to complain. But to continue your lesson; the next move is to assure Mr Moneybags that a sumptuous extravaganza can be shot on a budget of next to nothing, and you hurry him through the film's plot, leaving out anything controversial or intellectual. You can give him an abridged and bland copy of the screenplay, in case he opens it at random, but fortunately no backer has ever been known to read his way through an entire script. And that's the end of part one."

"Haven't you got the money yet?"

"A bit of it, but obviously you don't tell Mr Moneybags how much you're actually scheming to lift from his company's coffers. He'd have a heart attack on the spot, and that might hold up filming. No, you keep quiet until shooting begins, and then you inform Mr Moneybags that his original investment will sadly be lost, if the film has to be abandoned because of a few unforeseen additional expenses."

"And he's still listening to you?" inquired Hannah, amused by Nathan's smug air of complacency.

"This is the moment that separates the professional from the amateur. When Mr Moneybags objects to opening his cheque book for a second time, ask what colours he'd like for his screen credit, and suggest gold lettering on a crimson background. That generally gets him back in line."

"What if it doesn't?"

"You announce the inducement of all inducements, and reveal that the director chanced to say what a fascinating life Mr Moneybags has had so far, and how it'd be perfect material for a film. You then name a few ruggedly handsome stars who'd be ideal for the rôle of Mr Moneybags, and at this point, the sucker usually pays up with the meekness of a lamb. The strategy rarely fails."

"Even in a slump?"

"Luckily, the rich are always with us, as it doesn't say in the Bible, and of course I've already persuaded Mr Moneybags that entertainment booms when the country's bust, because people are desperate to escape their misery." Nathan smiled in self-congratulation, sat back, and drained yet another glass of wine in one gulp.

"Doesn't your prey later ask why his biography never got made?"

"Who cares? We've got the lolly and finished our film by then." Nathan went to stand, swayed a little, and sat down again.

"You must be well over the legal limit," said Hannah. "You won't be able to drive home."

"I haven't the least intention of driving anywhere, but a taxi across London on a Saturday night would bankrupt me. I'll stay at your place."

"Do I have any say about this arrangement?" demanded Hannah. Despite being flattered by a handsome man's attention, the Chisholm in her was adamant that an hour or so in a pub did not make a relationship advanced enough for Nathan to invite himself as an overnight guest, particularly when his breath would stink like a brewery.

"There'll be no dastardly attempt to sully your maiden virtue. I'm not used to drinking this much, so all I'll be able to do is pass out on your sofa, assuming you have a sofa."

"I've got a sofa," conceded Hannah, but she could hear her mother's voice refuting every word the scheming lecher said, and as Nathan and Hannah left the pub and walked out into the bitterness of the wind, Judith Thirlbeck née Chisholm refused to be left behind.

"All men are cheats and liars, Hannah. Just remember that, and you won't get conned." Judith's warning had been delivered in a matter-of-fact tone, wholly without resentment or cynicism. She was simply passing on information gleaned from experience, information that Hannah tried to ignore. Nathan was an exception to the rule, and her mother a hundred miles away.

After toiling up the many stairs of a Victorian house to Hannah's attic flat, Nathan proved himself to have been an accurate prophet. "The sofa! Thank God, it's Hannah's celebrated sofa," he said, the moment the door opened to reveal a small and shabby living-room, rather overpopulated by film posters. With a deep sigh of gratitude, Nathan stretched out, fully dressed, on the couch and was immediately asleep, not even stirring when Hannah covered him with a blanket. There was nothing else to do but leave Nathan where he slept, and then go chastely to her own bed, feeling spurned not to rate even a slight effort at seduction. Hannah had suspected that she was merely helping him to pass a few empty hours, and such emphatic confirmation reinforced the Hollywood message that romance was exclusively for the beautiful. The lesser attractive were comic relief, and she would be typecast as the clueless provincial, despite being in London, despite renting what was grandly described as a flat by her landlord. In actual fact, Hannah lived in one large room, with a wooden dividing wall to raise the place above the status of bedsit, and it seemed very full of Nathan's presence. Hannah, away from home for the first time, was still inclined to be woken by noises unfamiliar enough to startle her; but that night, reassured by somebody her mother would regard as a potential Lothario, she slept until unexpectedly disturbed by Nathan himself.

"Hannah, it's two in the morning, I've just been horribly sick, and I'm freezing cold." The touch of his hand on her shoulder felt icy, and he was shivering, even though fully dressed. "Do you have another blanket anywhere?"

"On top of the cupboard," said Hannah, struggling out of a dream, and uncertain which was the reality, talking to Nathan or being late for school. "Where have you been sick?"

"I managed to get to the bathroom, so don't worry. There's nothing to clean up." Nathan took a blanket, and then meekly went back to the sofa.

Hannah, finally awake, knew that her mother would refuse to believe in such chastity if the story were ever told; indeed, restraint might even be turned around and condemned, because Nathan Wyatt had doubtless insulted a daughter by considering her unworthy of his lascivious designs. Ruefully amused, Hannah tried to sleep again, but the effort to wake herself appeared to have succeeded only too well. And yet, she must have slept after all, because it seemed but minutes before her alarm clock started to buzz at seven. Soon it would begin to get light, and Nathan had told her to wake him early.

"It can't be morning," he mumbled.

"I'm afraid it is. Would you like something to eat?"

"Absolutely not." Nathan turned over on the sofa, coming perilously near to falling off altogether, and went back to sleep.

Judith would deem Nathan's complete lack of interest in seducing her daughter as a wily cover for an even more depraved intention, but Hannah accepted the situation. From their first meeting in the Farrenton office, she had not thought that Nathan could ever be attracted to her, and quite clearly he agreed. It was over before it had begun, and at least future solitude guaranteed that there would be no distraction from her goal of directing films. Resigned to a lonely yet creative fate, Hannah showered, dressed, had some breakfast, and then made another attempt to wake Nathan.

"You said that you had to go and see your father this morning."

"Don't remind me." Nathan sat up reluctantly, and although his clothes were creased, his hair remained tidily in place. Hannah had never seen anyone look less like the morning after the night before; even having been sick left no pallor or shakiness. Of course, the amount he had drunk did not rate as fantastically huge, nonetheless Nathan's recovery was quicker than she would have imagined in a normally abstemious associate producer. Her father needed much longer to rejoin the world after one of his bouts.

"We'll have to stop off at my place so that I can get changed," said Nathan. "I can't be seen at the paternal domain looking like this."

"You still want me to go with you?" Hannah had automatically assumed that, after their virtuous night together, Nathan would make his excuses and leave without a backward glance.

"I told you, a referee's essential," said Nathan, and he looked surprised that Hannah should think she was free. "It'll only be OK if you're there."

"Why should I have such a pacifying influence?"

"Because you're female; it's that simple. My father will hardly notice me if there's a girl in the vicinity. Five minutes of your time, ten at the most, is all I'm asking. Whatever details he didn't want to discuss over the telephone, the finer points can't possibly take longer than that. A few seconds, and my father's had more than enough of his son's company."

"Then how do you know that you dislike him?"

"Instinct, pure unadulterated instinct. Are you so well-balanced that you've managed to come through being abandoned without the slightest resentment?"

"My father never abandoned me. When Dad was at home, he didn't make a special effort to see me, but now I talk to him every day. The divorce cleared the air and simplified matters." If Nathan believed that, he would believe anything, but Hannah had no intention of saying more. Her mother never permitted an outsider to know that there was a problem, and Hannah had learnt the lesson well. Everything was a success, even a failed marriage, because no politician had a better grasp of spin than a Chisholm.

"It's nice to know that some people lead a civilized existence," said Nathan.

Hannah guessed that he had not accepted her version of events, but he allowed the topic to drop, for which she was grateful. Some memories were best ignored, in the hope that they would take a hint and go away of their own volition. "What time are you meant to be at your father's?" she asked, to move onto safer ground.

"Ten o'clock precisely, but he'll expect me to be late, and have a lecture on sloth all prepared, so punctuality would be a grievous disappointment to him." Nathan stood up, went to stretch, thought better of it, and added wearily, "This isn't going to be my lucky day, Hannah. I can sense it, and I'm not even psychic."

****

Nathan was more fidgety than dejected as they walked past the pub of the previous night to retrieve his car from a side street. Sunday morning, before the shops were open, meant that London was as quiet as a country village, with few cars, and footsteps often the loudest sound in the empty roads, yet Nathan seemed unaware of the peacefulness, and spoke stridently enough to be in a city centre at noon. The wind had cleared away traffic fumes, and Hannah could have fooled herself into believing that she had never left the East Anglian coast, although in her home town of low-wage seasonal jobs, nobody had money to buy the sort of car that Nathan drove. It was impractically large for London, and expensive, very expensive. Hannah's father, who had never owned a car in his life, would say that Nathan was out to make an impression. The same could have been said of Nathan's address.

"Farrenton Films must pay you really well," commented Hannah. "Obviously, I didn't make as bad a financial mistake as my mother's family predicted, when I chose to do a Mickey Mouse media studies course."

"It's not so much that I get paid well, it's more that I squander what money I have," said Nathan. "But my father will inform you of all this, so I don't need to elaborate now."

"Why bother visiting him, if it's such an ordeal? You should have claimed to be too busy."

"But he issued an order, and I can't stand up to him; I never could. The instant I hear his voice, I know I'm a failure and doomed to be one forever. You can't imagine what it's like."

"Oh, I think I can," said Hannah, her mother's voice taking the opportunity to make itself heard yet again.

15

"Are you sure you know what you're doing? It doesn't sound like a job with any security," Judith had said. "I wouldn't mind if the company made big films with big stars, but nobody's interested in miserable stuff about miserable people on miserable housing estates. If that's the sort of thing Romney Farrenton calls entertainment, you're not going to make much money. And they didn't even put your name on the list of credits at the end."

"That's because the film was shot before I went to work at Farrenton," explained Hannah.

"You mightn't have a job there long enough to get your name on anything." Judith was inclined to plumpness, but anxiety made her expression pinched and faded. The unruly brown hair, so like Hannah's, seemed absurdly frivolous and juvenile to frame a face that had suddenly acquired a hint of old age. "Film companies go broke all the time; everybody knows that."

"Romney started his company over twelve years ago, and it's still in business," protested Hannah.

"Probably close to its sell by date, then. You ought to be more sensible about the future."

"There are no secure jobs nowadays."

"What's wrong with teaching or the civil service?"

"Nothing, except that I'd die of boredom."

"I could be listening to your father all over again. You'll be talking next about the Oscar you're certain to win."

"People can make film their career, even in Britain." But Hannah had the uneasy feeling that Judith was right. Joel Thirlbeck's optimism was never based on reality, or anything that approached reality. "Anyway, I'm your daughter too, so there has to be a little commonsense mixed with the fecklessness."

Judith had laughed, but was not comforted, although she would assure her family that Hannah was creative and audacious, refreshingly different from the stick-in-the-mud Chisholm cousins with their dull jobs in retail or accountancy, and the deception forced on Judith made Hannah feel even guiltier at having let her mother down by chasing a dream.

"You can't possibly be a failure if you can afford to live here," Hannah told Nathan. He had been right to say that he squandered money, because his flat was spacious, with furniture that looked as though it might have left a shop only hours earlier, and everything seemed so pristine that Hannah sat on the edge of a chair while she waited for Nathan to change into fresh clothes. She could not relax among the unnatural tidiness, and felt that she had inadvertently wandered into a sterile photograph from a magazine rather than somebody's home. Nathan would probably remember the previous night as one spent in a slum, and there was no point in pretending otherwise. "I couldn't have dazzled you with the elegance of my rented room. This place must cost a fortune."

"Yes, but I'm not sensible enough to choose somewhere I can afford." Nathan emerged from his bedroom, struggling into the jacket of a dark suit that looked as costly as everything else in the flat. "I'm determined to project an image that says sophisticated and worldly, even when I don't have money to cover the bills. It's the only way of life I know. My mother juggled finance for years, so living beyond my means comes naturally to me."

Hannah's mother had also done a juggling act with money, because her ex-husband was a gambler convinced that the next horse, the next card, the next roll of the dice would bring the wealth that continually eluded him. That phantom fortune, still out of reach, had ended the marriage and caused Joel to live his adult life perilously near poverty, but absolute belief that, one day, his luck must turn never left him. Hannah's legacy from her father would be a reluctance to spend even a few pence on a raffle ticket. "I'd have thought that watching your mother battle with money would produce a miser, not a spendthrift," said Hannah, the Chisholm in her unwilling to admit that she spoke from experience.

"Life just isn't logical. Anyway, money's there to be spent, assuming it is there in the first place, of course. Yet despite being the eternal optimist when it comes to my finances, I'm a definite pessimist about today, but if I don't go and see my father as commanded, he's liable to show up on the doorstep here, and that's a far worse scenario." However, Nathan seemed to be trying to think of reasons to explain why the journey had to be made, as though Hannah needed to be convinced as well as him, and he added a bribe. "Once the dreary bit of the day's over and done with, we can go to a country pub for lunch."

"Fine by me," said Hannah, knowing that her mother would never believe the story of a man having lured Hannah into his flat, only to lead her straight out the front door again, without so much as a suggestion of a spot of debauchery. But that was precisely what happened and, as Nathan escorted Hannah back to his car, the Chisholm imagination would have run wild as it speculated on the depravity of his ultimate intention.

Even the warmth inside the car could not keep February at bay. The sky was gloomy with rain clouds, and when Hannah and Nathan began to leave London behind, suburban garden bushes were twisted in a wind that swirled plastic bags and sheets of newspaper along the road. Hannah, having grown up on the coast, accepted such weather as normal, but Nathan had become impatient with everything the day offered. "This is a complete and utter waste of a morning."

"Where does your father live?" asked Hannah. "I thought you said something about ten minutes of my time."

"Ten minutes, once we arrive," Nathan amended. "I didn't want to put you off altogether by admitting how long it'd take us to get there. A few years ago, my father got it into his head that he was the ideal country squire, and bought a shack situated in the middle of nowhere as proof."

"It's a day out when I didn't have anything planned. I don't mind where we go."

"But you haven't encountered my father yet. Though when you do, you'll wonder what I've been going on about, and probably even tell me that he seems OK, especially as he'll parade all his charm for you."

"It doesn't matter what I think," Hannah pointed out. "You're the one who has to live with him."

"Not literally, I hope," said Nathan. "I don't know which of us would scream louder in horror at the prospect."

Hannah smiled too, but understood more than she would have acknowledged. She was on fairly good terms with her mother, despite the Chisholm blood that charged belligerently through their veins, but returning home to live would be difficult after a taste of liberty. "If you tell me any other nightmare stories about your father, I'll refuse to leave the car."

"Good. I'll have an excuse to make a quick escape."

They were well into Surrey, and the remnants of city suburbs had started to give way to narrow country lanes when Nathan nodded in the direction of a flamboyantly Victoriana house at the top of a sloping garden that was tidily landscaped with drab lawns and regimented bushes. "There's the dump. It looks like some sort of institution to me, or the headquarters of a particularly bogus charity."

The house made Hannah think of a school, an old-fashioned boarding school, a place of midnight feasts and secret societies, incognito princesses and lowly scholarship girls, as described in books handed down from her Thirlbeck grandmother. There ought to be hidden passageways and buried treasure in such a house, and *The Grange* or *The Manor* emblazoned on high wrought-iron gates instead of a mere number. "If I'd come here as a child, I would have been very disappointed not to find myself in the middle of an adventure."

"An adventure?" repeated Nathan, but his mind was elsewhere. Vans had been parked on the grass verges at the side of the lane ahead, and it was plain exactly whose vans they were. "The police have caught up with my father at last. I knew that much money couldn't be legit."

"A cyclist's probably come off his bike."

"All those vans mean something more dramatic than that." Nathan began to slow his car as a policeman, gaudy in fluorescent jacket, stepped into the road and held up his hand. "They chose Sunday to catch my father off-guard."

"Why would they want him off-guard?" asked Hannah.

"To prevent him making a run for it, of course. I never realized the local plods were that intelligent. Unless I'm being stopped because one of my tyres looks a bit dodgy or the number-plate's fallen off, the law's decided to pounce on dear Dad." Nathan lowered his window as he spoke, and the policeman ambled to the car, the lack of urgency implying that he expected a genial chat. He was middle-aged, and had so mild an expression, Hannah thought it odd he should have been able to hold on to such placidity in a job presumably both stressful and unpleasant, but even his voice was relaxed.

"I'm afraid the road's closed. If you back for a minute or so, you'll come to a gateway and you can turn the car."

"I don't need to turn anywhere," said Nathan. "I've arrived."

"But you have to go back. This road will be closed for some time yet." The man spoke slowly and soothingly, as though Nathan were a fractious child who had to be pacified: a tone that Hannah was conscious of having utilized herself when fending off telephone inquiries from actors' agents and scriptwriters. "You'll only be able to continue your journey if you turn around."

"But there's no more journey for me to continue." The patronizing assumption that he required instruction made Nathan cantankerous, and he sighed impatiently. "This is my destination, or rather, that house is."

The policeman glanced over his shoulder, perhaps imagining that the single residence behind him might somehow have transformed itself into a vast collection of buildings while his attention had been diverted. "You want to go to *that* house?"

"Precisely," Nathan replied, with exaggerated forbearance. "I do hope you haven't any objection. You see, it's my father's house."

"Your father?" The man looked startled, and then worried. "Wait here for a moment, Mr Wyatt, and I'll get Inspector Quayle."

"Why? What's wrong?" asked Nathan, but the man was already hurrying off. "Oh well, I suppose even my father couldn't have expected his luck to last forever. The police are obviously here to nab him. How else would they know my surname?"

"That's far too melodramatic for a Sunday morning in the countryside," said Hannah. "There'll be a dull explanation. There always is."

"Not always," muttered Nathan, watching the policeman approach a couple of plain-clothed officers. There was a quick conference, during which all three turned their heads away, possibly fearing that either Nathan or Hannah might have lip-reading abilities, and then one man in a black overcoat detached himself from the group.

"This, presumably, is Inspector Quayle," said Nathan. "I think you're going to get that melodrama you mentioned."

"I hope not. My mother disapproves of melodrama."

"So does Romney Farrenton when it's not on stage or film. If my father's swindled his shareholders or embezzled the local Widows and Orphans charity, the chances of me keeping my job diminish with every step this Inspector takes towards us. Is it hubris or nemesis that clobbers you? I can never remember which way round they work."

Inspector Quayle did not look like an emissary of fate with the power to destroy anybody's career prospects. He was middle-aged, plump, plain, with dull brown hair, and he walked slowly, reluctant to reach Nathan's car. It was clear that the news he brought could not be good, but Nathan seemed petulant rather than apprehensive.

"I wish he'd get a move on. Why on earth is he dithering?"

Quayle was not dithering. He knew what had to be done, but evidently still needed a little preparation time, in spite of a job that should have accustomed him to being the bearer of bad tidings. Whatever he had to say was out of the ordinary, and Hannah longed to be somewhere else, anywhere else. She had enough problems in her own life to deal with, before other people's were added.

"These provincial policemen," muttered Nathan. "I suppose this is the biggest excitement he's ever known, and each minute has to be savoured."

"He doesn't appear to be enjoying himself all that much."

"Then he takes his pleasures solemnly."

The inspector paused to get an ID wallet out of his pocket and, thus shielded, he allowed his walk to become more resolute. "Detective Inspector Quayle," he announced, thrusting the proof into the car so abruptly that Nathan recoiled. "You're Owen Wyatt's son?"

"That's right. What's going on?"

Quayle hesitated, and looked at Hannah. "Are you a family member too?"

"She's a friend," said Nathan. "If you've got to tell me something, then tell me."

"It's bad, very bad."

"I've guessed that already." Nathan's irritability was turning into nervousness, and he pressed his fingers together to control their trembling.

"I'm afraid it concerns your father."

"I guessed that too." Nathan leaned against Hannah and clutched one of her hands, a gesture of intimacy that took her completely by surprise, and she hurriedly put an arm around his shoulders so as not to appear unfeeling in a time of need. And time of need it certainly was, despite Nathan's earlier breezy talk about the distant relationship he had with his father, but Hannah could understand Nathan's bewildered emotion. She had despised her own father often enough, only to have the exasperation fizzle out because Joel was able to adopt such a dejected air of helplessness, of being the bullied victim, that Hannah found herself compelled to pay his bills and buy him food, while knowing that she was merely averting a crisis bound to reoccur before the dent in her bank balance had been filled in. He was as shiftless and manipulative as her mother claimed, but Hannah could not abandon him as he had once abandoned her, and she assumed that Nathan must have a similar difficulty with his father.

"We're not sure of the details yet." Quayle was prevaricating, but he knew what words had to be said, and that he would have to say them. "Mr Wyatt was found in the garden this morning."

"What do you mean? Found?"

"One of your sisters —"

"Half-sisters," said Nathan.

"She didn't get an answer at the front door, and went to try the back. But at the side of the house —" Quayle stopped again, presumably realizing that silence would explain the situation as clearly as words. "She's very upset," he continued, after waiting in vain for a response from Nathan. "The shock, of course."

"Did he have a heart attack or something?" ventured Nathan. "Is he in hospital?"

Perhaps the same shock afflicting his half-sister had turned Nathan stupid. Hannah knew that so many police in the vicinity must mean a death, an unexplained one. The cold air rushing through the open window of the car made Hannah want to shiver, but that would look like parading an over-sensitivity to the fate of a stranger, and she willed herself not to tremble for fear of intruding into whatever Nathan experienced.

"I'm afraid it was too late to do anything. Your father's dead." Quayle began to speak more smoothly as soon as the bad news had been delivered, making it obvious that he preferred his job without the encumbrance of grieving relatives and their unpredictable reactions. "Would you go to your sister? She's a bit young to be on her own at a time like this."

"Where's Flora?" asked Nathan.

"Mrs Wyatt? I'm told she's in Switzerland."

"She would be," Nathan said balefully, and he sat up. Hannah was glad to be able to move her arm from its cramped position around his shoulders, and she felt callous to be aware of such minor discomfort, but any sorrow belonged to Nathan, not her.

"You'll have to leave the car here," said Quayle. "We're still checking a few things."

"OK. Come on, Hannah."

"I'll stay in the car." Like her father, Hannah was faint-hearted when it came to real life emotions, and she had no wish to deal with the grief of a stranger. "Don't bother your sister with introductions today."

"Half-sister," Nathan said again. "But you're going to have to rally round the flag, Hannah, because I can't cope without you."

Quayle would assume, from both words and attitude, that Nathan was very close to Hannah. Indeed, their relationship seemed to have taken a giant step forward minus any input from her, for Nathan spoke as if he had every right to expect support, whatever her own preference might be, and Hannah was as gratified as she was surprised that he should be so dependent on her, although she got out of the car with reluctance.

"Your half-sister's by the gate." Quayle signalled the direction with a wave of a hand, then turned to hurry off. But even he must have thought it too insouciant a way to treat the newly bereaved, because he glanced back to add, "We can't let anybody into the house or grounds at the moment."

"Why not?"

But Nathan's question was an automatic one that did not require an answer, and he clung to Hannah's arm while they walked toward a small, supposedly environment-friendly car that looked as expensive as Nathan's gas-guzzler. Ostentatious, Judith would say, a parade of wealth revealing nothing about the driver except bad taste, and certainly the white boiler suit that Tiffany Wyatt was wearing had no style whatsoever about it, with Wellington boots adding little to the ensemble; yet Tiffany had a fragile fair prettiness and a fashionably thin figure that made Hannah, already ill at ease to invade so private a meeting, feel intimidated.

Quayle's description of Nathan's half-sister as young and upset had caused Hannah to picture a sobbing teenager, but Tiffany was in her early twenties and gave the impression of being supremely in control. She leaned against her car, and spoke truculently, apparently expecting Nathan to start a quarrel. "Don't ask me what happened because I haven't a clue."

"This is Hannah," said Nathan, his voice matching Tiffany's enmity.

Hannah mumbled a few hackneyed words of condolence, but Tiffany regarded anyone with Nathan as an opponent, a Chisholm trait that Hannah recognized without resentment. Remembering the very different

Tiffany seen by Inspector Quayle, and knowing that her own first impulse in such a crisis would be to go running to Judith, Hannah asked, "Have you been able to contact your mother?"

"I left a message on her phone, but she hasn't rung back yet." For a split-second, Tiffany's façade almost crumbled, and Hannah caught a glimpse of the overwhelmed young girl Quayle had spotted. Then the poised coolness was back as Tiffany looked at Nathan. "What are you doing here? Why did the police bother to fetch you?"

"They didn't."

"Dad sent for you as well?" demanded Tiffany, astonished. "I don't believe it."

"Then don't, but Hannah can back me up. I insisted she came along as mediator. Why did he want to see you?"

"He didn't say. There was a phone message."

"I actually spoke to him. He said he was going to divorce Flora."

"Oh, this is too ridiculous," declared Tiffany, with sudden fury. "I don't believe any of it."

"Every single word I'm telling you is true," retorted Nathan. "Why on earth would I be here right now if I hadn't been summoned?"

"I didn't mean you, I meant —" Tiffany's hands swept out in arcs that encompassed the police, the house and the garden. "The whole thing's impossible. And what's Flora doing in Switzerland?"

"Giving herself an alibi perhaps? Dad was planning to dump her. He said she was a two-timing money grabber."

"That's been plain for ages," declared Tiffany. "Why did it take him so long to find out?"

"Because he was fat-headed enough to imagine that a young and beautiful woman could be attracted to him."

"Well, it doesn't matter now what he did or didn't imagine, but if he was going to divorce Flora, it could only have been because he'd met someone else." Tiffany sounded impatient, but talking was easier than thinking, and Hannah guessed that Tiffany had made up her mind not to weaken in front of Nathan.

Uncomfortable at being the outsider on so familial an occasion, Hannah backed a few paces away from Tiffany's car. A brick wall surrounded the house and its grounds, but the ploughed field on the other side of the lane was bordered by a ragged hedge dotted with gorse flowers, as yellow as buttercups in a summer meadow. To another person, the cold wind might have seemed incongruous as it buffeted such a forerunner of spring colour, but Hannah had grown up with coastal gales dominating each season, and she merely noted that the bare branches of a sycamore swaying against the February sky would make a dramatic opening shot for a film. The wind belonged everywhere; she was the one out of place, stranded in a country lane, surrounded by the aftermath of a stranger's death.

"Hannah works at Farrenton Films too," said Nathan, but he spoke simply to fill a gap, as his half-sister had not displayed any interest in Hannah's person or prospects.

"Oh," replied Tiffany. "There's no need to hang around here, Nathan. They can't want to talk to you."

"Inspector what's-his-name told me to stay with you."

"Why?"

"Presumably because he's sentimental about families, and doesn't realize that we hated each other at first sight, and never found a reason to change our minds. Why disillusion the poor man so cruelly?"

Tiffany forced a smile, but then said in bewilderment, "I've not been here in months. Why did it have to choose this morning to happen?"

"Because that's the way things like to happen," replied Nathan. "The cosmos isn't going to rearrange itself to accommodate your timetable."

And the cosmos did not seem inclined to give Hannah Thirlbeck a helping hand either. If she had been close to Nathan, she would have had a purpose, but a mere acquaintance was a trespasser, especially as Tiffany persisted in ignoring her with a thoroughness worthy of a Chisholm. Town-bred Hannah had always regarded the countryside as a wasteland, useful only for atmospheric background shots when filming on location, but the rural desolation around her was bleaker than even she had envisaged.

"Hannah and I met at work. She's our production assistant," said Nathan, as if answering a question from Tiffany. "Poor Hannah's job consists of whatever we haughty producers deem beneath our dignity. She books studios, writes letters, makes tea, and should a nuisance of a scriptwriter phone, she fobs the wretch off with a claim that everybody else is out of the office."

"That's a fairly accurate job description," commented Hannah.

"I have the most important task in the whole Farrenton Company, and that's to get my hands on the lolly," continued Nathan, "but I'm just talking for the sake of talking. Don't bother to listen."

"I'm not." Tiffany turned her back on the police activity, clearly looking for an escape route, but Hannah had already retreated into the refuge of fantasy. The scene before her was a carefully planned film shot, with the extras in place and a bonus of dark clouds scudding across a pallid sky to add an aura of foreboding to the take. Inspector Quayle had removed his overcoat, but, even from a distance, it was plain that his dumpy figure would belong to a supporting actor, not the lead. Nathan's appearance was better suited, much better suited, to a main character.

"Dad was covered in blood," Tiffany said abruptly, the revulsion in her voice startling Hannah out of the daydream.

"He probably hit his head when he fell. Try not to think about it." But Nathan was awkward in the rôle of comforter, and he hurried to change the subject, possibly more for his own sake than Tiffany's. "I wonder how good an actress Flora will turn out to be. I don't have her mobile number. Do you?"

"Why would I ever phone her?" Tiffany's question was a rhetorical one as she did not wait for a reply. "I've got to get away from here, Nathan. I want to go home."

"Then go. There's nothing you can do."

"But that Inspector said he had to talk to me."

Nathan was suddenly back in confident control. He only grovelled to the mega-rich, and that was on behalf of Farrenton Films. Petty officialdom could safely be despised, and he looked around to see Quayle, now in a white boiler suit, following similarly-clad cohorts through the gate and into the garden. With a jolt of revulsion, Hannah realized the significance of Tiffany's outfit. Her boiler suit was no botched fashion statement; the police evidence included the clothes she had arrived in.

"Why pander to Inspector Quayle?" asked Nathan. "It'd make him unbearably conceited. He can have his chat with you another time. Just get into your car and go. Hannah will drive you home."

"Actually, I can't. I never learned how to drive. Neither of my parents had a car."

Nathan stared at Hannah with such astonishment, she might have claimed that she had no idea how to post a letter or switch on a television. Evidently, Nathan had not encountered a car-less family before, and so dire a level of deprivation meant that he required several seconds to recover and find a solution to the dilemma. "I'll drive both of you home."

"I can drive myself." Tiffany spoke with pig-headed determination, and Nathan did not even try to argue.

"OK. Forego the delights of my company, but you still shouldn't be alone. Hannah's probably just as eager to vanish, so do her a favour and oblige as a taxi service. I'll make your excuses to Quayle."

Tiffany glanced at the gate, perhaps fearing that a horde of police might appear to foil her escape, but all activity had left the lane, and Nathan stacked the newly-placed traffic cones, then shifted the *road closed* sign to release Tiffany's car. It could have been their legal right to leave, but a surge of adrenalin made Hannah's heart thud at the prospect of outwitting pursuers, although the consequences of running away would not affect her, and she feigned calmness, waving to Nathan when the car passed him, but his attention was on the garden, and he failed to notice her.

Tiffany drove like a hunted fugitive, in her effort to outstrip the morning's events and leave them far behind. She ignored Hannah, but that might have been due less to antagonism than a mind centred on flight. To chat or not to chat? Silence, even though uncomfortable, was almost certainly better than a clumsy attempt at conversation when light topics would jar, decided Hannah; but the difficulty solved itself as they reached the outskirts of a village. Tiffany's hands began to shake, and then her whole body was trembling.

"Stop the car," said Hannah.

"I've got to get home," declared Tiffany, very near panic. "I've got to."

"Neither of us will go anywhere if you crash the car," Hannah pointed out, forcing composure into her voice. "You have to take a breather; you must know that yourself."

For a worrying couple of seconds, it seemed that Tiffany would be obstinate, but then she capitulated and parked at the kerbside without further argument. "Now what do we do?" she asked, with a tremulous smile.

"We wait until you get your breath back."

Tiffany pressed her hands together, bewildered not to be able to control them, and she tried to fake nonchalance. "It's stupid, behaving like this."

"No, it's a perfectly normal reaction. I'm the one who's stupid, never having forked out for a few driving lessons."

Tiffany, more perplexed than upset, barely registered Hannah's words. "I wasn't close to my father. In fact, when I heard the phone message he left, I was tempted to ignore it. I wish I had."

"Of course you do; anyone would." Exactly as Hannah wished that she had refused point blank to visit Nathan's father that morning.

"I didn't realize it before, but I hardly knew Dad. I don't even know where he grew up or went to school. We never had a proper talk, not once."

Perhaps because there was nothing that the father wanted to say to his children, as he shrugged them off without a backward glance. Tiffany's account was similar to the tale heard from Nathan, but on that particular day, an outsider could not possibly comment on Owen Wyatt's self-centred attitude. Hannah's rôle was primarily one of listener.

"I should have asked him about his childhood. I should have made him talk to me. I shouldn't have assumed it could wait, that there'd always be a tomorrow. Second chances aren't a right, and now they're gone forever." Then with a lightning change of mood, Tiffany was suddenly angry: angry with herself. "This is daft. I'm wallowing in self-pity."

"No, you're making sense," said Hannah, thinking of her own father. She had no idea when or why he started gambling, because she had never asked in spite of failing to understand how a man, who could be intelligent, affectionate and compassionate, was incapable of stopping the behaviour that he knew had wrecked much of his life.

"You're not like the standard run of Nathan's girlfriends," said Tiffany.

"Then they're obviously beautiful, sophisticated, elegant, and everything else I'm not." It was a relief to be flippant, and a greater relief that Tiffany had moved onto another topic.

"I meant, you're a real person, and Nathan usually goes in for phoneys. But then, he lives in a permanent fantasy world himself."

"That's an inevitable side-effect of working in films. The end product is always fantasy, even with a supposed documentary, I regret to say." It had been a student dream to be able to tell people that she worked in the film industry, and despite Hannah's lowly status at the Farrenton Company, she felt that if one ambition could be achieved, the chances of accomplishing her eventual goal were better. Someday she might be a director, and the thought comforted her. "Reality is the imitation of life, as far as I'm concerned. Give me any old Hollywood tinsel, and I'm perfectly content."

"I wish I could walk into some Hollywood mush right now, and stay there until I get my happy ending." Tiffany leaned back, closed her eyes, and for a moment, all tension seemed to drain away. Then she sighed, looked at Hannah, and said, "Nathan didn't want to listen, but I think somebody killed Dad. There was blood everywhere, like he'd been stabbed. I'd walked into it before I realized what — that's why the police took my clothes, but it was only on the shoes, not —" Tiffany shuddered, and clasped her hands together so tightly that they began to turn white. "He must have heard a noise, gone to investigate, and chased after them into the garden. Dad could be a total moron when he lost his temper."

"It might have been a heart attack or something," ventured Hannah, uncertain whether or not she ought to speak, but Tiffany's horrors cried out for reassurance.

"The blood could simply be the result of a fall, as Nathan said. You know how it can gush if you hit your nose."

"Yes." But Tiffany sounded tired and defeated, too old to believe in fairy tales. "Whatever happened, I think all this might have been easier if I'd actually loved Dad, but I didn't, and I can't get past feeling sorry for myself. I blame Dad for everything now, although when I was small, I didn't think that much about him. I'm a bigger phoney than Nathan. At least he openly admits to being a sham."

"Doesn't brooding on the past indicate hidden depths? Shallow people are able to brush things off without a second thought."

"Then I must be very, very deep," said Tiffany. "Sorry to lumber you with my whingeing, but I couldn't resist having a captive audience. I'm OK to drive now. I'll take you home."

"Nathan expected me to deliver you to your front door, so that's what I'll do, and then make my own way home. No need to bother about me." But Hannah might not have spoken with such fortitude had she realized exactly how far Tiffany's part of London was from her own.

2

Hannah had stopped noticing the cramped dinginess of the street she lived in, but after the Regency grace of Central London, she was aware of the empty cans in the gutter and the takeaway boxes dotted along the pavement. Then she saw the most desolate sight of all: her father sitting on the front step, with a weather-beaten suitcase on either side of him.

"Glenda kicked me out," said Joel, looking as if every one of his forty-five years weighed down on him. The smile, gently resigned with a touch of sadness in it, was the same; the dark-brown hair untidily hanging over his forehead was the same as well, so were the hunched shoulders and the entire situation.

"How did Glenda come to fall out of love?" asked Hannah.

"She suddenly realized that she was wasting her time on a good-for-nothing drunken gambler." Joel struggled to his feet, wearily submissive to fate. "How could anybody argue with that conclusion?"

"I could," said Hannah, his air of dejection making her want to comfort him, although she knew that whatever had happened was probably Joel's own fault.

"None of it matters when I'm with you. At least there's something in my life to be proud of: a wonderful, kind, caring, generous daughter."

"No need to overdo the flattery," said Hannah, smiling at the deluge of compliments. "I always fall for your hard luck stories. I'm your insurance policy and pension fund rolled into one."

Joel put his arms around Hannah, and pulled her close to him for a prolonged hug. "My luck can't be completely bad when I was fortunate enough to get you in life's lottery."

As a child, Hannah had felt safe in her father's arms. As an adult, she knew it was Joel who wanted to feel safe again. He thought that events tossed him around like a leaf in an autumn gale, but after a month or two with Hannah, he would once more start to believe in good luck, and that would be the beginning of his next catastrophe. Her father had become horribly predictable.

Joel followed Hannah into the dark and narrow hall that led to a flight of equally dark and narrow stairs. The house was originally intended to shelter a family in the days when there were children by the dozen, along with a miscellany of live-in servants, but since those more lavish times, both building and area had descended the social ladder with a thud onto the lowly plain of rented rooms, as jaded and unkempt as Joel looked. "Been out to lunch?" he asked.

"Don't worry; you'll get fed very soon. I haven't eaten for what feels like several days, and I'm ravenous." Hannah closed the front door, then took one of Joel's suitcases from him, and tried to sound cheerful as she added, "You give the impression of not having seen food in a year, but that's your normal appearance so I won't listen to any tales about the cruel Glenda starving you."

"She isn't cruel, and she's quite right to rid her life of me." Joel was visibly disheartened, in the sort of mood when he would promise Hannah never to let her down again, promise to avoid all forms of gambling, promise to become a teetotaller. The fever had abated, but would return because it always did.

"Oh, you're not that bad," said Hannah, hating to see him so demoralized, even though he was the cause of most of his problems.

"I'm the one who made a mess of everything, as I invariably do." Joel hauled himself up the stairs with a heavy reliance on the banister. Depression usually drained him of energy, but such out-and-out lethargy was exceptional. "I've been nothing but a curse to the people I love from the day I was born."

"Glenda must have been remarkably caustic indeed," commented Hannah.

"And left me feeling very sorry for myself," Joel acknowledged wryly. "But she's right. I'm a total failure."

"You're not a failure. You're just no good with money. Thousands of people get into difficulties because they waste their income on clothes and cars and flats they can't afford. It's pretty much the same sort of thing."

"No, it isn't."

Joel was not mistaken. He threw money away in futile attempts to get at more, and nothing would change, even in the unlikely event of him becoming a millionaire. There could be no ending because Joel would never be content with what he had. The elusive fortune that he chased was a mirage so enticing, its allure would haunt him as long as he breathed.

"Why do you go on gambling?" asked Hannah, recalling Tiffany's lost chance to talk to Owen Wyatt.

"Why do I go on gambling?" Joel paused, as though climbing stairs and thinking were too strenuous to be tackled simultaneously. "If I knew why I can't stop gambling, I might be freed from it. I'm so glad you take after your mother. Judith couldn't be anything but sensible if she tried."

Joel thought Hannah took after her mother, but Judith maintained that Hannah had turned out to be another Joel. Judith the sensible was correct, since only a gambler would take a job with an English film company in the hope that she might have a future as a director. "Did you start gambling because you wanted to get rich?" asked Hannah, conscious of how much money would have to be found if she were ever to achieve her ambition.

"I was rich. I simply didn't know it." But Joel spoke automatically. Ordinary life held little interest for him, just as it would never be enough for his daughter. The ability to live on hope was part of Hannah's genetic inheritance and would not be dislodged, any more than it could have been from her father.

"Aren't you feeling well?" Hannah had reached the door of her flat, but Joel was barely half-way up the stairs, and had again paused to rest.

"I'm merely old and decrepit. Pay no attention."

"You don't look after yourself," said Hannah, but she knew that Joel assumed other people were there to do whatever was necessary for his welfare. She also knew that Judith would claim Joel was deliberately exaggerating the pathos. "Are you back on the booze?"

"Drinking's far too expensive a pastime for me at the moment."

"One piece of good news then." Hannah went inside her flat, and the folded blankets still on the sofa reminded her of Nathan and his father. At least Joel, for all his failings, could be relied on to love Hannah unconditionally, and the thought of losing him was horrific. Forgotten promises were unimportant, and so was the money that she would undoubtedly have to shell out to get Joel back on track. While Judith did the worrying, he had made Hannah's childhood fun, and given her the unrealistic aims that ensured his daughter would never be trapped in a Chisholm desert of levelheadedness. Joel deserved his free board and lodging.

"Why are we discussing my useless existence?" asked Joel, finally appearing at the open door and putting down his suitcase with a sigh of relief. "What's happening to you? How's the job going?"

"Now I'm really suspicious. Why don't you want to talk about your own job?"

"You know me too well," said Joel, slumping onto the sofa, and clearly longing to pull the blankets over him and drift into a gentle world of sleep. "But, incredibly, for once I'm entirely blameless. There hasn't been much work outside the public sector lately, and not much in it either, so the firm's gone bust: no job, no redundancy payment, nothing. Glenda accused me of getting the sack or walking out, but I actually have documentary proof of my complete innocence, or rather, I did until she tore it up."

Judith would remark that Joel could still have brought the bits of paper along to corroborate his story, but Hannah ignored the cynical voice in her mind. Even when Joel was in work, she never expected any financial contribution from him toward food bills, or any bills. It had been a lesson learnt from her mother, and learnt well. "You hated designing shoebox houses anyway. Something will turn up. And I don't mean a racing tip."

"Why do you bother with me? I'm not worth it." Joel leaned back, apparently overwhelmed with misery: the look that Judith swore had been perfected in front of a mirror. "I'm a fool who's wrecked his life and doesn't deserve to be rewarded with a terrific daughter."

"Any more of this praise, and I'll become so smug, you won't be able to bear me. What's so amazing about letting you stay here? If I showed up on your front step, you wouldn't slam the door in my face."

"You're assuming I'd have a front step of my own. Everything's the wrong way around, and I'm ashamed of it. You ought to have a better life than supporting a shiftless father, who's even a jinx on the firm he worked for."

"Rubbish! The sole person you can jinx is yourself. Glenda's temporarily knocked the confidence out of you, that's all, and she made a big mistake when she booted you out. She won't find anybody more easy-going."

"Her big mistake was getting involved with me in the first place."

Hannah would never tell Joel, but she agreed with him. Glenda, a fluffy-headed manicurist, who once believed that love conquered all, had discovered to her cost that gambling was a greater rival for Joel's attention and bank balance than an avaricious other woman. He was an architect, often a well-paid architect, who lived in penury, and trusted that Glenda, or a similar soft touch, would provide his daily expenses. He knew what he was doing, and could genuinely despise himself, but turned to alcohol in an attempt to smother the thought of his behaviour, rather than endeavour to change it. Hannah was the safety-net, Joel's last resort when at rock-bottom, and she saw no way out. Joel was a gambler, always had been, perhaps always would be, and unfortunately Hannah accepted the responsibility for his life.

****

It was evening. Joel had fallen asleep on the sofa, when the front door entry phone buzzed, and Hannah found herself talking to Inspector Quayle, somebody she had never expected to encounter again.

"But Nathan isn't here," she said in bewilderment.

"Actually, it's you I need to speak to, just for a few minutes." Quayle sounded oddly apologetic for someone who could wield vigorous legal power should Hannah refuse, but he was even more diffident when he added, "I have to check something."

Nathan's whereabouts last night, thought Hannah. She had no other link with Quayle's investigation, and his journey to see her presumably meant Tiffany had been right to think that Owen Wyatt's death was not a matter of straightforward natural causes. To be asked to help a detective with his inquiries felt so like appearing in a film, Hannah had to remind herself that she was not being offered an opportunity to study police procedure, but had become entangled in a tragedy that included a real body, instead of an actor doused in fake blood while he earned the Equity minimum as a corpse. Ambition was laudable, but less praiseworthy when it caused her to view all events through a camera lens.

"What's happening?" Joel asked sleepily, roused by the one-sided conversation.

"A policeman's on his way up the stairs to talk to me."

"I haven't bounced any cheques of late, I swear," said Joel, reluctantly sitting upright. "My conscience is pristine, believe me."

"I do, especially as I know why this Inspector wants to see me. It's because a friend's father died."

"What's that got to do with you?"

"Nothing, but I suppose alibis are being checked."

"Why? Is my daughter acquainted with the sort of offspring who'd happily bump off a trusting father to get their eager little hands on an inheritance? At least I'm spared one of life's worries. Nobody's going to dispatch me because of my millions," said Joel, attempting to smooth his hair with one hand, but still looking drowsily dishevelled. "Lucky I'm here. This Inspector won't be able to bully you."

"I don't think he's planning to interrogate me," commented Hannah, amused that Joel's imagination should match her own.

"I hope your mother never hears that the police arrived on the doorstep minutes after I rolled up. She'd be certain the two events were somehow connected."

"I can vouch for your entire innocence."

"I'm innocent twice during the same weekend!" marvelled Joel. "As heart-warming as it's unexpected."

Hannah laughed, glad that Joel seemed to have shaken off the bleakness that had earlier surrounded him, but the sooner he recovered from his despondency, the sooner the compulsion to gamble would return. Suddenly dispirited, she opened the door of the flat to see Quayle, rugby-ball shaped in his thick overcoat, climb the last few stairs, and Hannah was surprised to note that he was shorter than her, a fact she had failed to register in the unpleasantness of the morning. Being on her own territory altered everything, and relegated the car ride with Nathan to a past so distant, it could have belonged to the previous year. The recurrent problem of Joel had taken over, and the Inspector was little more than a minor distraction.

Quayle had the option of sitting beside Joel on the sofa or standing, and he chose to stay on his feet, not bothering to remove his overcoat. Unwilling to feel like a child at school gazing up at a teacher, Hannah stood too, an action that would give an audience the impression she intended to defy Quayle. But the cameras were imaginary, Hannah reminded herself. The scene was a fleeting moment only experienced by those in the room, and if she never made her films, nobody in the future would know that she had once been alive.

"I just have a couple of questions," said Quayle, taking a notebook out of his coat pocket.

"Why?" demanded Joel. He considered himself so inadequate a father that when an occasion presented itself for him to demonstrate some devoted-parent credentials, he was inclined to overdo the protectiveness.

"It's simply routine," said Quayle. He turned in Hannah's direction, but fixed his attention on the notebook he held. "Was Nathan Wyatt with you last night?"

"Yes," Hannah said reluctantly, conscious of Joel's presence.

"What time did you meet Wyatt yesterday evening?" asked Quayle.

"Around 8:30."

"And he was with you from then on, until you both arrived at his father's house this morning?"

"That's right," Hannah agreed with even more reluctance. Quayle presumably had no daughters and was woodenly unimaginative, not able to guess that Joel might have considerably higher standards of decorum for Hannah than for himself. "Nathan drank a bit too much in the pub, and so naturally he couldn't drive home. He spent the night on my sofa."

The information was for the benefit of Joel, who had been staring at Hannah in shocked disbelief after the revelation that his daughter could shelter an overnight male while she lacked a wedding ring on her finger, but Quayle took the news in his stride and continued to scribble. "Wyatt was here all night?"

"Yes."

"How can you be sure of that?" Quayle glanced up at Hannah, as though he had spotted a glaring flaw in her account. "Were you awake the entire night?"

"No, I wasn't."

"So Wyatt stayed in here while you were alone in the bedroom, you say."

"If my daughter says that she was alone in her bedroom, then she was alone," stated Joel, incensed at the slur on Hannah's reputation. He had never once contemplated marrying Glenda, but of course that was different.

Quayle nodded, but failed to record Joel's assertion in his notebook. Either the Inspector refused to credit the possibility of restraint, which flatteringly meant that he deemed Hannah attractive enough to be irresistible, or he was waiting for her to acknowledge that she had no idea of Nathan's whereabouts for whole hours of the time supposedly spent together.

"Well, we arrived here sometime after 10:30, and I know Nathan was in the flat at two in the morning because that's when he was sick," said Hannah. "I got up around seven, but Nathan slept for another hour or so."

"On the sofa," Joel informed Quayle sternly.

"That's why there are still some blankets in here," added Hannah.

Quayle did not seem unduly impressed by the evidence on offer, and asked, "How do you know it was 2am when Wyatt took ill? Did you look at a clock?"

"No. Nathan mentioned the time when he woke me. He was cold, and wanted another blanket."

"So actually you don't know what time it was?" Quayle's words were more of a statement than a question.

"It was very dark, and felt like the middle of the night."

"Did Wyatt stay in the bedroom with you from then on?"

"No. He got a blanket and went back to the sofa." It sounded ludicrously weak, perhaps even a fable invented to pacify a strict father, and Hannah was not surprised that Quayle should appear sceptical.

"Then you wouldn't describe Wyatt as a close friend," he commented.

"Obviously not," snapped Joel.

"Nathan and I work for the same company: Farrenton Films." Hannah attempted a nonchalant tone, but she was talking about the first foothold in her career.

"If Nathan Wyatt's just a work colleague, why did he take you to meet his father?" It was probably automatic for Quayle to pick holes in an answer, but he could be recalling the way Nathan had clung to Hannah for support that morning. The Inspector must have seen people in every circumstance, and if he found such behaviour odd in mere casual acquaintances, it might indicate that Hannah was more important to Nathan than she had dared to think.

"It wasn't intended as a formal introduction to the family," Hannah said with an indifference that masked hope. "Nathan didn't want to visit his father by himself, so he asked me to go along."

"Why did he need somebody with him?" asked Quayle.

"That's a question for Nathan," replied Hannah, surprised the Inspector should apparently assume she would gossip behind a friend's back.

"He must have given a reason for not wanting to see his father alone."

"Why on earth are you interrogating Hannah?" demanded Joel. "It's quite plain that she can't help, and you must have spoken to this Nathan Wyatt already, or you wouldn't be here."

"I have to check what people tell me." It was difficult to picture Quayle dealing with conmen and thugs when a cross father could make him close his notebook and retreat, but retreat he did, not even waiting for an answer to his last question, so perhaps Quayle felt he had a power over criminals that was absent when he dealt with the general public. An exiled military dictator might have known the same frustration.

"Dreadful man! That two-bit authority's gone to his head," said Joel, the moment the door closed behind Quayle. "If I hadn't been on the scene, he'd have ranted and raved until he reduced you to tears."

It was a harsh depiction of Quayle's interview technique, but Joel needed to think well of himself, and Hannah smiled gratefully. "I wasn't bothered with you here."

"He had the nerve to imply that you were a slut, dragging the nearest available man into your bed." Joel wanted more praise for his successful rout of the slanderous detective, but he was still genuinely affronted at the insult to Hannah's virtue. "Quayle didn't believe a word you said."

"That was my impression too, but I've decided it's a compliment to be considered so alluring."

"He didn't intend it as a compliment," Joel declared grimly. "Who's this Nathan Wyatt, when he isn't carousing in pubs and being pursued by the police?"

As Joel spoke, the entry phone buzzed, and Hannah picked it up to hear the maligned Nathan's voice say, "I'm sorry to have muddled you up in all this."

"It's not your fault. Inspector Quayle put in an appearance, by the way, but he's just left."

"I know. I spotted him outside, and waited until he'd gone. Quayle favoured me with a visit earlier, and it was like trying to talk to a brick wall. Let me in, and we can compare notes."

"OK." Hannah replaced the phone, and noted Joel's tight-lipped suspicion. "Yes, Dad, that was Nathan, and he's on his way up the stairs, so here's your chance to meet the drunken wastrel in person. I hope you're not going to glare at him, and demand to know his intentions."

"Of course not. I'll be much more tempted to punch his sneaky face into the middle of next week. How dare he force himself in here and stay the night!"

"You sound as dubious about my virtue as Quayle was," Hannah remarked. "Nathan really did occupy the sofa, and we're not in the throes of a passionate affair. He hasn't even attempted to seduce me with his calculating wiles."

"In that case, Wyatt's got another girl somewhere."

"Why shouldn't he have one? We're not married." Hannah spoke without thinking, and was alarmed to see Joel immediately plunge into guilt.

"You blame me for deserting your mother."

"Absolutely," said Hannah, hoping to jolly him out of depression before it could take hold. "You abandoned me in a sea of Chisholms. There are crueller fates, but not many."

"Judith and I did nothing but quarrel, and it was getting worse. One day, you came in from school, heard us, and ran straight upstairs with your hands over your ears. I knew then that I couldn't bear to go on making you suffer." Joel sighed as he recalled the self-sacrifice involved when he had departed with one of Glenda's predecessors in an endeavour to spare his daughter pain.

"Well, I seem to have survived, and only developed the most mandatory of complexes. I understood that gambling was the problem. The thing I couldn't understand was why you didn't just stop."

"That's what I've never understood either." Joel spoke with such helpless resignation that Hannah longed to deliver an invigorating lecture on self-discipline and strength of mind, even though she knew that Joel's obsession was beyond his control.

"Well, you're not gambling today, and that's brilliant," declared Hannah, wishing she could believe what she said, but realism was too demoralizing for both of them. "You're not drinking either. This is a good day."

"It's always a good day when I'm with you, but I think that knock on the door means our evening is about to be ruined."

"Nathan's OK, and I don't want to lose my job, so please be nice to him. He's an associate producer."

"I hope he doesn't expect me to grovel with too much veneration," muttered Joel.

"Behave," Hannah said urgently, before opening the door.

"What a day!" Nathan was leaning against the wall, his attitude one of bewilderment rather than fatigue. "It feels like several centuries since this morning. Whatever's going to happen next?"

"Meeting my father," said Hannah, uncomfortably conscious of Nathan's bereaved state. "Dad was incredible, and sent Quayle packing the second he got officious." The lavish appreciation was intended to pacify Joel, who glared at Nathan with a frostiness that showed no sign of thawing. When Joel brooded, he could convince himself of anything, and what he saw entering the room was a scheming lecher determined to con Hannah.

Fortunately, Nathan regarded hostility as the norm before he launched into a spiel. He was used to worming his way into the unenthusiastic company of potential film backers, and could even face butlers without flinching. To somebody unfazed by rank, privilege and livery, Joel was no deterrent. "How nice to meet you at last," Nathan declared. "Hannah's told me so much about you."

Hannah had said very little to Nathan about her father, and Joel knew that she would not discuss his shortcomings with anyone except Judith, but he remained unappeased. "Quayle had a lot to say about you," commented Joel. And none of it good, his antagonistic tone implied.

"Our worthy Inspector looked taken aback when I said that I didn't get on with my father, but when somebody's not around much during your childhood, it's a bit difficult to regard him as family. Hannah's lucky to have a Dad who's always been on her side." Nathan sat down next to Joel, apparently considering their friendship firmly established.

"Yes, I'm lucky," agreed Hannah, although she could tell by Joel's frozen expression that Nathan's flattery had failed to make its usual impact.

"And I was lucky to have an alibi," said Nathan. "Quayle must belong to a sickeningly devoted family, because when I told him that, before today, I hadn't been near my father's house in weeks, our keen investigator appeared to consider it an admission of evil intent. Without Hannah, I bet I'd have been arrested."

"You *bet*?" queried a dour Joel.

"Spot on. I bet I'd now be languishing in a police cell."

"You seem very fond of betting," Joel remarked as austerely as a chapel elder, and Hannah had to fight back a smile.

"What did Quayle say?" she asked Nathan.

"Not much; it was more his attitude. He brought a dolt of a sergeant with him who didn't utter a word, but wrote down all I told them like every syllable had vital significance. And I bet nothing I said made sense, because I was still shell-shocked. What did you get asked, Hannah?"

"Just to confirm that you were here last night."

"And thank goodness you can. I couldn't take another bout of Quayle or the silent sergeant. Luckily, I left my car parked near a CCTV camera yesterday evening, so checking the footage should keep them busy. You see, Tiffany was right when she thought something awful had happened. It seems that my father got himself stabbed, so I guess he chased someone out of the house. He had a foul temper, and it could make him act stupidly."

"That's what Tiffany said too."

"We're united? That's a first." Nathan attempted a laugh, but it turned into a shiver instead.

"I'm sorry about your father." Any words would be inadequate, but Hannah felt compelled to say something.

"I hardly knew him," said Nathan, with a helpless shrug. "He was practically a stranger."

"You aren't close to your family then?" As the only member of the Thirlbeck family left to Joel was Hannah, and he had avoided the Chisholms throughout his marriage, he need not have been quite so disapproving.

"We'll be a close family when my father's third and final wife gets back from Switzerland. There's nothing like shared hatred to make people bond, and if Flora anticipates us bowing obsequiously before her, now that she's a rich widow, I'm afraid somebody's in for sad disillusionment."

It sounded very Chisholm-like to Hannah, because a family get-together was akin to tackling a court martial. If Joel's gambling had ever become known to her relatives, Judith would have emigrated, but she could keep a secret, and so could Hannah. "You're making me feel luckier and luckier, Nathan."

"You are; you definitely are." The day's events abruptly caught up with him, and Nathan blinked sleepily as he smothered a yawn.

"You shouldn't be driving when you're worn out," said Hannah.

"I'm OK," declared Nathan. "But I'd better leave now, or I'll fall asleep on your sofa again. This has been the longest day of my life."

"I'm so sorry," Hannah mumbled, trusting that Joel would not realize she was actually apologizing for him.

"It's all right." Nathan lurched to his feet, and smothered yet another yawn. "I'm in the midst of a vile dream and can't wake up, but I'll muddle through."

Hannah opened the door for him, and tried to think of comforting words that might help, but there were none. It would have been easier had Nathan mourned a loving parent, because all the clichéd phrases were even more trite when the father had chosen to be a distant figure.

Nathan could not grieve for an outsider who only belonged on the fringes of his life, and it was hypocritical to pretend otherwise.

"Thanks for everything," said Nathan, his gratitude taking Hannah by surprise.

"But I haven't done anything."

"You got me through today, and you'll never know how much I appreciate that."

The friendliness in his voice soothed Hannah's fear that Joel might have ended any chance of her being asked out again. Nathan was so confidently attractive, while she was merely half a Chisholm with an embarrassing father, but perhaps none of it mattered. Perhaps the snags and awkwardness would simply fade away. Perhaps she was at the start of the most important relationship of all.

"He's too old for you," decreed Joel, as Hannah shut the door. "Forty, if he's a day."

"Thirty."

"Only if the smarmy creep's altered his birth certificate."

"That sounds perilously close to something a Chisholm would say," warned Hannah.

"It just goes to prove how grotesque Nathan Wyatt is, changing me into a Chisholm. And the fool's left his wallet behind. Hardly the most awe-inspiring action of a mighty associate producer."

"His wallet?" demanded Hannah in alarm.

"Well. I presume it's his," said Joel, pointing disdainfully at a corner of the sofa. "It's certainly not mine. I've got better taste."

"I'll dash after him." Hannah grabbed her shoulder bag and snatched up the wallet, fear making her legs weak as she hurried out of the flat and down the stairs. Joel had been known to steal. In the past, Judith could never leave her purse unattended, and even Hannah's childhood piggy bank was kept under lock and key. If Joel had done a little pick-pocketing, if credit cards or money were missing from Nathan's wallet, Hannah felt that her world would end. She wanted to throw the wallet away, deny all knowledge of it when questions were asked, but that would make her as guilty as Joel. Nathan had to be faced, so did Joel, and only Hannah could sort out the mess.

Nathan was opening his car door, and looked around in surprise as Hannah rushed out into the darkness of the street, but then he smiled to see his wallet held aloft. "I'll forget my name next."

"Check it," said Hannah, as Nathan went to return the wallet to his coat pocket. "There might be something missing —hidden under the sofa or behind a cushion or somewhere."

Nathan turned toward the glow of a streetlamp, flipped his wallet open, and skimmed through the contents, while Hannah's heart pounded and lurched. "All present and correct," he reported.

"You're sure?" asked Hannah, not daring to believe him. "Maybe you should check again."

"No need to. Each credit card is a personal friend, and without them, I cease to exist. Thanks a lot."

"Don't mention it." Hannah struggled against tears of sheer relief, and put both hands behind her back so Nathan would not see that she was trembling.

"I won't show my gratitude by impetuously hugging you, because your father might glance out of a window, and I didn't make a pal this evening."

"He's under the impression that every man I meet is a boozy gambler, with a penchant for deceit, who's out to destroy my life."

"Then I'll get going before he appears armed with a horsewhip. Incidentally, you said Quayle became very officious, and your father got rid of him. What was that about?"

"I don't think the Inspector believed me."

Nathan stared at Hannah, his eyes wide with astonishment. "What's there not to believe? I drank too much and spent the night at your place. Why would anybody think you were lying?"

"It's the sofa bit that Quayle couldn't accept. He assumed we'd had a night of unbridled passion. My father promptly decided I'd been insulted, and got into a huff."

"That says more about Quayle's lascivious imagination than anything else," declared Nathan, smiling. "Take no notice."

"I didn't."

"Good. I'll phone tomorrow, if I don't see you."

Nathan's words would normally have thrilled Hannah, but Joel got in the way. The street was cold and windy, yet Hannah lingered there even after Nathan's car had vanished from sight. Joel would know why she had snatched up her shoulder bag, as well as the wallet, before leaving him alone in the flat. He would realize that she was unable to trust him with her purse, but neither of them would say anything, and so she could not tell him how thankful she felt that he seemed to have resisted temptation. It was Joel's success, although to congratulate him would be tactless, and perhaps incorrect, because there remained a chance he might have appropriated a banknote or two that Nathan had not missed. Joel regarded theft as a loan, to be paid back in full when the right horse came in first, the winning card was in his hand, or the roulette wheel obliged. Years of losing had simply made Joel certain that, mathematically, logically, he was more likely to win the next time, and even when he managed to fight his obsession for a week or a month, it still lurked in the background, waiting to overwhelm him yet again.

Rain began to mingle with the wind, making the pavement shine under the streetlamps, and there was no excuse for Hannah to stay out in the cold. Nathan's suggestion that Joel might be stationed at a window was enough of a possibility to send her indoors, because if her father had found the willpower to leave a neglected wallet untouched, any inkling that Hannah thought he could have stolen from Nathan might drive Joel into another alcoholic haze when his unemployment benefit was paid. He had to see a cheerfully trusting daughter to carry on the pretence that they had a carefree relationship, and Hannah forced a smile as she went back into the flat.

"Mission accomplished. Nathan's reunited with his wallet, and he told me to thank you for spotting it."

"He needs a minder following him about," commented Joel, unmoved by the fabricated gratitude. "And he actually had the nerve to check inside his wallet, as though he imagined you might have helped yourself to a handful of fifty pound notes. He's got a shifty mind."

"Naturally. He's a financier by trade. But you don't have to knock him, because I've already gathered that the charm of his character entirely passed you by."

"Don't blame me for being a father. It's my job to be suspicious of any twerp who so much as glances at you," said Joel, with a laugh that made him more relaxed than he had been since his arrival, and Hannah tried not to wonder whether the contents of Nathan's wallet were less intact than was believed. "Why did you stay out in the street after the dolt left? You must be half frozen. I knocked on the window, but couldn't make you hear. Did he upset you?"

"Of course not. I was looking at the way the pavements shone, and thought it'd be a good opening shot for a film. A quiet road on a wet night, monochrome except for the orange glow of streetlamps, the sound of Big Ben chiming in the distance, then suddenly —"

"Then suddenly what?"

"I don't know yet," said Hannah, pleased with the potential on offer. "Perhaps a ghost appears or a car explodes or someone dashes out of a house. I'll decide later. After all, there's plenty of time. I'm but a humble production assistant."

"You'll be more than that one day," Joel predicted with supreme confidence. "I have an instinct that tells me you'll succeed."

If the instinct chanced to be the same one that compelled Joel to pick horses that ambled rather than raced, his daughter's subsequent career did not look promising, but such unwavering faith never failed to encourage her. Joel could see the person Hannah wanted to become, and he was able to imagine those insubstantial future films with even greater clarity than she did. He gambled with money; she was prepared to gamble with her whole future.

3

The Farrenton Film Company was at the final editing stages of a television commissioned drama/documentary rather loosely based on the lives of Shelley and Byron, with considerably heavier emphasis on tangled love affairs than poetry. Hampshire, punching above its weight, represented the continent of Europe, while stock film footage of celebrated landmarks hopefully added a little verisimilitude to the saga of sex and drugs that lacked only a spot of rock 'n' roll. Some months earlier, at the end of the first production that Hannah worked on, she had felt a surge of accomplishment to be associated, even in a meagre capacity, with a film, but completion of the later project left her with a sense of loss, and a fear that another opportunity to be part of the process might never occur. The Farrenton track record was adequate, more muddling through than soaring on the uplift of smash hits, but to make bread and butter money in the precariousness of the British film industry was an achievement in itself.

Romney Farrenton had been an actor who discovered that the theatre was somewhat indifferent to his talents, but he managed to eke out a minor career in low-budget pictures. However, the uninspired scripts and on-autopilot attitude of the directors annoyed Romney, and resulted in an ambition to make his own films: films that would rival the intensity of the French cinema, yet capture Hollywood magic at its best. Romney's idea had not worked out exactly as foreseen, but his reality failed to prevent Hannah from making her own plan along similarly high-flown lines. Meanwhile, before that glorious time when backers wrote out million pound cheques, Hannah had a key to the half-glazed door that opened onto the premises of the Farrenton Film Company.

Officially production assistant, Hannah doubled as receptionist, and her desk barred the way to Romney

Farrenton's inner sanctum, as if he expected her to guard him from a horde of visitors, even though the postman was usually the only caller. The Company occupied the ground floor of a tall, thin building nearer Soho than Piccadilly, and no matter how often its walls were decorated, the place retained the traditional dinginess associated with small-time show business. However, there was no need for Romney to acquire a more expensive address, despite Nathan's continual urging for a better background, because only prospective investors had to be impressed, and they were entertained in hotels and restaurants. Everybody else was a Company insider who knew the truth.

"Anything interesting in the mail?" It was Romney Farrenton's first question every morning, delivered in the resonant stage voice that would have projected itself to the back row of any theatre had he been given his chance. Romney was dark-haired, tall and portly, but even in middle age, he hung onto traces of the handsome juvenile lead he had once aspired to be, and that frustrated dramatic impulse coloured all Romney did, making him appear to act the rôle of film producer rather than be one in reality.

"There's a script," said Hannah, "but I've only had time to glance at it."

"And that glance tells you —?"

"There seems to be a lot of action, mainly on board a navy ship during the Napoleonic Wars."

"Galleons! Costumes!" exclaimed Romney, with a doom-laden theatrical groan. "Expense, and more expense."

"It gets worse. There's an explosion in the opening scene, and five sailors are blasted overboard, while the rest fight a fire."

"Stuntmen, divers on standby in lifeboats, health and safety, firemen —!" Romney shuddered at the prospect, overdoing the horror. "We'd have spent the entire budget in the first few minutes, with still another hour or so to shoot. And being the Napoleonic wars, I suppose there's a sea battle at some point, with ships sinking all over the place, and half the cast floundering around in water. Why can't I ever find an exciting script, full of tension and wit, that's set in a modern hotel room throughout?"

"Because it'd be a stage play," said Hannah, "and you'd tell the scriptwriter to add flashbacks to liven it up when he did the screen adaptation."

"Very true," agreed Romney, sighing. "I don't need one-scene scripts; I need bigger budgets. I'll have to give Nathan a pep talk. Has he put in an appearance yet?"

"I don't think you'll see him this week. Something awful happened yesterday." But the journey to Owen Wyatt's house seemed to belong much further in the past than the previous morning. Hannah was back in her real life, with her real problems, many of which centred on Joel. "Nathan's father died."

"A heart attack?" demanded Romney.

"A robbery gone wrong. He was stabbed."

"Dreadful! Dreadful!" But Romney looked more reassured than shocked, and it occurred to Hannah that, as his son had been at school with Nathan, Romney was likely to be a similar age to Owen Wyatt, and news of a heart attack would constitute a reminder of mortality that Romney was glad to avoid. A random killing gave him a reprieve. "Arrange for flowers to be sent to the funeral from the Company. But first, make me some coffee."

Romney hurried into his office, leaving the death of a contemporary firmly outside with Hannah. She switched on the electric kettle, but it was pointless to order flowers when she had no idea where they should be sent, and instead Hannah printed a copy of the standard rejection letter that claimed the submitted script had been closely studied, but unfortunately the cost of a lavish production, necessary to do justice to the screenplay, ruled out the Farrenton Company's involvement. Feeling sympathy for the disappointed writer, whose ambitions probably matched her own, she forged Romney's signature on the letter, then poured out a mug of coffee, and as though its aroma had summoned him, the next generation of the Farrenton Film Company arrived.

Plain, with light-brown hair and a reedy figure, Lionel Farrenton had not inherited his father's imposing appearance. He was overshadowed by Romney in every way, but Lionel seemed content to drift through life with an amiable smile on his face, which certainly made him an agreeable colleague, but one with a complete lack of drive. He would, at some future date, become the head of Farrenton Films, yet the Company might just as well have produced cardboard boxes for all the interest Lionel displayed in its purpose. Being an associate producer was merely a job in the family firm, and his insouciance amazed Hannah, for whom the chance to control an established film company would be most of her daydreams come true. She was at the office early and left late, even when she had little to do, but Lionel strolled in and out, using a sporadic timetable that relied on Hannah to produce much of the work expected of him: a mutually beneficial system, as Hannah welcomed any opportunity to gain more knowledge of film-making. Although unenthusiastic about the job, Lionel got on well with Romney, especially as he obligingly agreed with every word his father said, making Romney believe that he had an astute son rather than an echo. Such passivity could have been a reaction against Romney's thespian temperament, but Hannah suspected that Lionel had simply been born with an easy-going nature.

"Any more coffee around?" asked Lionel. "I've been here since nine o'clock, by the way."

"And then you went out for something," Hannah instructed him, "because your father arrived a few minutes ago."

"Thanks for the warning. Not that he'd care much, as there's nothing for me to do right now." At the thought of his empty schedule, Lionel could not be said to have relaxed, because he was never stressed, but he sat on Hannah's desk and remarked, "It's going to be difficult in a slump, wangling finance for the next Farrenton spectacular, but if anybody can do it, Nathan will."

"His father died yesterday," said Hannah, again feeling that she spoke of a long distant past.

"How awful." Lionel's smile faded, and he looked troubled, obviously imagining the pain his own father's death would cause him. "Poor Nathan."

"I don't think the Wyatt family could be described as a close one," Hannah said, to console Lionel.

"I know, but it's sad, all the same. I feel dreadful now, about being late. I'll go and tell Dad that it's totally my fault because I just turned over when I heard the alarm clock."

"Owning up is doubtless the worthy thing to do, but it won't help Nathan."

"But I'll be able to bask in a glow of nauseating self-righteousness." Lionel picked up two mugs of coffee, and used an elbow to push down the door handle of Romney's office. "This is my chance to pose as a martyr."

Morally superior or not, Lionel had been right in one thing; there was little to do that morning, but Hannah could have happily made work for herself at a desk all day, if the desk belonged to a film company. She tidied files, did email checks, and sorted out the backlog of scripts that had accumulated during busier times. Hannah always had the hope that she might discover a screenplay so intriguing, it would transform the insignificant Farrenton Company into a big player, and result in a grateful Romney eventually giving her an opportunity to direct, but the miracle failed to materialize that day. Even Hannah, with her limited knowledge of film-making, could work out that the cost of production for the scripts she read would be greater than any likely profit. She wrote a few synopses for Romney, but there were too many exotic locations and too many elaborate costumes to please him, and enough characters shinning down precipices, leaping out of moving cars, and vaulting onto runaway horses to chill a Health and Safety heart, as well as sending the production insurance into the stratosphere. Hollywood could get to grips with such extravaganzas, but the Farrenton Film Company had to be more circumspect, despite Nathan's fund-raising skills. All the scripts would probably be returned with thanks, and Hannah was rooting for padded envelopes when the street door opened. She glanced up, and then stared in surprise.

"Yes, I know I'm supposed to be a devastated pulp," said Nathan, "but it's better to be honestly cold-hearted than a fraud. Besides, I was getting bored by myself."

"You'll be just as bored here. Nothing much is happening."

"Romney still hasn't decided on our next effort to storm the big time?" asked Nathan, then added, "Stupid question. I've only missed a few hours this morning, but I feel like it's been several months."

It was exactly how Hannah felt, although she could hardly chime in, whatever Nathan's feelings for his father. Hypocrisy was a strict taskmaster. "Romney's in his office with Lionel. They'll be discussing options now."

"Discussing? Our revered boss hasn't quite grasped the concept of discussion, any more than an autocratic czar of all the Russias could. But before I tackle Romney's overcooked condolences, I want to ask you something." Nathan hesitated, but it was a pause for effect, not apprehension that he might be refused. "I can't cope with the assembled family on my own. Could I entice you with an invite to a funeral? I'll need someone on my side, even more than when I thought I'd have to confront my father."

"Of course I'll go, if you want me to," replied Hannah, attempting to mask reluctance, because it had to be a compliment that he should choose her.

"It's not fair to make you promise when you don't know what an ordeal a gathering of Wyatts can be. You'll never speak to me again afterwards."

"Don't worry. My mother's family provided excellent training. They could teach the Borgias a thing or two." It was surely another compliment that Nathan should talk so freely, and Hannah wanted to feel that they were exchanging confidences, but he clearly had no interest in Chisholms, past or present.

"You're being terrific," declared Nathan, with real gratitude in his voice, unusual in somebody who preferred to sound trite. "I'd never have managed to get through yesterday, if you hadn't been there. That reminds me, I hope the police aren't still bothering you."

"There's no reason for them to. Have they been chasing after you?"

"An amble rather than a chase. That Inspector left a message on my phone about something or other, but I'm not calling back. It'd only make him even more overbearing than he already is. Anyway, I don't want to rehash the weekend yet again. And there's no need to tell me that the man's merely doing his job."

"I wasn't going to, but Quayle's paid to talk to people who don't want to talk to him."

"I suppose so," Nathan admitted grudgingly, "but he shouldn't make it a habit. There's such a thing as restraint."

"What detail does Quayle want to check?"

"Ask him; that's his department, not mine. I expect he's an obsessive-compulsive who has to do all his work over and over again."

"Rather a good trait in a policeman, I'd have thought," commented Hannah, deciding that the situation could be used in a film, with an obsessive-compulsive detective conducting a personal vendetta against Nathan. The reason why Quayle was so bitter hardly mattered; perhaps Owen Wyatt had once cheated him or eloped with the detective's wife, although, in either circumstance,

Quayle might have been more inclined to leniency toward the killer. Easier to have Quayle owing Wyatt a debt of gratitude that made the deluded detective believe a great and good man had been slaughtered by an estranged son. Or there could be an element of national security brought in, with Owen Wyatt a government minister and Quayle the police bodyguard who discovered that secrets were being leaked for cash. Quayle had gone to Wyatt's house to blackmail him, but there was a fight to the death, and the detective managed to get himself put in charge of the murder investigation so that he could control evidence and make sure someone else got the blame. Nathan, the alienated son, was the perfect patsy.

"I'll go and get Romney's commiserations over and done with," said Nathan, mercifully unaware that he now featured as persecuted hero in Hannah's scenario. "It'd help if I had some real work. I think I'll start my own company, invent a film project, and try to raise money, just for something to do."

"Good idea. Much better to run around in useless circles than brood."

"And why should my circling be described as useless?" protested Nathan, pleased to return to his usual glibness. "You ought to have more faith in the magnetic attraction I have for money. Nobody else could have found backers for our disastrous re-make of *The Immortal Hour*. Without me, Romney would be reduced to directing television adverts for toothpaste."

There was some truth in Nathan's claim, because the Farrenton Company certainly had found itself a little better financed after Nathan applied his talents to boosting capital. He enjoyed the challenge of prising open the tight fists of the wealthy, and liked the idea of himself as the most essential person in the production team, without whose labours there was no film. Somebody so conscious of his worth had no need to pretend diffidence, and after the most cursory of knocks on the door, Nathan strolled into Romney's office, knowing that he would be a welcome sight, despite the conventional urge that was going to force Romney to suggest a week or two's holiday in view of the circumstances. Nathan's refusal would be greeted with relief because he was invaluable to the Company, and Hannah, who could easily be replaced at any time, envied him.

****

"I've had a lousy day," announced Joel, the moment Hannah opened the door of her flat. He was reclining on the sofa, and had an exhausted air about him that might have been genuine but was more likely manufactured to get her sympathy. "I went to sign on unemployed, and a twelve-year-old with orange streaks in his hair, understandably protected by a sheet of bullet-proof glass, had the effrontery to ask me if I could read and write."

"Probably because his own literacy skills leave something to be desired," suggested Hannah. "Did you find any interesting jobs?"

"The illiterate, cowering behind his security screen, came up with one vacancy: part-time on check-out at some DIY place. He said an architect ought to know about paint and putting up shelves," reported Joel in disgust. "The half-wit had no idea that architects never see hammer or nail, let alone cans of emulsion."

"I'm sure he's now aware of the gap in his knowledge," said Hannah, glad that haughtiness had taken over from Joel's defeated mood. If he could muster sufficient instinct to fight, there might be less chance of him sinking into a lengthy depression, a depression that Joel would try to relieve with alcohol as soon as he got his hands on some money. "The ignoramus won't mistake an architect for a shelf-stacker again."

"I did rant on a bit," conceded Joel, "and then the idiot had the nerve to say that, if I refused to go to a job interview, I'd be penalized. Penalized! It's national insurance, not national charity, I informed him. No adolescent, who looks as though a tin of spaghetti exploded on his head, informs me that I'm only good enough to sit at a till in a warehouse."

"It doesn't matter if they won't fork out." Hannah knew all too well that any money going into Joel's bank account shot straight out again, and not in the direction of rent or food, because the winnings that he so confidently expected would take care of minor details. Should Joel decide to scorn the benefit system, it would actually be a bonus, as only complete lack of funds had the power to control him, and Hannah coped better with privation than his drinking. "You don't need money when you're staying with me; you know that."

"Of course I'll pay my way." Joel undoubtedly believed what he said, and Hannah smiled in a show of appreciation, but discounted the words. He had always been generous, indeed munificent, with his promises. "The bust-up with Glenda has really got me thinking. It's all change from now on, I'm determined."

"That's good." Hannah's response was automatic, a reply she had often made before, and would probably say again after the next crisis convinced Joel that he was a reformed man. Perhaps, one day, his resolve would last, but Hannah had very little optimism. "When did you start to gamble?" she asked, hoping to discover a reason for Joel's behaviour that would help her to deal with it.

"It was my father's fault, in a way. He used to get me to pick horses for him. Not that he was much of a gambler. The National, the Derby and a few races on television during wet Saturday afternoons were plenty for him. But it was fun, picking a name out of the list of runners, and then watching the nag win." Joel smiled at the memory, before adding ruefully, "And my horses always won in those days. I'd get a hunch the moment I read a certain name, and knew that'd be the one. It never failed. I couldn't figure out why my father stuck with a job that bored him, when it'd be so easy to make loads of money through betting."

"When did your horses begin to lose?"

"When I was desperate for them to win. There'd been no pressure as a child, but the minute I really needed some cash, my hunches went haywire. The absolute certainty had gone, yet the chance of going from poverty to riches in a split-second was still there, as well as the chance to forget all my problems for a few incredible moments." Joel laughed at the sudden enthusiasm in his voice, and then sighed. "I hope you don't understand what I'm on about."

"Can't you just watch the telly, and pick winners for fun like in the old days?" asked Hannah. "Does money have to be involved?"

"Good. You don't understand. I'd hate to think I'd passed on some hereditary tendencies toward stupid and self-destructive behaviour. I'm afraid money has to be involved, because there's nothing to compare with the excitement of risking everything. That instant before the dice fall or when the horses go into the final length — you've no idea what it's like. The rush of adrenalin, or whatever it is —" Joel laughed again, and shook his head. "No, I'm not explaining any more. There might be something infectious you could catch."

"I think I'm probably immune."

"Yes. The only thing I've done right in my life is produce a sane and sensible daughter."

A sane and sensible daughter who wanted to spend millions of pounds directing a film. If she ever got the opportunity, Hannah could throw away more money in one go, than Joel would squander over years. Such ambition was neither sane nor sensible.

"But from now on, it's all going to be very different," declared Joel, his instinct as out of touch with reality as when he awaited fortune's blessing. "I've been a fool most of my life, and it's time I got a grip. Other people don't make a mess of everything, and there's no reason why I should, especially as I'm not in denial about my problems, and that's meant to be the first step in sorting yourself out. It's just a matter of willpower."

Hannah tried to look equally positive, because if Joel guessed that she no longer believed his promises, gloom would envelop him with the cold dankness of a sea mist. Hannah knew that he was incapable of helping himself, and she had no idea what could stop her father repeating the behaviour he despised. She was able to ensure that Joel had food and shelter, but the rest of his existence remained a worry with no apparent solution. Joel deserved better than to be ruled by compulsions that might not be his fault, but the strength to resist had to come from him. Nobody else could alter a thing.

"I'll get back on my feet somehow. Glenda isn't going to wreck my prospects. I'm absolutely determined that this time it'll be different." The telephone rang as Joel spoke, and he snatched up the receiver, entirely forgetting his customary wariness of unknown callers. Then he made a face at Hannah, and said, less buoyantly, "Oh, hello, Judy."

Hannah had been hoping to keep Joel's latest upheaval a secret from her mother for as long as possible, aware what the reaction would be, and she took the phone from Joel with reluctance. "Hello, Mum. How are things?"

"Why is he at your place?" Judith's voice was filled with exasperation, and she had no need to wait for a reply. "He's sponging off you again, isn't he? I suppose the latest airhead kicked him out, and that means he's lost another job, so his only answer is to freeload, as always. Get rid of him."

"I'm glad everything's OK," said Hannah, although Joel would probably deduce what the other side of the conversation actually was. "How's Aunt Pam? Any better?"

"Boot him out into the street," ordered Judith. "Boot him out at once. If you don't, he'll leech until you're drained dry. You know what he's like. You must know by now."

"'I'm doing OK at work," Hannah continued valiantly. "How's your job?"

"Why do you listen to his whining self-pity? He's no victim, and he doesn't care about anybody. The only things that interest Joel are gambling and boozing."

"The weather's OK here too — well, for February."

"He cons you every time." The belligerence was suddenly gone as Judith accepted defeat, and tears sounded horribly close. "I know that lost and alone image he projects, but it's simply a façade to get his own way. You can't protect him; nobody can. He's going to break your heart."

It was probably true, but to Hannah's relief, the entry phone began to buzz, and she seized the chance to escape. "I'll have to ring you back. There's someone at the door."

"No doubt a loan shark chasing your father," declared Judith, experience adding distinct sourness to her words. "He's been sacked, hasn't he?"

"The slump's affecting everyone," said Hannah, a little too defensively. "Romney Farrenton hasn't got a new project up and running yet, so it's a case of fingers crossed about my own job."

"Joel doesn't need a slump to find himself out of work," retorted Judith. "He only has to turn up drunk, or not turn up at all, and employers get the picture."

An undeniable fact, but one that Hannah tried to ignore as she looked across the room at her father, who was replacing the entry phone with an impatient shove. "That detective nuisance has turned up again," Joel reported indignantly. "He says he's got to check a detail, and check it this very minute, for some obscure reason."

"Sorry, Mum, but I really do have to ring off," said Hannah, astonished to have cause to be grateful to Quayle. "The police are here to talk to me."

"What's Joel done now? Another spot of embezzlement? It'd solve everything if your father got locked up, though he'd find a means of gambling in solitary confinement." Judith was resigned, not sarcastic, and Hannah wanted to protest, but then remembered her own assumption about Joel and the contents of Nathan's wallet. Her father was difficult to defend.

"A detective's here because of a friend of mine — well, not him exactly — oh, it's too complicated, and there's no time. I'll call back and explain later."

"And it better be a good explanation if the police are hammering on the door, seconds after Joel arrives. Don't believe a syllable your father utters. He deserves what happens to him, and has got to sort his own life out. You have to let him go."

Judith's advice was sound, but Hannah could not imagine herself ever developing the mental strength required to condemn Joel to exile, no matter how it might benefit him later on. He would remain her problem because the danger of Joel sinking without trace was too great to risk.

"Judith's on the warpath," commented Joel, as Hannah put the telephone down. "I suppose it didn't even occur to your mother that I might just have dropped in for a chat. She's got a suspicious mind."

"Not without reason," said Hannah, forcing a smile. "Why does Inspector Quayle want to see me again? What's the detail that's so vital?"

"Who knows? Who cares? He must have assumed I wouldn't be here, but I am, and so he's not going to browbeat you. I won't allow it." Joel sounded proud to be the scourge of the police, liking the idea of himself as strong and undaunted. He could cope with the exceptional circumstance; it was everyday life that defeated him. "I suppose Judith jumped to the conclusion that Quayle's on his way up the stairs to arrest me."

"Of course she didn't," declared Hannah, laughing as though Joel had made a silly joke, but she was thankful that Quayle's knock on the door immediately distracted her father.

"I'll let him in," stated Joel, determined that his intimidating presence should he felt from the start.

Still swathed in his dark overcoat, Quayle seemed unaware that he had been foiled, and sat down on Joel's vacated sofa without an invitation to do so, apparently regarding the acquaintanceship with the Thirlbecks now advanced enough for minor civilities to be ignored. The expression on his round, plain face was more relaxed than before, and although Hannah had difficulty in believing that a man of Quayle's age could be uncomfortable with strangers, it was a possible explanation for the ease of manner that even Joel's bellicose attitude failed to disturb.

"My daughter's told you everything you need to know," declared Joel, closing the door with an unnecessary slam. "Hannah doesn't have a word to add."

"Yes, but I want to get a few details clear in my mind." Quayle spoke apologetically, as if he were at fault because of an inability to grasp simple statements first time round, and Joel smirked in victory.

"Then you should have asked Hannah more questions yesterday, instead of bothering her again."

"I had to check something, before I could do a recheck with Hannah, and make sure I'm on the right track." The implication was that Quayle could only trust Hannah's version of events, and a mollified Joel smiled again.

"You're checking Nathan Wyatt's story, of course."

"I couldn't possibly comment," said Quayle, but his bland tone was the confirmation Joel sought, and Hannah suspected that a deliberate attempt had been made to appease her father. Certainly Quayle seemed to be managing Joel with more shrewdness than on the previous visit.

"I don't trust men like Wyatt who work with other people's money," stated Joel, "especially when they hide behind a company name, and control the accounts. You never know what's being siphoned off."

"The rich don't get rich by letting anyone siphon so much as a penny off them," said Hannah.

"But when they're up against someone entirely without scruples, it's different," argued Joel.

"My father only met Nathan once, and that was just for a few minutes," Hannah told Quayle. "It's amazing how astutely Dad spotted a warped Machiavellian nature."

"OK, I know nothing about Wyatt except that he spent a night in my daughter's flat," admitted Joel. "But I consider it reason enough to hate him."

"As Nathan wouldn't drive home after drinking a bit too much wine, surely that indicates a responsible and law-abiding character," said Hannah.

"How drunk was he?" asked Quayle.

"Hardly at all. He was sick in the night, but fine the next morning: no hangover."

"And how much did you drink?"

"My daughter's never been drunk in her life," protested Joel.

"No one said I was," Hannah pointed out.

"Wine makes me sleep," commented Quayle, as though he were throwing a chance remark into casual conversation. "Does it have that effect on you?"

"I don't drink enough to know, but I generally go out like a light anyway."

"A clear conscience," said Joel, for Quayle's instruction.

"So you slept soundly that night, apart from when Nathan woke you up?"

"Yes." Hannah realized that Quayle wanted her to say she was unable to guarantee Nathan's presence in the flat throughout Saturday night, and as Nathan had abandoned the sofa, been sick in the bathroom, and still had to wake Hannah to get her attention, Quayle might have a point.

"You're certain you didn't look at a clock, when Wyatt said it was two in the morning?" continued Quayle.

"Why would I bother? Nathan had told me the time."

"He wanted to establish an alibi," declared Joel. "It's quite obvious."

"Not to me," said Hannah.

"Nor to me," added Quayle. "But you can't be sure that Wyatt was here all night, can you?"

"I could have woken at any time and realized he'd left the flat, assuming Nathan did go out."

"He'll have wrapped a bolster in the blankets to make you think he was still on the sofa," decided Joel.

"But Nathan didn't chance to be lugging a bolster around with him that night," said Hannah.

"He used the cushions then, or perhaps he drugged your wine to make you sleep," suggested Joel, not to be vanquished.

"A Nathan that diabolically cunning could get away with anything," Hannah declared, smiling.

"OK, perhaps I've watched too many movies," conceded Joel, "but Wyatt went out of his way to set up an alibi for the night, yet he could have been roaming around half the country for all you know."

"Do you always leave your keys in the lock?" asked Quayle, studying the door.

"It means I know where they are," replied Hannah, sensing criticism.

"That's how Wyatt was able to come and go so easily," said Joel. "He doped your wine, and watched to see where you left the keys. Then the moment you slipped into unconsciousness, he was off."

"Wouldn't I have noticed the after-effects of being drugged to a stupor? Anyhow, I didn't actually have a drink in the pub. Nathan did get me a glass of wine, but if he bunged anything in it, he must have been astonished at my immunity, because I only pretended to sip at it. You know I've got stupidly childish tastes, Dad, and prefer coca-cola to the greatest French vintage." In front of Joel, Hannah could not admit that the mere smell of drink repulsed her, as he would guess that his problem with alcohol was the reason for the revulsion.

"Whatever Wyatt did or didn't do, I'd like to know why he was so determined to place himself in here at 2am precisely," said Joel. "Was that when his father died?"

"The exact time isn't established yet," replied Quayle.

"Nathan only mentioned 2am in passing," said Hannah, "and I could have forgotten. He didn't remind me in the morning."

"And it felt like 2am; that's what you told me," said Quayle. "What did you mean?"

Hannah was silent for a moment, trying to recall a trivial incident that might have escaped her memory but for subsequent events. "I was in the middle of a dream, and couldn't work out what was real. When the alarm clock goes off in the morning, I'm awake straight away, and usually know that I'm awake."

"Usually, but not always?"

"Not always, although I don't go back to sleep again, and I must have that night, because the next thing I knew, it was seven o'clock."

"Why was he sick?" asked Quayle.

"Nathan said he wasn't used to drinking that much."

"But he'd only had a few glasses of wine."

"I guess that's a lot for him."

"The paragon of all the virtues," muttered Joel.

****

"Wyatt's plainly the chief suspect," Joel declared, a hint of triumph in his voice. Quayle had gone, but left Nathan behind as the inevitable topic of conversation.

"A bit premature to gloat over Nathan's downfall," said Hannah.

"I'm not gloating," protested Joel.

"Yes, you are."

"Well, perhaps just a little," conceded Joel. "But you have to admit I've been proved right about him. I can recognize another gambler when I see one. It's a kind of sixth sense."

"Nathan doesn't gamble."

"How do you know?"

"I've never heard him mention horses or visiting a casino or anything like that, and he walked right past the fruit machine in the pub without a second glance."

"So do I, when I want to impress somebody," argued Joel. "Wyatt's not going to let you suspect that he's got a problem."

"Nathan hasn't tried to impress me," said Hannah, pleased with her father's unshakeable belief that his daughter was constantly pursued by men. "You're thinking of your own strategy for targeting a female. Nathan doesn't pretend."

"Nor do I. You know that I told Glenda all about my problems when the relationship got serious, exactly as I'd told Melanie. And Celia too. And Fern as well. Nobody can say I'm not straightforward." Joel looked proud, convinced that candour was the only thing required of him. It was up to the other person to do any adapting necessary. Joel had done his bit.

"Nathan doesn't pretend because there's nothing for him to pretend about. He was quite happy to tell me that he didn't get on with his father, when there wasn't the slightest call for him to say a word."

"Then there wasn't the slightest call for him to burble on, maligning his poor dead father. You've had a lucky escape."

"There's no need to escape when you're not trapped, and Nathan didn't know that his father was going to die so soon," said Hannah, but Joel was too captivated by his depiction of Nathan as scheming deceiver to listen to reason.

"At any rate, Quayle's seen right through him." Joel's opinion of people could change with the fickleness of a breeze, and the formerly despised Inspector was now a colleague who had done a brilliant piece of detection. "Wait until Wyatt discovers that he's no longer got a convenient alibi for 2am."

"Nathan won't care. If there's one thing he doesn't do, it's worry."

"Quayle's going to make him worry," predicted Joel, relishing the prospect.

Hannah might have been tempted to argue, but the telephone rang, and she and her father were suddenly allies again.

"Judith," declared Joel.

"I know," Hannah said apprehensively.

4

If Hannah had been able to manufacture an excuse, she might have used it to avoid Owen Wyatt's funeral, even though the result would be to let Nathan down. However, Romney decided that she was to represent the Farrenton Company at the service, and as Romney could hold the key that opened a door leading to her dream future, his wishes were commands. Therefore, on the suitably dark and bleak day of the funeral, Hannah searched her wardrobe for the type of sombre clothing that would be restrained, and yet not make her look like she planned to hijack the mourning for a man she had never met.

"You're being used," declared Joel, officially on a job hunt, but in reality stretched out on the sofa while he watched an old movie on television. "You're the patsy."

"I know, but Romney told me to represent him," said Hannah, deliberately misunderstanding. "And I don't blame Romney in the least. I'd delegate someone else, given half a chance, but even Lionel isn't easy-going enough to get lumbered with this duty."

"It's actually Nathan Wyatt who wants you on parade. Why?"

"I can't imagine. Of course, it's utterly unthinkable that he might value my support at a difficult time in his life."

"He wants your support all right." Joel made the motive sound sinister, and only to be expected from somebody with the most evil of intentions. "He wants you to be convinced that he's above-board, so that you can sway Quayle's opinion."

"I haven't got the power to influence a policeman. Forget Quayle. Is this jacket OK? And, more importantly, what am I going to do about my hair?"

"What's wrong with it?"

"It just isn't funereal."

"No reason why it should be."

"I suppose not." But Hannah made another unsuccessful attempt to subdue the thick brown mass.

"Leave it," said Joel. "You might be attending the service under duress, but that's no reason to bully your hair. Besides, it's Chisholm hair, and so there isn't a force on earth strong enough to quell it."

"Yes, sometimes you have to admit defeat," Hannah acknowledged. "No one will be looking at me, anyway. I'm simply an extra in the background."

"Then why bother putting in an appearance? Farrenton's not going to know you weren't there."

But Nathan would. Temptation had to be crushed, and duty done. "It's no big deal. I'll be OK."

Before Hannah finished speaking, the telephone rang, as it had rung at frequent intervals since Judith discovered that the wastrel ex-husband was living at her daughter's expense. "I'm not here," Joel announced.

"Coward," said Hannah.

"Absolutely craven when Judith's in belligerent mood. Tell her I'm out seeking gainful employment. She can't prove otherwise."

"Unless she's phoning from the street below."

"In that case, I've every intention of barricading the front door."

"Do you really think a mere barricade could repel Mum?" Hannah picked up the telephone receiver and, as expected, heard her mother's voice.

"I want a word with that layabout."

"Dad isn't here," lied Hannah, with the fluency of long practice. "He's at a job interview, and I've got to represent Romney at a funeral today, so I'm half-way out the door."

"Then why can I hear your television?"

"Because I've been watching *His Girl Friday* to try and cheer myself up."

"I know your father's there." Judith gave a sigh, more weary than cross. The situation had occurred before, and she knew that it would occur again. "Put Joel on the phone. There's something I want to say to him."

"He's out; I told you. And I have to leave this minute."

"You're always on his side. It doesn't seem to matter how often he lets you down. I sometimes think he's got hypnotic powers." Judith attempted a laugh, but it turned into another sigh. "Of course, I was the nagging parent and Joel was the fun parent. I couldn't compete. I can't compete."

"It's not like that at all." But Hannah knew Judith was right. A Chisholm mother had lectured on working hard at school and aiming for a secure job with pension attached, while a gambler father taught Hannah that a spot of good luck would solve everything.

"You've got to listen to me this time," urged Judith, "or he'll sponge off you forever."

"I have to go," said Hannah. "I'll call you back later."

"But you never do," Judith pointed out.

****

"This is all so phoney," Nathan muttered to Hannah, although the service at the crematorium was functional rather than ornate, minus flowers, eulogies, solemn music and any excesses of grief; a suitably business-like occasion for the no-nonsense type of man that Hannah imagined Owen Wyatt to have been.

Nathan had distanced himself from the others in the room by ushering Hannah to the chairs nearest the door, even though a dozen empty rows separated them from the platform, where an unadorned coffin awaited its final journey. A school assembly hall at the start of a new term could not have shone more pristinely, or smelt more cloyingly of polish, or made Hannah feel more apprehensive. Measles had caused her to miss the first few weeks of official education, at the age of five, and afterwards Hannah felt that the other children belonged to the school and understood its rules in a way forever denied her. It was a feeling that had accompanied Hannah into adult life, but never more so than in the sickeningly over-perfumed room.

Tiffany was in the first row, next to a slightly younger girl, whose fair hair and muted clothes made Hannah assume that she was looking at Tiffany's sister, and the rake-thin, dyed-blonde in deepest black, a haggard version of the two girls, had to be their mother. Further down the row, sitting by herself, was a brunette, presumably the third wife, Flora. She appeared to be only a few years older than Hannah, but there any resemblance ceased with humbling abruptness, because Flora was beautiful, with a face and figure that belonged in a Hollywood film rather than the everyday world. According to Nathan, Flora had wrenched a wedding ring out of Owen Wyatt by unadulterated guile, but Hannah could understand how easily a man might be ensnared. Flora need not work to be admired; she simply had to exist. Certainly, the moment the unceremonious ceremonials ended, the dark-suited collection of men in the second row took no notice of anyone else, and gravitated to her side.

"A handful of business acquaintances, and a family who prefer never to meet," commented Nathan, slumping back in his chair as the tension in the room began to slacken. "It's not much to show for having lived. I suppose I ought to feel some regret that there wasn't the slightest hint of father-son bonding, but I'm still too angry at the way he treated my mother to think of anything else, even now."

"Better to be honest than pretend," said Hannah, but she was uncomfortable with Nathan's bluntness, so close to the Chisholm determination to point out other people's faults while ignoring their own. Hannah felt more at home in Joel's fantasy world.

"That raddled blonde is the second wife, Candace. Simple and sweet Candace, more gushing than a fountain, latched onto a wealthy man after realizing that work wasn't for her. Much easier to replace the woman who'd married my father when he had nothing, and stuck with him during the difficult times." Nathan made an attempt to sound wryly jocular, but his resentment was very real and very bitter. "However, I'm pleased to report that dear Dad got his comeuppance. A year of Candace's cackling laugh, steam-whistle shriek, and bleating voice was enough to send him into the arms of a string of gold-diggers, although none dug quite as deeply as Candace did at the divorce. Two pregnancies might have been disastrous for her figure, yet Candace spared no effort to guarantee that she'd always have some money in her sticky-fingered clutches. But perhaps you think I sound a trifle cynical?"

"No more than I do when I'm on the subject of my father's bimbo girlfriends," replied Hannah, glad to be distracted from the memory of a coffin's slow disappearance into a furnace. "I suppose the brunette's Flora. She's very good-looking."

"Flora! Now I can really get eloquent," said Nathan. "But I see by your face that you don't approve of me wittering on like this, right after a funeral, and yet you're the one who told me it was better to be honest than pretend."

"I'm a hypocrite," admitted Hannah. "Anyway, you're only talking to stop yourself thinking, aren't you?"

"How right you are. You'll never know how right you are." Nathan stood up and hurried from the room, suddenly as eager as Hannah to seek daylight and fresh air again. She followed him, even though it seemed rather abrupt to turn her back on the others without the slightest acknowledgement of their presence. However, Tiffany seized the chance to make her own escape, catching up with Nathan and Hannah in the car park.

"Gruesomely bland, wasn't it? Flora maintained that Dad wouldn't want a fuss made. She knew him even less than we did." There was anger in Tiffany's voice, perhaps a method of avoiding condolences that she had no wish to hear.

"It wouldn't have been Flora's decision what happened today, if Dad had been able to hang around long enough to divorce her. His death was very conveniently timed for the third Mrs Wyatt," said Nathan, in control of himself again after his momentary weakness inside the crematorium.

Tiffany tried to smile at Hannah. "You must think we're horrible."

"That's because we are horrible," declared Nathan. "There's no arguing with genetics. Not that Hannah will understand. Her father's normal, and he likes his daughter."

"I'm lucky," said Hannah, astonished that anyone could describe Joel as normal, although the Chisholm in her was pleased with a successful façade. "My parents did get a divorce, but it was all very civilized."

"That's why Hannah turned out level-headed, while we're foul-tempered miseries." The cold wind circulating the car park had revived Nathan, and he began to speak briskly once more. "Come on, Hannah; let's get going. The further away from this place I am, the better I'll feel."

"You've got to come to the pub with us," protested Tiffany. "You have to be there, Nathan, if only to keep Mum from punching Flora."

"Why would I want to stop that delightful occurrence? And what pub are you talking about, anyway?"

"Flora's decreed that Dad would choose a pub as the perfect aftermath to his funeral." The anger returned, and Tiffany struggled to keep back the tears suddenly choking her voice. "When did Dad ever go inside a pub?"

"He might have frequented them on a daily basis for all I know." Nathan shrugged, clearly uncomfortable with Tiffany's vehemence, and he tried to move back to his habitual smoothness. "What does it matter?"

"It just does," stated Tiffany. "Besides, I remember Dad once telling Mum that he hated bar bores droning on with their half-baked political opinions."

"That might have been because the bar bores wouldn't let him drone on about his own half-baked opinions," suggested Nathan. "Why worry? After today, you won't have to see Flora again. It's over."

"Yes, it's over." The idea brought no comfort to Tiffany. She needed to be angry with someone, possibly her father, and the third wife was a good substitute. "You can't desert us now. You've got to put Flora down with one of your snide remarks. That grieving widow pose is merely for show."

"Flora's entire life is merely for show," said Nathan. "Hannah, could you face another half-hour of family hatred?"

"No problem." But Hannah's words were an attempt to encourage herself. She wanted to leave the taint of bereavement far behind, as though staying close to its presence with people already infected would somehow contaminate her own life. Commonsense informed Hannah that death was not a disease that might be passed onto Joel, yet instinct urged her to take flight, because if somebody else's father had died unexpectedly, it followed that Joel could as well. He was a liar and a thief, but also the only person in the world who believed that Hannah would achieve all her goals. She was as dependent on Joel as he was on her.

****

Nathan's unwillingness to remain in the vicinity of the crematorium meant that Tiffany was left to wait for her mother and sister, while Nathan drove Hannah through suburban streets as if chased by memories that could be outrun. He was clearly more affected by the service than he had anticipated, and Hannah, so often trapped between her conflicting emotions about Joel, imagined that she could guess something of what he felt.

As Nathan parked his car outside the pub, he demanded, "Why do we all collude in these empty rituals?"

"Because they're rituals, I suppose, and it's easier to go along with them than blaze an original trail," replied Hannah, uncertain whether Nathan expected or wanted an answer.

"I don't care what anybody thinks of me, and yet I'm here. Why?"

"Because Tiffany asked, and you didn't let her down."

"How very fraternal of me," Nathan said gloomily, getting out of the car.

The pub appeared to have been decorated around the word *quaint*, with false beams on its brick exterior and an abundance of empty casks that presumably doubled as flower tubs in more clement months. Inside, additional fake beams stretched across the ceiling, with replica carriage lanterns and pewter tankards hanging perilously near head-level. A plethora of horse brasses and rosettes straggled down the walls to wooden benches, while flecks of gold paint on the bare floor presumably symbolized the sawdust considered too messy to be there in reality.

"Flora chose well," commented Nathan. "This is the ideal venue."

"Is it?" queried Hannah in surprise. "I'd have said bogus ale-house that even a Hollywood recreation of Merrie England would spurn."

"Exactly. It's phoney enough to match everything else about today, and precisely the sort of place that my father would have recoiled from: cheap, tawdry and altogether pointless." The thought seemed to cheer Nathan up, and he led Hannah to the bench nearest the door, their footsteps loud on creaking boards.

It was too early for regulars to be clustered in front of the bar, but still Hannah found the atmosphere of the pub intimidating. She wanted to go home and forget the events of the afternoon, and she also wanted to cry because one day, one day soon if Joel failed to curb his drinking, she might have to face her father's death. Generally, she could pretend, with all of Joel's ability: fool herself into believing that he was immortal, and so his alcoholic lapses hardly mattered, but they did, and she had no means of protecting Joel from himself. He would live life his way. All she could do was watch.

The door opened, and Tiffany's black-clad, emaciated, dyed-blonde mother paused on the threshold for a few minutes, perhaps expecting Nathan to escort her to a place of honour, but he ignored Candace's entrance, and headed towards the bar instead.

"Hannah! I'm so pleased to meet you at last," Candace declared with such delight that Hannah was taken aback. "I've heard all about you from Tiffany."

Tiffany could not have been very eloquent, as her knowledge of Hannah Thirlbeck's life and times was somewhat limited, but Candace rushed to embrace the new acquaintance with childish enthusiasm. "It's nice to meet you too," Hannah said lamely, reminded of the way that Joel's girlfriends gushed over his daughter before the novelty of romance with a penniless gambling drunk wore off.

"I never thought you'd be so sensible, Nathan," Candace remarked to his back. "You always seemed to go for glamorous minxes."

"Yes, it's a great change for Nathan to be seen with somebody run-of-the-mill," agreed Hannah, amused at the bluntness.

"I didn't mean that," protested Candace. "I didn't mean that at all. Oh, I'm such a scatterbrain. It's just that Nathan doesn't normally pick ordinary girls — no, I don't mean that either. You can't be in the least ordinary if choosy Nathan's decided you're the one for him."

What on earth had Tiffany said to her mother? Hannah glanced at Nathan's back, but he failed to react, although he must have heard. "Would you like a drink, Candace?" asked Hannah, for something to say.

"We'll have champagne, Nathan," announced Candace. "It's definitely a champagne sort of day."

"A celebration, in fact," said Nathan, voice expressionless, meaning clear.

"You're always so determined to misunderstand me," Candace complained, pouting like a teenager. "You know I open my mouth, and the words fall out before I can stop them. Don't listen to a syllable he says about me, Hannah."

"Too late," said Nathan. "Hannah already knows the worst."

"Then she knows that I'm the complete dunderhead. You'll simply have to accept me as I am, Hannah." But Candace spoke complacently, with the confidence of someone who could still rely on looks to guarantee approval, and it explained why middle-age and beyond had to be fought to submission. Candace's identity would remain youthful and attractive, her mind incapable of acknowledging any other persona. It was a trait that Joel shared in his own way, as girlfriends became progressively younger, enabling him to remain in a juvenile world where immaturity and heedlessness could be considered normal behaviour. Perhaps Candace valued that same excuse.

"I'm not forking out for champagne," said Nathan, "not with my overdraft. You'll have to foot the bill, Candace, but that shouldn't be a problem, even though the alimony's been stopped rather abruptly. After all, you hardly came in second at your divorce."

Candace laughed, untroubled by Nathan's attitude, possibly untroubled by anyone's attitude while she had a thin figure and expensive clothes. "OK, I'll cough up, unless I can off-load the tab onto Flora, but I'll probably be out of luck. I bet we're congregating in a pub because she's tight-fisted enough to expect everybody to pay for their own drinks, and that won't be good news for you, Nathan. I suppose you're on the verge of bankruptcy as usual. Don't ever trust him with money, Hannah. It trickles through his fingers like water."

"And never lend him so much as a penny," Tiffany added, from the doorway. "You won't get it back."

"Yes, do join in the denigration," said Nathan. "Amber, have you anything to contribute in this attempt to frighten off Hannah?"

"Of course I'll do my bit. Nathan sulks, and still throws the occasional tantrum." If Tiffany's sister resembled an eighteen-year-old Candace, Hannah could imagine a wandering husband being lured from his marriage. Tiffany was attractive, but surpassed by her younger sister's exceptional prettiness. Amber might have looked as bland as a yellow-haired china doll but for the liveliness of her expression: lively and inappropriately over-cheerful, doubtless in an effort to relegate the ordeal of the funeral to the past. "Find somebody else, Hannah. Nathan's a spoilt brat, convinced that he's the most important person in the universe."

"I can always rely on Amber to keep me informed of my defects," said Nathan.

"Let me finish. I haven't got to your selfishness yet, or the snide way you talk about people behind their backs."

"While Amber broadcasts her opinion to their faces," Tiffany commented to Hannah. "There are times when I'm very tempted to gag her."

"Amber takes after me. I speak before I think too," said Candace, apparently congratulating herself on an achievement.

"The trouble with Amber is that she does think, but still feels compelled to proclaim her views," declared Nathan.

"No need to be anxious, Hannah," said Amber. "I like you."

"You don't know me," Hannah pointed out.

"I practically do. I've heard all about you from Tiffany."

"She can't have told you a great deal."

"But what she said, I liked, and once I've decided to approve of somebody, it's too much hassle to change my mind, so we'll be good friends. You're wasted on Nathan."

"I think it's time for Hannah and me to bid farewell to the lot of you," said Nathan. "I'm rapidly passing my endurance threshold."

"No, you simply must stay here," urged Tiffany. "You've got to tackle Flora. It'll be the only way to get through this. If she takes centre stage, I don't know what'll happen."

"I do," said Amber. "Mum will slug her in the mouth."

"And why not?" asked Candace. "There isn't a more deserving person for the rôle of slugee. That floozy broke up my marriage."

"Dad had gone AWOL long before he met Flora," said Tiffany.

"But I'd have got Owen back, if she hadn't leeched onto him."

"Exactly as you leeched onto him when he was married to my mother," said Nathan. "Isn't it a case of the kettle and the pot?"

"Oh, don't start all that, Nathan," pleaded Tiffany.

"Why not?" asked Amber. "Let's have a terrific family row, and take our minds off today. Then, when Flora condescends to put in an appearance, we can unite in pure hatred to attack her *en masse*."

"I wonder how many besotted men she'll have trailing after her," said Candace, a sour expression making her look distinctly older. "You note that she didn't offer to introduce any of us to the coterie around her. She's probably still trying to work out which of them is the richest, before she faces competition for their attention."

"Don't underestimate the marvels of your lipo suction and botox treatment," said Nathan. "There,

Amber, a snide observation, and I've addressed it right to your mother's face. Even you couldn't be that outspoken."

"I accept the challenge," Amber announced.

"You don't need to be challenged," said Tiffany. "You already carry brutal plain speaking to its heights, or rather its depths."

"Besides, I've never had anything to do with lipo suction or botox," objected Candace, overdoing the mock indignation. "You're not only snide, Nathan, you're slanderous as well — at the moment, anyway. Who knows what my future could include?"

"Stop looking at me like that, Tiffany," protested Amber. "I didn't say a word."

"But you will, you will."

"Glad you're an only child, Hannah?" asked Nathan.

"An only child," repeated Tiffany, the envy in her voice not altogether an attempt to joke. "It must be heaven."

"Far too dull for me," declared Amber. "I like having somebody around to argue with."

"Don't I know it," said Tiffany.

A sister might have been a help in dealing with Joel, unless that sister had turned out to be as scathing as Judith, and the thought of facing an alliance, united in disapproval of Hannah's weakness, was too daunting to contemplate. Fate had clearly known what it was doing in presenting Joel Thirlbeck with an only child, because another family member against him would have made Joel even more dependent on Hannah.

"Now it gets totally unbearable," muttered Tiffany, as the pub door opened and Flora strolled inside, escorted by her group of attentive men, but to Hannah the influx represented escape. Although Flora's entourage merely added eight extra to the gathering, the room now felt crowded, which meant that the departure of two people might pass unnoticed. Hannah glanced at Nathan, expecting him to signal to her as he started to back towards the door, but it seemed that Nathan was prepared to obey Tiffany's instruction, and he approached Flora.

"You haven't met Hannah yet," said Nathan, his tone implying that Flora was at fault for not acquainting herself with Hannah at the earliest opportunity. "You haven't even acknowledged her existence."

"Then I really must acknowledge Hannah right now," declared Flora. Her smile was so perfectly judged, preoccupied yet brave, that Hannah found it difficult to believe in Flora's sincerity. Most people were clumsy when emotion was on public display, but Flora looked poised enough to be following a script that told her she was a young widow, bewildered by the abrupt collapse of her world, but with the fortitude to control excesses of grief until she could be alone. Then Hannah felt ashamed of her cynicism. A part of Flora's life had come to an end, and it would take courage to start again, no matter how deep or shallow the widow's feelings were for the departed husband.

As Flora crossed the room to speak to Hannah, Tiffany and Amber walked away with a brusqueness as cold as Nathan's words had been. Candace also seized the chance to head for the bar, where Flora's deserted retinue gathered. Owen Wyatt's former business colleagues did not appear particularly alluring to Hannah, but Candace addressed them with a kitten-like playfulness that had the effect of emphasizing her actual age, and making the attempt to preserve her looks even more manufactured, especially in contrast to Flora's relaxed elegance. Brown hair tied straight back, as though arranging it would have been too much of an effort that day, Flora had used a minimum of make-up, a restraint that drew attention to the natural beauty of her face. In a film, such careful casualness would establish her character's resolve to endure a bad time without fuss. But it was not a film shoot, Hannah reminded herself, and she ought to stop seeing real people as actors moving through a pretence of life.

"Hannah, you're the first girlfriend Nathan's condescended to introduce to me." Flora's innocuous tone was surely too innocuous, and made her appear to be smirking inwardly at a private joke that nobody else could share. Without Nathan's input, Hannah might never have doubted Flora's sincerity, but he had spoken, and Hannah persuaded herself that she could sense duplicity in each word Flora said. "I wish we'd met on a happier day."

"Not that bad a day for you, Flora," remarked Nathan.

Flora ignored him, and her blank reaction could have meant that everything about the afternoon was insignificant in comparison to the loss she had experienced, but it might also mean that Nathan's opinion of her was unimportant, because Flora felt that she had the upper hand. "It's good of you to be here, Hannah. I appreciate the thought."

There had been no thought involved, only a wish to please both Nathan and Romney, a fact that made Hannah feel guilty to have questioned Flora's genuineness, and even guiltier to go on questioning it. Hannah tried to tell herself that Nathan had fuelled a prejudice, yet something about Flora jarred. The widow was softly spoken, mutedly gracious, sensibly controlled, but such perfect behaviour continued to jar, if only because perfection was so rarely encountered.

"We'll talk properly another time," said Flora. "I can't think straight today." The calmness of her tone hardly matched the words as she turned around to accept a drink offered by one of the men who had arrived at the pub with her. In his late twenties, with light-brown hair, he was plain and thin. He was also unaware that anyone but Flora existed at that moment.

"You're so kind, Hugo; everybody is so kind." Flora sounded suddenly weary, as though her courage would evaporate at any second, but then she was smiling bravely again. "Have you met Hannah? She's a friend of Nathan's."

An invisible friend of Nathan's, as far as Hugo was concerned. He nodded in Hannah's direction without taking his eyes off Flora, then put an arm around the widow's shoulders and led her towards a quiet corner.

"Flora's giving a really polished performance," said Nathan. "You have to admire the attention to detail. And now she's decided to nab Hugo Portham, whose father practically owns Oxfordshire. Not a bad haul, when she's only had a few days to get going again."

"Isn't that a bit harsh?" ventured Hannah, but conscious of her own doubts. "Flora might be genuinely upset."

"And Romney Farrenton might direct an Oscar winning film."

"No, that's what I'm going to do."

"Then you'd better follow Flora's shrewd example, and start vamping Hugo Portham," said Nathan. "And while we're on the topic of riches, who gains from all this? Who gets my father's loot?"

"You're about to tell me that it goes to Flora."

"Right down to the very last penny."

"Lucky Flora, in that case," said Hannah, knowing what conclusion Nathan wanted her to reach even before he spelt it out.

"I bet you anything that Flora's behind the whole shemozzle: Dad's death, her inheritance, the works."

"I never bet."

"No risk involved. This one's a cert, with the winnings as good as in your hand. And don't bother pointing out that Flora chanced to be in another country at precisely the right time. It just shows how cleverly she planned her little scheme."

"You can't prove any of this."

"That doesn't mean it's untrue."

The scenario was a bit too dramatic for Hannah's commonsense, but not for the film running through her mind. A beautiful and ruthless woman, a rich husband on the verge of divorcing her, then the unexpected and convenient death; of course the villainess must have had something to do with the murder. Nathan's script would be logical on a screen, where there was a reason for every word and action: no random happenings, no loose ends. The director would have a shot of Flora sitting in a corner of the pub with co-conspirator Hugo's comforting arm around her shoulders, then cut to Tiffany and Amber as they approached their half-brother.

"No need to issue any more commands on the subject of cornering Flora," said Nathan. "She's fully occupied cornering Hugo Portham."

"With a smile so sweet, it's a month's calories in one nauseating dollop," added Amber. "I hope that Hugo's pancreas is in full working order, or we might have to send out for some insulin."

"It'll be too late for medical help, if he doesn't do a runner soon." Nathan sighed and shook his head: a close shot, of course, with his key-light flattering an already handsome face. The camera would love Nathan, just as it would approve of both Tiffany and Amber. The director's appearance did not matter. Hannah's place was on the other side of the studio.

"Doesn't look like Hugo's planning to go anywhere in the near future," said Amber. "His own stupid fault if he's conned by Flora."

"Yes, he should remember that Flora's already dispatched one husband, so bumping off a second is hardly going to daunt her."

"Shut up, Nathan," snapped Tiffany. "Just shut up."

"Surely you're not going to turn into Flora's defender?" Amber asked incredulously.

"And you can shut up as well."

It had not previously occurred to Hannah that Tiffany was the only one in the pub for whom the day held stark reality, because she alone had seen the dead Owen Wyatt. Nathan and Amber could talk flippantly, get themselves through by pretending they were unaffected, but no such choice was offered to Tiffany. She knew the truth. A life had ended, and the memory of Sunday morning would come between her and any attempt to dismiss what had happened. Tiffany was alone, and nothing could alter that.

"I've been standing here long enough to parade my hypocrisy," said Nathan, cutting into the silence that followed Tiffany's outburst. "Come on, Hannah. I bet you've no wish to linger."

"We're going as well," announced Tiffany. "Get Mum, Amber."

"I'll never persuade her to leave all those men to Flora."

"Then you'll have to walk home. I'm out of here right now." Not bothering to say goodbye, Tiffany hurried off in an effort to end a day that could never really end for her.

"Why do people with driving licences think the sole alternative to a car is walking?" asked Amber. "I could easily get a bus."

"And your mother could easily find an obliging man to act as chauffeur," said Nathan.

"And you could save me the bus fare by offering to be my chauffeur, if Dictator Tiffany has actually gone."

The blast of cold air, swirling through the pub as the door slammed, made Candace look around, and then cross the room to solve the mystery. "Where's Tiffany off to in such a rush?"

"Home," replied Amber. "Are you ready to hit the road?"

"We can't leave yet," protested Candace.

"Why not?" asked Nathan. "Duty's done, Flora's consoling herself with the thought of Hugo Portham's bank balance, and everything's been said that gets said on these occasions."

"I think I'll stay a bit longer though," Candace decided, glancing back at her deserted audience. "Hannah, you must come to dinner. And your parents as well."

"My parents?" repeated Hannah, startled.

"I want to meet them. Give me your phone number, and we'll arrange a date."

"My parents can't possibly go anywhere together," said Hannah, so dazed by the invitation that she forgot her Chisholm spin. "It's not a good idea to have them at the same table, if you value your crockery."

"Then come to dinner twice, and bring a different parent each time."

"You'll like Hannah's father, Candace," said Nathan. "He's a tall, dark-haired, handsome architect who loathes me. In fact, you'll adore him."

"Absolutely," agreed Candace, ignoring Nathan's barbed tone. "My mother always told me that you can't know too many architects, especially handsome ones."

"Wisdom to guide you through life, Amber," said Nathan.

****

"I've never been more glad to leave a pub in my life," declared Nathan, as he led the way into the car park.

"I don't like pubs much," said Amber: "too boring."

"And too noisy," added Hannah.

"The noise is the best part," said Nathan. "Stops you thinking."

"Thinking what?" asked Amber.

"Thinking in general. The world has been spared another philosopher because of my penchant for background music."

Tiffany was sitting in her car, the engine already running, and Amber sighed. "I'd better go, or she'll be in a mood for ages. I suppose nothing like that should matter now, but I can't cope with anything more. This is the end."

"The start," said Nathan. "We're moving further away with every second. A month, two months, and today's ancient history."

"That much time won't ever pass." Amber sighed again, as Tiffany's car horn blared out in impatient staccato. "Bye, Hannah. See you at Mum's dinner."

"Is that dinner really going to happen?" Hannah asked, watching Amber hurry across the car park.

"Correction: are *those* dinners really going to happen," said Nathan. "One for your father, one for your mother, remember. I think you can safely assume that Joel will be offered a meal, because Candace won't deny herself the opportunity to meet yet another man. She'll be less determined to bond with your mother."

Amber got into her sister's car, and Tiffany drove away as though fearing pursuit, but she would be unable to shake off what was actually pursuing her. Nathan had been too optimistic when he told Amber that their lives were about to start again. "Should Tiffany be driving at the moment?" asked Hannah.

"Well, I'm not tearing after her to debate the question. Anyway, most of the cars on the road are driven by people who ought to be banned, and no one does a thing about them."

"That makes the thought of Tiffany driving worse, not better."

"It's her decision. Why the concern?"

"Because today's been more difficult for Tiffany than for anybody else."

"Perhaps." However, Nathan had no interest in discussing Tiffany or her feelings. He wanted to convince himself that he could coast through the rest of the week, go back to work, forget what had happened, but a death had happened, and he was unable to escape so easily. "Has that Inspector bothered you again?"

"Not lately. Why should he?"

"Just wondering. You said he wasn't convinced by your story, and it confirms what I've always suspected: that virtue's a mistake. Merely because I chance to be the complete gentleman who respects a lady, particularly when I'm too drunk to do anything worth mentioning, half the Surrey police are on my trail. It simply goes to show the low standards of behaviour they must have."

"Their problem, not yours."

"They seem determined to make it my problem. Let's hope our hot-shot detective isn't so thrilled with the brilliance of his sleuthing that he decides to plant a little evidence to help the investigation along."

"Quayle didn't appear that devious to me, or that determined," said Hannah. "Bad casting."

"Don't be so sure. He insisted I handed over the clothes I was wearing on Saturday night."

"Why on earth would he do that?" But Hannah knew the answer to her question as she spoke, and added. "I imagine it's routine, rather than a plot to frame you."

"That same routine compelled them to take my car as well."

"Your car?" said Hannah, looking in surprise at the vehicle in front of her.

"You're not hallucinating. They returned it yesterday."

"But why couldn't they simply go through the CCTV footage? Didn't you tell them that the car was parked by a camera on Saturday night?"

"Only from 8:30 — 8:39, to be exact. They'd already checked."

"Then you're eliminated from the inquiry, as they say in films."

"I'm still awaiting the return of my clothes though, and it'll be pointless getting them back, if they aren't sent soon. Fashions change so quickly." Nathan tried to sound amused at Quayle's thoroughness, but more than a trace of arrogance lingered in his voice, and that would not go down well with any policeman interviewing him, and might even make Nathan likelier to be hassled.

"It must be awful, having to deal with officialdom as well as the rest," said Hannah. "I wish I could do something to help."

"You're more help than you'll ever know. Don't worry. I'll survive. And so will our relationship."

But what relationship? Hannah got into Nathan's car, conscious of the forensic investigators who must have worked their way through the vehicle, and she attempted to pigeonhole the so-called relationship. Nathan implied that they were close, while showing no desire at all to seduce her, or even kiss her, yet he had given his family the impression that Hannah was an important addition to his life. It appeared to be some type of bluff, and meant that Nathan wanted to parade a convenient girlfriend, perhaps because he was unwilling to acknowledge in public the existence of an inconvenient one, who might actually be a boyfriend. It was conceited to decide that a man must be gay when he had no interest in her; however, if Nathan did prefer men, the camouflage explained itself, but not the reason for such reticence. He cared nothing for his family's opinion of him, and nobody in the film industry would consider being gay a problem, therefore the difficulty was presumably one that Nathan had with himself. He needed to blend in with the majority, to be invisible in a crowd. He feared being different; he even feared gossip.

"Will Joel be at home?" asked Nathan, as he braked his car outside Hannah's flat.

"I expect so."

"Then I won't distress him by going inside with you. I'll do Joel a favour and make something good happen for somebody today."

"He'll appreciate your thoughtfulness." Hannah smiled too, but she was saddened by the avoidance tactic. The Nathan who had never been hers was lost forever, as if that Nathan were the one dead rather than his father. The replacement Nathan could be a friend, but not yet a close one who felt that he was able to trade confidences, and there seemed no reason why he ever should. Total honesty left people unprotected, and Nathan's flippant approach to conversation was a cloak that proved how cagey he preferred to be.

"I'll see you at the office." Nathan sounded cheerful, clearly glad that Hannah accepted his excuse without objection.

"Don't rush back to work before you're ready."

"I'm ready now. Besides, my money-garnering ability is the sole explanation of Romney's shaky foothold in the film world. If I don't get some backing for his next venture, you could find yourself unemployed in the not too distant future."

"Then I won't attempt to persuade you to have more time off." Hannah got out of the car and, despite the dusk of the late afternoon, saw Joel's face at the window of her flat. She waved, but he had already moved behind the shelter of a curtain.

It was pointless for Joel to brood on his daughter's abhorrent suitor, but if Nathan wanted a smokescreen, Hannah had no right to clear the air, especially as Joel was hardly the most discreet of men, and would regard any information about Nathan's sexuality as belonging to the public domain. It was Nathan's secret, if secret it had to be, and should remain so.

Joel was sprawled out on the sofa, as Hannah opened the door, and his show of surprise would have been convincing had she not seen him at the window. "Oh, it's you, Hannah."

"Who else did you expect?"

"I didn't realize how late it was. I know you won't have had an easy time, but I hope it wasn't too bad."

"It's over, and that's the only good thing to be said about this afternoon." The telephone rang as Hannah spoke, and she left it to ring. With any luck, Judith might assume the flat was empty, and give Hannah a breathing space before the next lecture.

"Are you going out again?" asked Joel, also ignoring the phone.

"I'm not in the mood to go anywhere."

"I suppose the devoted boyfriend, so desperate for your company on an official occasion, dumped you in the street, and sped off to his real life."

"Actually, it was the thought of my hostile father that sent Nathan scudding away."

Joel smiled as though he had been given a compliment. "I can't bear to see you being fooled by a conman, and he's definitely a two-faced charlatan. I've got an instinct that makes me sense these things, having been a bit of a con artist myself at times — times now in the past, of course."

"Nathan will be very disappointed if he's hoping to con money out of me. I haven't got enough to interest the most desperate of gigolos."

"I'm not talking about money."

"Nathan's just a friend, nothing more serious, and never will be." Hannah felt a pang of regret, but she would have to accept the situation, because no alternative offered itself. Her Nathan had been imaginary, and that was that. "Incidentally, you might get an invite to meet his father's second wife plus second wife's daughters."

"Why?" demanded Joel. "So that the conman can exhibit his official girlfriend yet again? Do you know what a ringer is?"

"Someone who looks like somebody else."

"Not exactly. A ringer is someone who's passed off as somebody else. It's a racing term."

"It would be," said Hannah.

"A horse gets entered in a race, but an identical horse turns up at the track, and that's what's happening here. You're being run under the name of girlfriend."

"What makes you think that?" asked Hannah, wary of Joel's unexpected astuteness.

"It's obvious Wyatt can't trot out the real girlfriend before the family, so he's using you: having his cake and eating it as well."

Nathan was definitely not having cake with Hannah, but to point out the fact might put Joel on the right track, and that would be close to betrayal. "It's Nathan's business what he does, not mine. He hasn't made any vows of exclusive devotion to me; not that they're exactly regarded as binding these days."

"You blame me for walking out on your mother," declared Joel, alert as always to the slightest hint of criticism, real or imagined. "I know you blame me, and you're right."

"I spend half my life maintaining that I've never blamed you for anything." Hannah could only hope that, yet again, she sounded convincing, and it was fortunate that Joel wanted to believe her, despite his constant need of reassurance. "When I was at school, practically all the parents were divorced. We regarded it as the norm."

But Joel was determined to wallow in self-pity for a little longer, knowing that he could rely on Hannah to rescue him before he sank into a quagmire of gloom. "I put myself first. I was totally callous, and simply abandoned you. I can't bear to think of the pain I must have inflicted. Why don't you turf me out into the street as I deserve?"

"Because of a sanctimonious nature so nauseating, it's a wonder you aren't fleeing in horror from me. You know quite well that I didn't have a traumatic childhood. I was far too busy having a good time." Hannah had been five years old when a school friend put doubts in her mind concerning the existence of Santa Claus, and she found herself using the same comforting tone as Joel had, when he assured her that Father Christmas did indeed live at the North Pole with his reindeer and workforce of toy-making elves.

"You never seemed angry with me," Joel said cautiously, already on the way to the tranquil conscience that he knew Hannah would restore.

"Mum complains that you were the fun parent, and she's right because you didn't tell me to work hard at school or be sensible. You took me to the beach, read story books, told jokes, and fed me junk food. It was wonderful." As though Judith could hear what had been said, the telephone immediately began to ring again, and made Hannah feel guilty.

"Judith won't give up," warned Joel. "You'll have to answer soon or disconnect the phone."

"Mum can't be certain that I'm back yet."

"Don't underestimate Judith," said Joel. "She knows everything."

****

It was late evening when Hannah finally capitulated, and steeled herself for the inevitable lecture. She had been so convinced that Judith was on the other end of the phone line, Hannah felt dumbfounded to hear an entirely different voice.

"It's Candace. I've got to have something to look forward to, after this horrible day, so take pity on me and come to dinner tomorrow. Oh, and bring your father." The words were added too emphatically to be a mere afterthought; they were an instruction.

"I'm not sure if Dad's free tomorrow."

"Persuade him to cancel anything else. I'm so longing to meet him —and to see you again, of course. It's marvellous that Nathan's settling down at last."

Nathan certainly wanted his camouflage, and it seemed odd that such a confident man should be so determined to hide what was a simple fact about himself. Perhaps the dead father had been rabidly homophobic, and listening to his rants made the teenage Nathan ashamed of his feelings. A resultant fear of being outed could easily linger, because childhood memories were able to outwit any amount of adult rationale, as Hannah herself knew only too well.

"Nathan's ordered me to fulfil all his social obligations in one fell swoop," Candace continued. "Even the Farrentons are to be invited, so it'll be quite a party, but just what I need to take my mind off everything, as Nathan said."

"Nathan said that?" Hannah queried in surprise before she could stop herself.

"Ignore the way he talks to me in public," replied Candace, her laughter a shrill girlish merriment that failed to ring entirely true. "We get on well, and he actually came to live with me and the girls for a while after his mother died. Nathan's problem was always Owen. Nobody could hate silly me."

It was surely the Candace version of events, as Nathan's hostility toward the second wife had seemed very real to Hannah, and very bitter. Lack of money might have forced a young Nathan to live in a pretence of family at the home of the woman he blamed for ousting his mother, but the moment circumstances permitted, he would move out. Hannah could be certain of that. The thought of having to share a flat with one of Joel's girlfriends appalled her.

"I can't make commitments for Dad," said Hannah, hoping to keep Joel and Nathan as far apart as possible.

"I'm sure your father will think that meeting Nathan's family is more important than any other invitation. I'll expect you both at seven." The discussion was at an end. Joel and Hannah were to cancel whatever plans they might have; Candace had spoken.

"What am I not committed to?" asked Joel, as Hannah put the phone down. "And what did Nathan Wyatt say that so surprised you?"

"He's organized a dinner party in your honour: or rather, he's ordered his father's second wife to arrange one. I thought he couldn't bear to be in the same room as Candace."

"A dinner party?" Joel looked torn between his instinct to grab free food and drink from any source, and his disapproval of the Nathan connection.

"It'll be a real gathering, apparently. Romney Farrenton's invited as well."

"So the ringer's being trotted out before family and boss. They won't know you from the genuine article before long. Will you?"

"If anyone knows the truth, it's the ringer," said Hannah.

"Tell Wyatt to take a running jump. He's going to hurt you badly."

"Not when the ringer's been put on her guard by a racing expert. There's no need to go anywhere. I'll say you're busy."

"Oh yes, my diary's so full, I've no time to take a breath these days. Don't bother about me. There's probably an old film or something on television, and I'd better get used to being on my own. After all, nobody's going to want a middle-aged failure, without money or prospects."

"For goodness sake!" protested Hannah, laughing. "Let's commit suicide, and have done. Are you telling me that you'd like to go to this dinner?"

"Not particularly, but what's the alternative? You'll go anyway, and I'll be stuck here, completely alone."

"Do you plan to glare at Nathan the entire evening?"

"Naturally," declared Joel. "It's no more than a father's duty."

5

When Joel was down, he needed to impress, and he looked so well-groomed in his best suit that Hannah felt drab in comparison. The mistake of her life had been to resemble the Chisholms, instead of the Thirlbecks, but she was stuck with her appearance, and it made dithering in front of a mirror pointless. She should have known from the start that a man as handsome as Nathan would never be attracted to her, Hannah thought gloomily as she frowned at her reflection; the wonder was that he had been able to fool his family about the ringer.

The spendthrift Joel yearned for a taxi, although even he had to admit that it would be a waste of Hannah's money when buses were available, but pride still had to be served. "If anyone asks, we came by cab," Joel instructed Hannah, when they arrived in the Regency elegance of lamp-lit Central London. "And I'm freelance, not unemployed."

"Of course you are."

However, cross-city journeys and career status were not foremost in Wyatt minds that evening. When Amber opened the front door in a graceful Georgian terrace, Candace's voice, high-pitched with incredulity, spilled out to the darkness of the street. "But my car simply can't be full of his blood; it just can't be. I don't believe a word you're saying."

"The police are here," whispered Amber, breathless in her impatience to pass on the news. "An inspector's practically on the brink of arresting Mum for murder."

"Perhaps we should go home," said Hannah, startled by the abrupt plunge into drama. She glanced at Joel for guidance, but he was smiling in appreciation of Amber's prettiness. If his girlfriends got any younger, he'd be the one arrested, thought Hannah.

"Don't go anywhere." Amber grabbed Joel's arm and hauled him inside the house. "Mum will feel much better with a man at her side. Come and tell Inspector Quayle that he's being a total moron."

"Of course he is," Joel said comfortingly, an even more comforting arm around Amber as she hurried him down the narrow hall. Hannah was left to close the door and then follow the sound of voices to the front room, where Quayle sat in a chair, and watched impassively as Candace paced up and down in bewildered fury.

"Are you claiming that I killed my husband?" she demanded. "How can you be so absurd?"

"He just said there was a trace of blood in your car, Mum," said Tiffany, plainly worried despite her attempt to sound calm. "It must have come off the boots I was wearing."

"But you haven't been in Mum's car for ages," said Amber.

"I drove it to the chemist's that Sunday afternoon," declared Tiffany, gazing steadily at Amber and daring her to argue with the statement. "Mum had a headache. Don't you remember?"

"Yes, that's right," Amber agreed obligingly. "We didn't have any aspirin in the house, so you said you'd get some. I remember now."

"I had to go back to my car when I was at Dad's to phone for help. The blood must — must have got inside, and then transferred itself onto those boots —" Tiffany's voice faltered at the memory of that Sunday morning, but Quayle continued regardless.

"Why not drive to the chemist's in your own car?"

"I couldn't bear to get inside it again."

"Why didn't you change into your own shoes when you got home?"

"I don't know. I couldn't think straight." But Tiffany was making up for any previous lack of quick-wittedness. "The blood must have got into Mum's car because of those boots— yes, it was those boots."

"You see," Candace informed Quayle in triumph. "You shouldn't go around making wild accusations."

"I didn't accuse anyone of anything," said Quayle. "It's my job to ask how those traces of blood came to be in your car."

"You could have asked with more sensitivity, instead of upsetting everybody in such a brutal fashion," declared Joel, arm still firmly around Amber. "If this harassment continues, you'll be reported to the Chief Constable."

Candace's attention immediately fixed itself on Joel, and Quayle no longer existed as far as she was concerned. "Thank you so much for coming to my rescue. I don't know what would have happened, if you hadn't been here."

"I've no intention of standing by when defenceless women are being bullied." Joel had forgotten that he was unemployed and dependent on his daughter. He had now become the hero of the scene, Amber's masterful protector, the man who sent detective inspectors scurrying away.

"I've got a few further questions to —" began Quayle.

"Questions that can be asked at a more appropriate time," decreed Joel.

To Hannah's surprise, Quayle meekly stood up. She had expected him to remind Joel that a murder inquiry outranked a dinner party, as well as the sensibilities of the people interviewed, but Quayle put his notebook into a pocket, and Joel released Amber to escort him from the premises.

"Oh, Hannah, your father's wonderful," said Candace, sighing in admiration. "He simply withered that atrocious man. I thought I'd be thrown into the nearest dungeon at any second."

"It was actually Tiffany and me who saved your bacon," Amber pointed out.

"But that appalling Inspector wouldn't have listened to a word, if Hannah's father hadn't been so decisive. I'll never forget the way he swept in and took control."

Hannah stored the words in her memory for use the next time that Joel felt worthless and defeated. It was a rare moment of glory for a man regularly pushed around by events: events that were usually his own fault. "My father won't tolerate minor officialdom throwing its weight about," said Hannah, hoping to glean more praise for Joel.

"He's incredible, amazing. I don't know what I'd have done if the two of you hadn't showed up when you did." Candace sank onto a chair, only to spring to her feet again as Joel returned. "How can I ever thank you? That ludicrous policeman virtually accused me of murder."

"Take no notice of him," said Joel, still in full commanding mode. "Quayle expected to intimidate you. It was mere bluster."

"But so frightening," declared Candace, although she appeared to be relishing the excitement. "Your arrival was a miracle of perfect timing."

Joel shook his head in deprecation, while lapping up all the flattery he could get. The rôle of hero might not come his way again, and he savoured every moment, even if Candace rather than Amber insisted on monopolizing his attention. Tiffany, he ignored. She still looked worried, and Joel avoided females who were inclined to mope, mainly because he suspected they could be brooding on his defects. On that occasion he was wrong, very wrong.

Tiffany had lied to Quayle. Hannah's instinct told her that Tiffany had lied. The Inspector would check and re-check the story of the drive to the chemist's, because it was plain that Tiffany invented the journey to protect her mother. However the traces of blood found their way into Candace's car, they had not arrived there via Tiffany. Amber knew it too, and so did Candace. The three had closed ranks against Quayle, and also against Owen Wyatt.

"We can relax now that it's all sorted out," announced Joel, casting himself as the party's expansive host.

"Yes, let the revelries begin," said Amber. "Well, let them begin as soon as the others arrive."

"Others?" Candace repeated absently, as she gazed at Joel.

Romney Farrenton always turned up at the last minute to make his entrance more effective, especially when he could breeze into a drawing-room resplendently clad in full evening dress like a character from a 1930s comedy. The need to act was so strong in him that Romney seemed to be doing an imitation of a grand old man of the Edwardian theatre that evening, a performance he alternated with his portrayal of an eminent film producer. "Hello, everybody. I do hope I'm not late."

"You are, but it doesn't matter," said Amber. "Nathan and Lionel aren't here yet."

Romney looked disappointed that his appearance failed to be the one that signalled the start of the action, but then he rallied. "It still feels odd to go out to dinner alone, but Nathan assured me that there'd be a plethora of beautiful ladies present, and how right he was."

Romney's ponderous gallantry made Hannah cringe, but Candace accepted all compliments as her due. "You nearly lost one of your ladies," she said. "A detective came here to arrest me for murder. Some people have no sensitivity."

"He didn't say anything about arresting you." Tiffany had been genuinely upset by her father's death, but the shock was manifesting itself as irritability that night. "Why make a bigger story than it already is?"

"It's a big enough story for me," said Candace.

"And there are times when stories need a little help," added Amber, her tone deliberately bland as she glanced at Tiffany.

"You won't credit it, Romney, but the wretched Inspector pretended he'd found evidence that incriminated me. Me!" Candace affected a puzzled smile, and held out both hands in bewilderment. "How can people be so heartless?"

"It backfired on Quayle though," said Joel, eager for more adulation. "I threw him out into the street."

"You could make a film about everything that's happened to me lately," Candace declared.

"Write a treatment, and have it on my desk Monday." Romney instructed Hannah, expecting her to smile at Candace's exaggeration. Although so keen to rant in stage tragedy, Romney preferred to distance himself from real life drama. Lacking a script to follow, distraught women were an embarrassment, liable to cling when at their least attractive, with swollen eyes, ruined make-up, and a tendency to sniffle. His high standard for female self-control had been formed by his wife Imogen, a poised and crystal-vowelled actress who spent a minor television career typecast, first as upper-class girlfriends and then as upper-class wives: rôles so close to her reality, she barely had to act. Imogen's death meant that Romney was left with the memory of a saint, whose perfection could never be matched by the flawed examples of womankind he encountered, and Candace of the streaked hair, adolescent clothes and jarring voice came nowhere near his recollection of Imogen's dignified composure.

"I won't be in the slightest bit surprised if Quayle's deliberately planted evidence to frame me," said Candace.

"Yes, making an arrest is all he'll care about, and it doesn't matter who his victim chances to be." Joel tried to sound cynically astute, and Hannah wished that he had kept quiet. Backing Candace's highly-coloured embellishments would not impress Romney, who might dismiss Joel as a paranoid fool.

"There's obviously been some mistake," said Hannah. "The forensic people will sort it out."

"I certainly hope they do," sighed Candace, but she was determined not to have her histrionics quelled by commonsense. "It won't stop that awful Inspector charging back here tomorrow with more of his wild accusations though."

"He can't accuse you of anything," declared Tiffany. "I've explained what happened, and that's the end of it. Let's have dinner now. Nathan and Lionel can eat leftovers, if either of them bothers to show up."

Nathan and Lionel. Hannah's mind did a detour, wondering if the automatic pairing of names held a significance that she had previously not registered. Possible? Anything was possible. Probable? Whatever the relationship between Nathan and Lionel, it concerned nobody but them. She should not speculate; she would not speculate. Yet, despite such lofty resolve, Hannah found herself reviewing the times she had seen Nathan and Lionel together, as she waited for the opportunity to observe them in a new light.

The opportunity was denied Hannah that evening. Lionel sauntered in alone, apparently unaware that an apology for his lateness would be appropriate, and Nathan entirely failed to put in an appearance.

"Typical of Nathan," said Candace. "He orders me to arrange a dinner party for him, and then doesn't make the effort to meet his own guests."

"He's missing an excellent dinner." Romney leaned back in his chair as though he had physically expanded so much, it was now difficult to sit close to the table, and he could not have sounded more grateful for a banquet.

"If Nathan's busy currying favour with the money, he won't think about anything else," said Lionel. "You really will have to find him a script to push before much longer, Dad, or he'll carry out his threat and start financing a phantom film of his own."

"Nobody's more eager than me to discover our next smash hit, but we mustn't bore our lovely hostess by talking shop." Romney raised his wine glass to Candace, and Hannah felt embarrassed for him, although Candace simpered like an ingénue and glanced at Joel in the hope that he would second the toast, but she was to be disappointed. Joel, sitting between Candace and Amber, preferred to devote himself to the pretty young girl rather than the mother.

"Are you sure you won't have any wine, Joel?" asked Candace, to remind him of her existence.

"It's his strict Methodist upbringing," Hannah said quickly, before Joel had time even to consider succumbing to temptation. "You can avoid chapel easily enough, but you can't get away from your conditioning about the demon drink."

"Inescapable," agreed Joel, amused to have a private joke that only he and Hannah could share. "If I drank strong liquor or gambled, I'd expect the gates of hell to fling themselves open in front of me."

"It's so nice to meet a man with principles," declared Candace.

"You haven't. You've met a man who's lumbered with childhood indoctrination," said Amber. "That's very different."

"I understand you, Joel, because I come from a religious background myself," Candace claimed, ignoring the incredulous look that crossed Amber's face. "I couldn't cope without my belief in miracles."

"There are no miracles," said Tiffany.

"Don't be so defeatist." Candace laughed, too loudly and too shrilly, in her effort to sound girlish. "You'll be saying next that life's nothing but problems and bills. The world's a magical place, full of chance meetings and poetry and music."

"Especially if you get your hands on a bit of money," added Amber.

"I don't know how a dreamer like me managed to rear such down-to-earth daughters." Candace laughed again, and Hannah guessed that Joel found the screech as irritating as she did, particularly when he wanted to concentrate on Amber, but Candace was determined to be the leading lady of the evening. "I'm the only person in the family who sees the brighter side of life."

Lionel glanced at Tiffany, who was staring at the table, and then he turned to Hannah. "Where do you think Nathan is? Did he mention having to meet somebody? It clearly led onto whatever he's doing now."

"You'll have to ask him for details," said Hannah. "I've no idea where he is."

"No one will ever be able to pin Nathan down." Lionel smiled, and Hannah wondered if he had given her a warning. Whether involved with Nathan or not, Lionel had known him since childhood, and might be offering Hannah a sound piece of advice.

"Nathan doesn't appreciate how lucky he is to have a nice girl like Hannah in his life." Candace pressed Joel's hand to show how much she admired his daughter, his *nice* daughter: a damning adjective.

"Nathan never appreciates anyone." Either Lionel spoke from personal experience, or Hannah was reading between lines that were simply not there.

"It's unfair to criticize somebody who's absent," said Hannah.

"The best time to pull someone's character to bits, I'd have thought," commented Romney. "You don't have to bother about truth or charitableness, and both spoil a discussion so."

"My opinion exactly," said Amber. "Let's disillusion Hannah before it's too late."

Too late? The loss of Hannah's fantasy Nathan had already happened, and there was no choice but to accept the fact, move on, and recover.

****

As they said goodbye at the front door, Candace put her arms around Joel and kissed him before he escaped into the darkness of night. "I could have been locked away for life by now, if you hadn't rushed to my rescue. I'll never forget the way you routed that dreadful Inspector. I can't thank you enough and I feel that I've been surrounded by true friends this evening: people who'd stand by me through anything." But the only true friend she addressed was Joel. The others were ignored, and left unkissed.

"Bye," called Amber as the guests trooped out into the cold wind, but Joel was the person she waved to, just as Candace did.

Even if Hannah had not suspected that Owen Wyatt went unmourned, she would have known it then. Tiffany remained in shock, but that was not the same thing as grieving. Owen Wyatt's presence or absence evidently made little difference to his family, because he had left them behind years earlier.

"Damsels in distress used to be tied to railway lines rather than charged with murder, but villains have obviously widened their range," said Romney, crossing the pavement to his car. Hannah was apt to dismiss her boss as a poseur who seldom touched reality, but he could be astute when he chose, and even though Romney had played up to Candace's image of herself, he was aware of having done so. "I must keep your phone number to hand, Joel, in case I'm ever the target of a police raid."

"An inspector's nightmare is that I'll be at the scene of an arrest. You couldn't do better than call on me for protection," boasted Joel, laughing at his own conceit. To the benefit of Hannah's finances, Romney had offered them a lift home, despite Joel's airy talk of taxis, and she hoped that her father's craving to show off would moderate, now that he was separated from Amber, although his need to brag never seemed to abate.

"I don't think I've eaten a meal that depressed me more," said Romney, as he started his car. "Nobody appeared to care two hoots for their dear departed. When

I'm summoned to the great hereafter, will you throw a dinner party, Lionel?"

"Of course not. I'll be far too busy wailing and whining, especially if I've just found out that you disinherited me. Actually, I think it must be Owen Wyatt's fault his kids aren't too upset. A child isn't born hating its parents."

"And Wyatt never did a single school sports day," added Romney, "not even to make a fool of himself in a parental sack race."

"I was once felled, deliberately felled, during a fathers' egg-and-spoon race," claimed Joel, not to be outdone by Romney's paternal efforts, although Hannah could not recall her father ever putting in an appearance at any school event. "It was my brutal introduction to the cut-throat world of pushy parents."

"I've known Nathan since we were five, and yet I only saw his father once or twice in all those years," remarked Lionel.

"When somebody knows Hannah, they know me as well," maintained Joel, happy to distance himself from Owen Wyatt's inadequacies.

"I always felt sorry for Nathan," said Lionel. "That sounds ridiculous, because he did nothing but pass exams and win prizes."

"It isn't in the least ridiculous," declared Joel. "Family's the most important thing. The rest — money, career, awards — merely dross."

"Don't try to talk Romney out of having a career, Dad. I'll be unemployed if you succeed," said Hannah. She doubted that Joel was making a good impression, even though most people seemed to like him at first: an opinion that usually changed on better acquaintance.

"I'm not retiring until I've won a BAFTA," announced Romney.

"The film business must be akin to gambling," said Joel, smiling to prove that his words were a joke. "Is there a Film Producers Anonymous?"

"If there isn't, there ought to be one," replied Romney.

Fantasists Anonymous, thought Hannah; that was where she belonged.

****

"Those girls weren't telling the truth when they said Tiffany was in Candace's car that day," Joel remarked, as he and Hannah climbed the stairs to her flat.

"I know."

"Quayle probably knows it as well. He'll get hold of all the CCTV footage he can find, and check what journeys Candace's car actually made."

"It might not matter. Candace wouldn't bump off her ex-husband and let the third wife inherit," said Hannah. "She'd be more likely to eliminate Flora, given a chance. Candace is spoilt rotten, and convinced that she gets her own way in the end, so watch out."

"It's my fatal attraction," Joel smirked in self-congratulation, before adding, "Her daughters seem to believe that she's in need of back-up."

"It was an automatic response. Doesn't mean they suspect their mother of anything." Hannah opened the door of her flat, pleased that the evening was over, and especially pleased that Joel had been forced to stay sober.

"Would you protect Judith if she did me in?" asked Joel, flinging his coat onto the back of the sofa, and loosening his shirt collar with a grunt of relief. "Would you lie to the police to stop her getting caught?"

"There'd be no point in lying. Mum's a Chisholm, remember, and they can't do anything by stealth. Her fingerprints would be all over the smoking gun."

"But whose side would you be on?" demanded Joel, waiting to be hurt.

"Yours, of course. I'd shop Mum without the slightest hesitation."

"But would you forgive her?" persisted Joel.

"Not a chance. She'd have had her last Christmas card from me."

"Well, I suppose I can't ask for anything more," said Joel, so reluctant to abandon the subject that Hannah knew it would be rehashed before long. "And while we're on the topic of supporting me, couldn't you have come up with a livelier excuse than teetotal Methodism? It's very principled of me to have such high-minded ethics, but I'd prefer a more dashing reason to shun alcohol."

"I'll think up a better story," promised Hannah. "But there's no need to bother with Candace again, if you don't want to, so her opinion of you isn't important."

"How that screeching phoney managed to produce such a lovely daughter is beyond me."

"She produced two lovely daughters, although I suppose Tiffany's a bit on the elderly side for a cradle-snatcher like you."

"Can I help it if beautiful young girls find me irresistible?" Joel's would-be weary tone was jokily false, but not the complacency. He could take pride in being attractive to women, and few areas in his life were worth crowing about.

"At least it means you won't be able to criticize me if I ever fall for an ancient Lothario," said Hannah.

"Criticize? There'd be no time for criticism. I'd be fully occupied knocking his block off. I can't bear to think of my daughter being seduced by some foul lecher. The sooner you get rid of that Nathan Wyatt, the better."

"He's neither old nor a lecher. Nathan hasn't even tried to seduce me."

"Then what's wrong with him?" demanded Joel.

"More likely there's something wrong with me. I clearly didn't inherit your magnetism, because Nathan's been the perfect gentleman."

Joel laughed cynically. "You're his ringer; I told you. Why is he letting his family assume the pair of you are about to take a trip to the nearest registry office? He's a conniving fraud."

"You're sounding more and more like Mum."

"I'm your father, and that's worse. I've got even higher standards for you than Judith has, and it's quite plain to me that Wyatt's involved with somebody who isn't you. Why else would he miss the chance of an evening in your company, especially as he knew that I'd be there as well?"

"Perhaps you've just hit on the reason for Nathan's absence," suggested Hannah. "If you and Mum join forces, he'll probably flee the country."

"He'd be no loss," said Joel.

****

"Yes, I'm late again, but I've got a really good excuse for once," declared Lionel, as he strolled into the Farrenton Film Company's office. "Incidentally, I liked your father."

"Everyone does, except my mother," said Hannah, looking up from the script she held. "Could you believe in an MP who's a serial killer in his spare time?"

"Yes, of course. It merely confirms what any taxpayer already suspects. Who does he serially bump off?"

"He starts with his wife to get the sympathy vote as a bereft widower, then he eliminates a secretary who tries to blackmail him over an affair, and next the chairman of his constituency party bites the dust for reasons I haven't got to yet."

"I didn't know that MPs were quite so diligent," Lionel remarked. "Any idea what Nathan's doing today?"

"Not a clue," replied Hannah, registering the fact that Lionel and Nathan had presumably spent the night apart. "I'll try ringing his mobile if you want to locate him."

"No, it doesn't matter. Why did he miss his dinner party? Has he latched onto somebody with access to millions?"

"Let's hope so."

"Hasn't he phoned you to explain?" Lionel looked surprised, and Hannah was equally surprised that he appeared to imagine Nathan was in constant communication with her, although a possibility existed that Lionel was merely attempting to add to Nathan's camouflage as part of the same bluff.

"I think any explanations ought to go to Candace. I'd be a bit miffed if someone ordered me to arrange a dinner party, and then didn't make the effort to show up. Not that Candace seemed troubled about it," said Hannah. "What's your really good excuse for being late this morning?"

"I was assisting the police with their inquiries," announced Lionel.

"Whatever for?"

"The same reason you had to talk to Inspector Quayle: Owen Wyatt."

"How could you shed light on anything?" asked Hannah, wondering if Quayle's interest could be taken as evidence of a liaison between Lionel and Nathan.

"Don't you know about me and Flora?" Lionel was clearly puzzled by Hannah's lack of knowledge, and he shook his head in bafflement. "There was poor me, all self-conscious, under the impression that everybody in the world knew I'd been dumped by Flora when she latched onto Owen Wyatt. Did Nathan really not tell you, or are you being tactful?"

"He's never uttered a syllable about you and Flora," said Hannah, uncertain whether her hypothesis was now totally discredited, or if Flora had been Lionel's personal smokescreen.

"It wasn't that earth-shattering a trauma. I don't blame Flora for ditching me. She wants an awful lot from life, and I'm content just to drift along." Lionel might claim not to think badly of Flora, but there was still an undertone of bitterness in his voice, for all he hoped to pose as easy-going.

"Why would Quayle bother to dig up your long-past history?"

"He apparently thinks I might be as vicious as an MP, because I was asked if I had an alibi for Saturday night. Quayle's plainly under the impression that I could have dispatched Flora's husband in a jealous rage," said Lionel, smiling at the idea. "The beautiful girlfriend walks off, I brood on the catastrophe of my life, and then resolve the situation by eliminating the rival. I was rather stunned to be considered so ruthless."

"Quayle's clutching at straws."

"I suppose he has to dream up all possible scenarios, but it's certainly a revelation to look at myself through his eyes. When I told him I only had a dog for an alibi, I thought he was going to arrest me on the spot." But Lionel was making a better story than the actual truth, and Hannah smiled as well.

"Is your dog now being questioned?"

"He isn't my dog at all. I was simply doing a favour for a friend, who asked me to be his dog-sitter. The damning point is that I stayed at Gideon's house, and Gideon's house is a lot nearer Mr Wyatt's place than my flat. I could practically hear the Inspector's brain ticking as he pictured me mulling over the doomed affair with Flora, while I consoled myself with a glass or two of strong liquor, before hurtling out into the dark to slay her husband."

"A lesson to us all: never do a favour for a friend."

"The silly thing is that I almost had Nathan as an alibi."

"Nathan?" queried Hannah, wondering if she would get confirmation from Lionel himself about his relationship with Nathan.

"He rang me up on the Saturday morning to ask if he could stay the night at my flat, because the paint fumes in his own place were making him sick."

"What paint fumes?"

"The decorators moved out on the Friday, and of course Nathan felt lousy after spending a night there. I told him he was welcome to join me and the hound, but it turns out that Nathan's allergic to dogs. I offered him the keys to my place, but he said he couldn't be bothered driving into deepest Surrey when he was so queasy. And that's the sad story of how a mutt named Algernon chanced to be my Saturday night alibi."

"Did you cite Nathan as an almost-alibi to Quayle?"

"What would be the point? I'm stuck with Algernon, and if he refuses to back up my story, I'm in big trouble."

Nathan must have been burdened with an extraordinarily acute sense of smell, because Hannah could not recall detecting the slightest odour of new paint in his flat on Sunday morning. Either the fumes managed to evaporate, despite the closed door and windows, or Nathan wanted to ensure that he had company throughout Saturday night: ensure he had an alibi, in fact. Quayle's suspicious mind was evidently contagious, Hannah told herself, but she was still compelled to ask, "What time did Nathan phone you on the Saturday?"

"Early. Algernon objected to my choice of ring-tone, and he woke me with an impressive range of operatic high notes. I think it was around eight o'clock. Why?"

"Just examining the minutiae of your story like the fussy inspector," replied Hannah, aware that Quayle would be interested to learn that, shortly after the call to Lionel, Nathan had phoned Hannah to ask her out for a drink: a drink that led to his Saturday night alibi.

"Anyway, you took pity on him, luckily for Nathan, so he doesn't have a detective inspector going through the dregs of his life."

And Lionel's dregs were rather murky. Flora was supposed to have ditched him, but the situation could be less straightforward. Nathan had remarked that his father's death came at a very convenient time for the third wife, because Flora's husband was planning to divorce her, yet she, irreproachably in Switzerland, was about to inherit his entire estate. If she had a hand in Owen Wyatt's fate, there must have been an accomplice in England, and that accomplice could be Lionel, fortuitously placed in Surrey for the weekend.

"I've read too many scripts," Hannah said in amusement. "I now view the whole world as one vast conspiracy. Algernon the Wonder Dog is almost certainly the culprit, and you're covering for him. That's why you told Quayle about Flora being your ex-girlfriend: to throw the Inspector off Algernon's track."

"I didn't say a word about my rejection. Flora spilled the beans, so if anybody's in league with Algernon, it's her." Lionel had recovered his usual cheerfulness, and Hannah began to think that she must have imagined the resentment in his voice, but then it was back. "She'll get caught though. Flora's never been much of an actress. She's got the looks of a film star, but not the talent."

"I didn't know she acted."

"She tried to. Plenty of ambition, but that isn't enough. I suppose she thought it would help her career if she went around with a film producer's son. Must have been quite a blow when she realized that the Farrenton Film Company isn't exactly a ticket to Hollywood."

"Where did you meet Flora?" asked Hannah, again noting Lionel's uncharacteristic sourness.

"She did a screen test for a bit part in Dad's remake of *Grace and Favour*, didn't get the job, but the cameraman invited her to a party. I was there too, unfortunately." Lionel had no more talent for acting than Flora, and his attempt at a light laugh had an unmistakeably false ring to it. "Poor gullible me had no idea that it'd lead onto police questioning a year or so later. I don't know what Dad's going to say when he hears."

"He'll tell you that any publicity is good publicity."

"Yes, of course." Lionel made a second attempt at carefree laughter, but it was no more successful than his first try. "What did you think of Flora?"

"I never got to talk to her."

"Was she upset by Owen Wyatt's death?"

"There weren't any tears, but no one cried. She was probably still in shock."

"You're very charitable," Lionel commented. "Either that, or I'm so conceited, I can't believe a woman could be attracted by another man when she's got the chance to bed me. Therefore, in my arrogant opinion, Flora had to be chasing money when she took off after Nathan's father."

Was Lionel perhaps overdoing the spurned lover? But the question belonged to Inspector Quayle, not Hannah, and she should be earning her wages instead of allowing scenarios to run through an imagination that featured the boss's son as murderer in league with a fortune-hunting wife. It might be a commonplace situation in the scripts she read, but on a cold February day in a London office, the plot was unconvincing, especially with Lionel in the rôle of co-conspirator. He could be a dupe, Hannah conceded, but not one prepared to kill an inconvenient husband.

"Oh well, I suppose I should make an effort to do some work this morning and justify my existence," remarked Lionel, reluctantly picking up a script from the pile on Hannah's desk. "I'll tackle this one."

"Thanks," said Hannah, glad that Lionel could never know the speculation wandering through her mind about him. "You might be holding the screenplay of a smash hit."

"And I might not be." Lionel opened the script, started to read its synopsis, and sighed. "The palace at Versailles in the eighteenth century. Fat chance, when the usual Farrenton budget barely covers a shoot in present-day Finchley. I don't think I've found our winner."

****

The street door opened, and as Hannah glanced up, she was astonished to see Candace saunter into the Farrenton office.

"I tried to phone you early this morning to suggest lunch, but I wasn't early enough. You and Joel must leave for work in the middle of the night."

"It feels like it, at this time of year," said Hannah, suspecting that the dawn target for Candace's invitation had actually been Joel, who would ignore any ring of the phone in case Judith might be on the rampage.

"Is your father's office nearby?" asked Candace, too casually. "I thought we could surprise him."

"He said something about going to inspect a site today. I've no idea where he is at the moment." Both of Hannah's statements were untrue. She was fairly certain that Joel, without money, would spend the whole day in her flat watching television.

"Then it's just you and me," announced Candace. "Where do you normally lunch?"

"Right here. I bring sandwiches in with me. Somebody has to stand by to answer the phone." It sounded gloriously important, as though the Farrenton number was constantly dialled, but in fact Hannah chose to stay, simply because it made her feel more a part of the film world than going out to a café, where she was merely another office worker on a lunch hour.

"Then I'll get some sandwiches too, and we can have a long gossip in here," said Candace, refusing to be discouraged. "I won't be a minute, so switch the kettle on."

Candace was not dressed to perch on a desk and eat sandwiches. She wore a short skirt and low-necked top, despite the February chill, and had probably hoped to ensnare Joel with the youthfully fashionable clothes that only served to emphasize her actual age. Hannah was unenthusiastic at the prospect of a quiet lunch hour being disturbed, and she wished that she could produce Joel to accept or rebuff Candace's interest in him. But he was miles away, and Candace swiftly returned with a few morsels of diet food that shamed Hannah into hiding three-quarters of her own lunch in a drawer.

"It's so nice, getting to know each other like this," said Candace. "I want you to tell me everything about yourself."

Candace meant everything about Joel, and Hannah provided her with a fairy tale. "My parents got divorced, but it was all very civilized: no scenes, no arguments, no recriminations. My father came to London because of a job, and he's lived here ever since."

"He never got married again?"

"No." Joel had not felt the need to tie himself down, as he drifted from one obligingly susceptible female to the next. "No, he didn't remarry."

"That's so like me. I couldn't get over divorce either. It's awful, being sensitive." Candace sighed, and pecked at a sandwich to demonstrate the sorrow that had quite removed her appetite. "When I got married, I married for life."

However, Candace ought to have known that Owen Wyatt hardly deemed matrimony to be a permanent state, considering that she was his second wife and the reason for the first Mrs Wyatt's displacement, according to Nathan. "It must have been terrible for you," said Hannah, as Candace paused for sympathy.

"It was all Flora's fault," declared Candace, rancour abruptly overriding wistful sadness. "She got her claws into Owen, and wouldn't let go."

"How did they meet?" asked Hannah, remembering Lionel's story.

"You won't believe it, because I still can't myself, but I introduced them. Yes, I was the person who introduced them. Nathan told me to invite Romney and Lionel over for Christmas, because it's been a difficult time for them since Imogen's death, and Lionel's girlfriend showed up with him: Lionel's girlfriend Flora. I organized the whole party, did all the work single-handedly, and invited the Farrentons out of sheer goodness of heart, and that grasping harpy walked off with my husband. Owen thought Christmas was a complete bore, but I insisted he put in an appearance, if only for a few minutes, to give the girls their presents. I actually insisted he was there. Talk about insult added to injury." Candace forgot to nibble dejectedly, and took a savage bite out of the sandwich that she held.

Any comment was superfluous, and Hannah left a silence that she hoped would appear tactful rather than callous, but there was something repellent about Candace, and it seemed odd that Owen Wyatt should have been fool enough to marry someone so self-centred. Perhaps Nathan had prejudiced her mind, but Hannah thought that she would have come to the same conclusion without any previous input, and was glad that Joel had been distracted by Amber. The contrast between mother and daughter ought to keep him immune to Candace, even without the little matter of an ex-husband's blood in her car, and the lies told about how the traces came to be there.

"Flora gets everything: every last penny. What am I meant to do?" demanded Candace. "How can I pay the bills when my money runs out?"

Look for a job, thought Hannah; but that was unlikely to be the advice Candace wanted to hear. "Perhaps you should talk to a solicitor."

"I already have, and he says it's a case of contesting the will. After all, I'm as much of a dependant as Amber and Tiffany. Owen shouldn't have tried to duck his obligations, leaving the whole lot to Flora."

Presumably Owen Wyatt had not anticipated crossing the great abyss with such speed, and imagined that his daughters would no longer be a financial responsibility then, while Candace could fend for herself. It was the will of a man who thought he would always be in control of his life, even to the extent of its length, because random events happened to the powerless; the rich were never buffeted around by chance.

"I told the solicitor all about Owen divorcing Flora, and that Nathan's quite prepared to repeat under oath exactly what his father said to him during their phone call. That divorce is an established fact, but Flora denies the whole thing, of course. So like Owen not to live long enough to change his will. He was the most inconsiderate man you could meet."

If Joel got involved with Candace, Hannah resolved to follow her mother's advice and kick him out for good. However, there was a possibility that Candace might be the person who did the slinging out, should Joel's perennial insolvency come to her attention, because she believed that she was in pursuit of another wealthy man. "What did you do before you were married?" asked Hannah, in an attempt to stop Candace's petulant whine.

"I was a model, and a very successful one. I can't count the number of catalogues that had my picture in them, and I was on TV as well: a commercial for leg wax." The memory of her former glory made Candace smile, and the sulkiness was replaced with pride. "I'd have probably gone into films, but I'm the old-fashioned type. When I became a wife and mother, I devoted myself to family. It was a sacrifice, of course, but I've always put other people first. You wouldn't catch me leaving my daughters penniless. I know my duty."

It was clear that all roads led back to Rome or, more accurately, to Owen Wyatt. Hannah had never before realized how lucky her parents were to have no money worth fighting over, because divorce was nasty enough without greed thrown into the mix. Judith and Joel had been able to keep a modicum of dignity between them, if only in one area. "Is Amber still at school?"

"She's in her first year at university. That's the worst of marrying young; you have such elderly children when you're little more than a girl yourself," Candace declared, making a face to prove how very youthful she was. "Tiffany does her finals this summer, and then I'll have a graduate for a daughter; me, who never had a brain cell to my credit, as proved by the fact I let that money-grubber into my house. Flora thinks she's got away with it, but she can think again. I haven't the slightest intention of being swindled."

They were back to money, and Hannah resigned herself to being a trapped audience for the tirade against ex-husbands negligent enough to get themselves murdered before finalizing divorces from avaricious third wives. Life, always unfair, seemed to have gone out of its way to be particularly unfair to Hannah that lunchtime.

****

"If you ever shack up with that appalling Candace, I'll disown you," Hannah informed Joel, as she opened the door of her flat.

"What brought that decree on?" asked Joel, still lounging on the sofa in front of the television.

"Candace arrived in the office at lunchtime and stayed most of the afternoon, complaining about her ex-husband's meanness in dying at the wrong time. I'm sure Mr Wyatt never made a more sensible decision in his life than when he divorced Candace."

"She must have been gorgeous when she was young, if Amber's anything to go by. I suppose Wyatt stopped seeing the looks, and started to hear the voice instead. There's no danger I'd be fooled like that."

Unless Amber targeted him, thought Hannah. Her father assumed that he had described Owen Wyatt's weak spot, but seeing only the appearance, and mistaking it for the complete woman, was Joel's constant blunder. "Candace wanted to have lunch with you, not me. I was meant to lead her to your office."

"She wanted to have lunch with a successful architect," Joel said gloomily. "I'm a fraud."

"So is Candace. I said you were working on a site out of town. That's the story if she rings, and you need an avoidance strategy."

"I've stopped answering the phone. It's the best avoidance strategy of all."

"Then I'd better check for messages." Hannah sounded cheerful, but when Joel was both lethargic and defeated, his remedy was usually an alcoholic one, and she dreaded the arrival of the first unemployment payment. She would have to persuade him to give her any bank cards he had, and hope that such a lack of trust did not send Joel deeper into depression.

"All messages will be from Judith. Why bother checking?" Joel tried to laugh, but ended up sighing instead. "Today has definitely not been a good day."

"You'll feel better after something to eat."

"I'd have done a meal for you, but I didn't know what time you'd be in." Joel was making a lame excuse, and he knew it.

"No problem. I'll bung a packet into the microwave, and we'll be fed within minutes." Hannah dialled the message service and, as Joel had predicted, heard Judith's voice ordering her daughter to return the call, but the second message was much more welcome.

"Hi, Hannah; it's Nathan. You must be thinking I'd fled the country, but I've got an explanation for deserting you: a rather feeble explanation, anyway. What about meeting at that pub near your place? See you around seven, if you're still speaking to me."

The thought of getting away from Joel's despondency was so heartening that Hannah immediately felt guilty because, as she had often told herself, Joel needed support, not abandonment, and she ought to be more understanding. But perhaps the trouble was that she did understand, understood him only too well, and doubted that he would ever be able to tackle the problems wrecking his life, no matter how many resolutions he made when floundering out of his depth.

"I suppose there were a dozen messages from Judith, every single one telling you to boot me out, which is exactly what you ought to do," said Joel, fully aware that Hannah would do nothing of the sort.

"Mum just asked me to phone her when I've got a minute. That's all."

Joel looked unconvinced, and he was right to be sceptical, but both messages were safely deleted, so he could not check her story. "I know why Judith wants you to phone her, and you know as well."

"Mum will simply complain that I never listen to her. What else can she do?"

"Make you see the same man she does," replied Joel.

****

Nathan's eagerness to retain his camouflage had him waiting outside the pub for Hannah, and she was amused to think how well circumstances condescended to favour him. With Joel in residence, Nathan had a good excuse not to go back to her flat, and therefore an hour in a pub with the ringer would be all that was required before he returned to his real life, under the impression that Hannah had not worked out her rôle.

"I hope you aren't too livid with me for abandoning you to the boredom of a Candace dinner party," said

Nathan, the moment he saw Hannah walking towards him. "Heaps of apologies, sack-cloth and ashes, but I simply couldn't face it."

"Nothing to apologize for. I'd have been surprised to see you."

Nathan had clearly expected to have to pacify an indignant ringer, and his smile became one of relief. "Was it as dreary as usual, with Candace whining on and on about money?"

"It started off more dramatically than that, because Inspector Quayle was there when Dad and I arrived. Candace thought she was about to be arrested, and got a bit hysterical."

"She makes a song and a dance over nothing, merely to get attention," said Nathan, opening the pub door. Light, warmth and the stale smell of beer enveloped them, along with the glare of an elderly man who sat at the nearest table and resented the cold draught of night air. Blasts of music, that nobody was listening to, forced the drinkers into shouted conversation, and made Nathan pause on the threshold. "I've suddenly gone old. That music's too loud, and I know I'll get a headache. Would you regard me as impossibly middle-aged if I suggest we find a quiet café instead?"

"Fine by me. I've never liked the bogus jollity of pubs." But it was not the ambience that Hannah objected to; the smell of any alcoholic drink reminded her to be anxious about Joel, and she wanted time-out from worry.

There was a café further down the street, and Nathan led the way as though they were making an escape. Hannah suspected that his father's death troubled him more than he would admit, and noisy strangers were an intrusion when he was feeling isolated. The falseness of his relationship with her would not help either, and it might be time for Nathan to consider being honest because the strain of concealment was beginning to show. However, inside the café, Nathan had apparently reached safety, and could start to relax. He ordered coffee, chose a table in an alcove far from the other customers, and then asked, "What were you saying about Candace and hysterics? Why was she even crazier than usual?"

"Quayle had the results of a test done on her car," said Hannah, wishing that she had kept quiet about Candace. It was blunderingly tactless to talk of blood and DNA to Nathan, no matter how alienated he had been from his father.

"Why would tests make Candace screech? She knew they were being done, exactly as they were on my car. It's routine."

"I suppose so," agreed Hannah, and hoped Nathan would assume that there was nothing further to say, leaving somebody else to reveal a fuller story to him, but he was more astute than she had realized.

"What don't you want to tell me?"

"Well, according to Quayle, there was some blood in Candace's car: your father's blood," Hannah said reluctantly. "That's why she overreacted."

"No wonder Candace shrieked," commented Nathan, looking astonished.

"It was all explained," Hannah said, before Nathan could brood on the revelation. "Tiffany told Quayle she drove the car that Sunday afternoon, and was still wearing the boots the police gave her. She must have transferred some — well, it's sorted out, anyway."

"For one startling moment, I thought Candace was even more vicious than I'd imagined." Nathan attempted a laugh that failed to convince, and then he continued, "Why wasn't Tiffany driving her own car?"

"You'll have to ask Tiffany," Hannah replied, hoping that her answer ended the topic.

"It's unimportant, if the Inspector's happy." Although Nathan's words were not a question, he looked inquiringly at Hannah.

"Quayle left, so I guess he's content." But Hannah was fairly certain that, as she and Joel knew Tiffany had lied, a policeman would know as well. A return visit was all too probable, especially after Quayle checked the actual journeys of Candace's car on local CCTV footage.

"It's just so stupid," declared Nathan, suddenly impatient. "I don't feel that I'm the same person anymore, living the same life. I have to get back to work, think about something else, talk about something else. Tell me, has Romney found his ideal script yet?"

"Not even a close runner-up," said Hannah, only too pleased to change the subject.

"He should compromise on second-best, or even third-best. We need to do another feature film. Half-hour TV commissions are too safe, too predictable, and security leads to stagnation," Nathan decreed, before shaking his head in disbelief at the pomposity. "Does that sound as pedantic as I suspect it does?"

"No, it sounds right. We have to take chances in life."

"Yes, we do; we definitely do," Nathan agreed emphatically, but added more lightly, "I'm seriously tempted to start my own company, if only to get away from Romney's rut. It'd be easy to make a film on the cheap that looked good. Persuade a celeb that the lead rôle would be an artistic challenge or some such waffle, get the actors to wear their own clothes, use a hand-held camera —"

"And give the audience a terrible bout of sea-sickness as the picture wobbles all over the screen. Anyway, it's not money that makes a good film, it's the script. The rest is cosmetic," declared Hannah, glad to be back in the world that she wanted to make her own, in which Nathan's father could be forgotten, and even Joel temporarily pushed to the far recesses of her mind. "You can't make an interesting film out of a dull script."

"You're as bad as Romney. People watch any rubbish as long as there are enough famously beautiful bodies around."

"That's why Romney will have you raising finance, rather than directing the Farrenton *magnum opus*."

"Oh dear, someone else who wants to talk about art rather than profit," said Nathan, sighing with exaggerated weariness. "It's called the film industry, remember, and industry is supposed to make money, as much money as possible. Hollywood isn't run as a charity."

"But good films make money too, in the long run."

"We don't live in the long run," Nathan pointed out, a statement that brought them straight back to Owen Wyatt's death. There could be no avoiding the memories, and Nathan decided that it was futile to pretend otherwise. "I'm a complete misery tonight, determined to bring any conversation juddering to a halt, yet I despised the man and he couldn't stand me. There's nothing to regret, no reason to feel down in the dumps. I don't even have Candace's fever to lift money off Flora, although that's not magnanimity; it's because I've got the sense to realize I'd be wasting my time."

"I didn't know until today that Flora had been Lionel's girlfriend," said Hannah, curious to see Nathan's reaction to her words.

"Lionel took being ditched quite badly, and I've no idea why. You'd think he'd be happy to escape after Flora revealed her true colours by chasing gold, but Lionel acted like a rank amateur throughout." Nathan spoke patronizingly, but he was always inclined to mistake an affable temperament for weakness. Hannah, who had hoped to distract Nathan from his gloom, found that she had succeeded better than anticipated. Without Flora, Nathan might have had a share of his father's wealth, but Flora existed and so did the will in her favour. Resentment, indignation, acerbity, all mingled in Nathan's voice, and it would be difficult to pinpoint which was the strongest. "Don't get me going on the subject of Flora. I knew my father was a nasty piece of work, but I hadn't suspected that he could be a fool as well. If only he'd come to his senses a bit earlier — but when you begin that 'if only' business, you can go on forever."

"Yes." If only Joel had never gambled, he might not have started drinking. If only, having started to drink, he had been able to stop. If only Hannah could develop the strength of mind to make him recognize that he had to sort out his problems, and soon. "You're right; that 'if only' route's got no end, and the Floras of this world usually win anyhow."

"You're right. Born-lucky Flora's got it all."

"She hasn't," objected Hannah. "Lionel told me that she wants to act, but hasn't the talent. Money can't buy her that, so she'll never achieve one ambition."

"Ambitions can change. Anyway, Flora's got the looks, and that's more important in film than anything else."

"Only if she plays a statue."

"Flora doesn't aim at the Royal Shakespeare or the National. The camera loves her, and film careers have been built on less."

"But not great careers."

"Flora merely wants her fifteen minutes of fame. Acting isn't a passion, just a means to an end, and that end is her picture in all the papers. She hasn't got your puritanical work ethic."

"I don't think the Puritans would have had much truck with cinema."

"They still don't." Nathan smiled, perhaps considering that his camouflage was securely re-established, because he then complained of being exhausted and in need of an early night. The ringer's hour was up.

6

"The ringer wasn't kept out for long this time," commented Joel, as Hannah walked into the flat. "Wyatt's getting overconfident. That'll be his downfall."

"I thought you'd be pleased to see me returned so speedily."

"I am, but I hate to think of you being treated like a fool." As Joel spoke, the phone began to buzz, and he sighed. "It's been practically non-stop for the last twenty minutes. Judith's really in a mood."

"So would I be, if I had an ungrateful daughter avoiding me." Hannah braced herself for the inevitable reproaches, and picked up the receiver, certain that she would hear Judith; but the piercingly unmistakeable voice, already half-way through its first sentence, belonged to someone else.

"—and just won't listen to a word I say," fumed Candace. "I've told him and told him that his silly cameras are wrong. Gadgets always go haywire, exactly like the door on my washing machine: soaking wet clothes all over the kitchen floor."

"Cameras?" queried Hannah, her mind automatically picturing a film set. "What cameras?"

"CCTV. The police ought to know better than to trust contraptions like that. When do they ever go right?" demanded Candace, more peevish than alarmed. "I have to talk to Joel."

"My father?" Hannah looked at Joel, who shook his head decidedly. "Sorry, Candace, I'm afraid he's out."

"But I want to talk to Joel," said Candace, apparently convinced that she merely had to state a wish for it to be fulfilled. "He's got to come here and get rid of the police."

"Wouldn't a solicitor be better?" Hannah suggested tentatively.

"I don't need one. I'm innocent, completely innocent. Tiffany was in my car on Sunday afternoon, no matter what those useless cameras show." Either Candace now believed every word of the story that Hannah was fairly sure had been invented, or the police were listening. Either way, things did not look good for Candace.

"Where are you?" Hannah asked, hoping that Candace was not wasting her one telephone call before a cell door clanged shut behind her.

"I'm at home. Tell Joel to get here as soon as he can. It's all absolutely ridiculous, but he'll sort it out for me; I know he will."

"Is Inspector Quayle there?"

"Yes, and talking a load of rubbish. This is a free country, not a police state, and we have rights. Tell Joel I need him."

"I'll try and contact him," said Hannah. "Are Tiffany and Amber with you?"

"No, they're out somewhere." A touch of helplessness crept into Candace's voice. She was evidently unused to being on her own, and real fear lurked underneath the performance. Candace knew perfectly well that the car journey to the chemist's never happened, and also that her infantile stubbornness to admit the truth would not be enough to send Quayle away. "I just need Joel."

"Don't say anything to anyone," ordered Hannah forgetting, in the urge to protect, that her mother was several years younger than Candace. "If I can't locate Dad, I'll come to your house myself."

"Try and get Joel," pleaded Candace, in whose opinion no female could ever be an acceptable substitute for a man, even in an emergency, and Hannah's only use was as a link to Joel.

"Why on earth did you promise to go tearing across London to that screecher's house?" demanded Joel, the second Hannah put the phone down.

"The police are there, and they know that Tiffany lied about being in her mother's car. I'll ring Nathan and tell him what's happening. He might go to Candace's, and save me a journey."

"It's not your problem."

"But I can't just sit here and do nothing." Hannah rifled through the notebook by her telephone, found Nathan's mobile number, and dialled, but as always in a crisis, there was no answer and she could only leave a message.

"He's switched the phone off because he doesn't want to be disturbed now that he's with his dodgy girlfriend: the one who can't be paraded in public, unlike the ringer," Joel declared sourly.

"Oh well, whatever's occupying Nathan, I did promise Candace to rush to her side, and someone has to be there."

"Why?"

"Because she's on her own."

"So what?"

"She's silly, and won't get a solicitor unless somebody persuades her to, and Tiffany and Amber might need help, if the police arrest Candace."

"You can't go careering around London by yourself late at night, and it's bound to be very late by the time Candace gets carted off," declared Joel, but it was mention of Amber, not Hannah's safety, that had altered the situation for him. "If you insist on this mad journey, I'll go with you."

"Amber isn't there at the moment," warned Hannah. "It's just Candace."

"Don't sully the generous impulse that's going to force me out of a warm flat on a cold night, and race to the rescue of a woman who, for all I know, bumped off her ex-husband."

"If she did, Candace would have made sure her car really was driven by Tiffany on the Sunday afternoon."

"Is Candace that intelligent?" Joel looked sceptical, but then smiled. "However, I'm glad to note that my quick-witted daughter wouldn't be at a loss if she wanted to mislead the police."

"It must be inherited quick wits, so congratulate yourself."

"No, such a useful inheritance comes straight from your mother. Judith wouldn't be fazed by a little DNA. It's a shame she didn't help Candace with the planning."

"I don't think Candace would deliberately end her source of alimony." But Hannah felt uncomfortable with so cynical a comment, and tried to ease her conscience by adding, "We'd better hurry, and make sure a lawyer gets called before it's too late."

"The police have to tell people their rights."

"If they've done that, we're already too late."

****

"Joel! Oh, Joel!" Candace abandoned the hallway's warmth for the misty chill of the street, flinging her arms around Joel as though they were reunited lovers. "I knew you wouldn't let me down; I knew it."

"Are the police still here?" asked Joel, staggering back a step or two under the onslaught of emotion.

"I haven't said a word to them," Candace announced between frantic kisses, "just as you told me."

"It was actually Hannah who gave you the sensible advice," said Joel, trying to ignore the excess of ardour. If it had been Amber throwing herself at him, his reaction would be very different, and Hannah felt ashamed of Joel's shallowness, although it was common enough in men. Females were, and perhaps always would be, judged by appearance, and Candace's main fault, in Joel's opinion, was that she had lost the youthful beauty seen in her daughter.

"The police are being so stupid, but I'm not worried now that you're with me," declared Candace. "You'll get rid of that silly Inspector again."

"It might be a bit more difficult this time," ventured Hannah.

"But Joel can do it. He can do anything." Candace spoke with absolute confidence, her attempt at a girlish voice making the words sound doubly exaggerated, like a jokey imitation of Shirley Temple.

"You have to get a solicitor," urged Hannah.

"I don't need anyone but Joel."

Despite his disdain of Candace, Joel was gratified to be the recipient of unbounded praise, and he escorted her into the house with the air of a grandee conferring an honour. Whatever else resulted from Candace's tribulations, at least Joel's ego had been given an unanticipated boost.

Inspector Quayle must have felt that he required back-up, as he had brought a second officer with him, but the rôle of Detective Sergeant Erith seemed to be merely secretarial because he held a notebook, already open. He was in his early thirties, had light-brown hair and a tall, thin build that, next to Quayle's stoutness and medium height, made the pair of them resemble a comedy duo. However, there was no humour in either face as they watched Candace wilt against Joel, the tight grip that she had on his arm suggesting a guard and her prisoner, rather than moral support.

"And are you now prepared to answer a few questions, Mrs Wyatt?" Quayle's tone was expressionless, but Candace's refusal to talk had probably been interpreted as guilt.

"Shouldn't she have a lawyer?" asked Hannah, determined not to be intimidated, and reminding herself that the police were servants of society, not the masters.

"It's Mrs Wyatt's decision whether or not she wants a solicitor present." Quayle and Erith looked at

Candace, both men apparently expecting a reply from her that would reveal something of significance to them.

"I don't need anyone now that Joel's here." Candace clutched his arm even more firmly, while she tried to act the wide-eyed innocent. "You can't really think I'd hurt my own husband, Inspector."

"Your ex-husband," said Quayle.

"I couldn't hurt anybody. Joel, tell him that I just couldn't."

Joel sidestepped the command, unable to bring himself to oblige Candace with a character reference, even though her dependence on him was again bringing out the masterful personality that he would have liked to be permanently his. "What questions do you want to ask, Inspector?"

"Mrs Wyatt's daughter Tiffany told me that she drove —"

"Here we go again," Candace wailed, clinging to Joel. If he sat down, she would probably squeeze into the same chair or perch on his knee. "Inspector Quayle seems to believe that I'm the most outrageous liar."

"Your car didn't go anywhere on Sunday afternoon," said Quayle, "yet you told me —"

"On Sunday afternoon, I'd just learnt that my husband was dead. How can I possibly remember what I did or didn't do, after news like that?" Candace sighed plaintively, and rested her head on Joel's shoulder. "I bet your silly cameras are on the blink anyway."

"They're working," said Quayle. "And the Saturday night footage shows somebody going into the car park at the end of the road —"

"This is all too stupid," declared Candace, speaking over Quayle's endeavour to take control. "You won't credit it, Joel, but they have the weird idea that somebody stole my car, and then kindly returned it at three in the morning. Have you ever heard of anything dafter?"

"The car wasn't broken into." Quayle stated a fact, cold and unarguable, but Candace refused to be daunted.

"And that proves my car wasn't stolen. The keys have never gone missing."

"Whoever took the car was able to open the door immediately and then drive off," said Quayle. "He or she had the keys."

"Nonsense!" retorted Candace, forgetting to droop against Joel. "Your cameras filmed the wrong car."

"There's no mistake," insisted Quayle. "When the car returned, it was parked in a different space. Didn't you notice?"

"Of course not, because none of this happened." Candace pressed her lips together, under the impression that blank denial could change events that had already occurred. "Tell him, Joel."

"We've been able to track the car out of London on Saturday night," said Quayle.

"I suppose you'll claim next that it was driven to my husband's place," remarked Candace, shaking her head in exasperation.

"It certainly went in that direction, and came back from there as well. Who has keys to your car?"

"Who do you think?" Wheedling had failed to work, and therefore Candace resorted to peevishness. "Isn't this completely absurd, Joel?"

"You said something about 'he or she' getting into the car, Inspector." Joel was so clearly reluctant to defend Candace that he had probably convicted her in his mind of Owen Wyatt's murder, but the wish to be a dynamic hero persisted. "The CCTV film must be pretty poor if you can't even tell whether you're watching a man or a woman."

"Exactly," said Candace in triumph. "How clever you are, Joel. It's such an awful picture that nobody can tell my car from any other. It's how the mistake was made."

139

Quayle and Erith exchanged glances, and Hannah was irritated by their superior air of knowing more than anyone else in the room. "Why can't you enhance the image?" she asked, to prove that she knew something about cameras, and therefore would not be palmed off with vagueness that was, perhaps, deliberately designed to unnerve Candace. Getting a lawyer seemed more than ever a good idea.

"It's not a matter of enhancing images. We can't say whether the figure's male or female, because he or she is wearing a baggy track suit with the jacket hood pulled down low over the face," said Quayle, as though explaining to slow-witted children.

"I wouldn't be seen dead in a baggy track suit," Candace declared indignantly. "You can go through my entire wardrobe, and you won't find anything like that, and my daughters wouldn't wear a track suit either. You'll be saying next that we go around in scruffy trainers." The idea appeared to offend Candace more than the earlier insinuation that she could have driven her car to Owen Wyatt's house on the night he died, and Hannah began to wonder if Candace might actually be a lot brighter than assumed under her dumb-blonde façade.

Quayle ignored the invitation to search Candace's wardrobe, no doubt aware that if a track suit existed, shapeless or otherwise, and had been used as a disguise, the incriminating clothes would long since have left the premises. "So the problem is how the baggy track suit managed to get hold of car keys that were never missing," continued Quayle. "And I can assure you that he or she had the keys. I can also assure you that your car was driven out of London just before midnight on Saturday, and returned early Sunday morning. Is it only you and your daughters who have access to the keys, or is there somebody else?" As he spoke, Quayle looked speculatively at Joel.

"I don't go in for baggy track suits either," said Joel with patronizing amusement.

"I won't stand here and listen to my friends being insulted," announced Candace. "Joel's taste in clothes is impeccable."

"My father hadn't met Candace before yesterday evening, Inspector," Hannah said, hoping to prevent any police checks on Joel's background that would reveal a credit history or, more accurately, a discredit history as it included bounced cheques and several County Court Judgments. When dubious characters with a connection to the Wyatt family were being sought, Joel's name would almost certainly go onto the list of suspects, if his past became known to Quayle.

"Oh, this is absolute harassment," declared Candace. "I'm slandered, my daughters are slandered, and now a dear friend gets slandered, all because some duff cameras filmed the wrong car."

"Mrs Wyatt, could anyone have taken the car keys on Saturday afternoon, and then been able to return them before Monday morning?" Erith looked up from his notebook, and Candace was at once diverted by the attention of a man, a comparatively young man. "Who visited your house over that weekend?"

"Lots of people; we're very popular," said Candace, and she smiled, trying to charm Erith and make him an ally against Quayle. Candace's stupidity had to be an act, thought Hannah; no one could really be that dense.

"Was there a Saturday visitor who returned on Sunday or Monday?"

Hannah's movie-obsessed imagination promptly decided that the detectives were attempting to play a Good Cop Bad Cop scenario. Erith's voice was quietly relaxed, doubtless deliberately so, because Candace had to be offered an escape route that might later turn into an ambush, and there was something abhorrent in the idea of a trap, even though Candace thoroughly deserved to be caught if she had killed her ex-husband.

Candace stared unseeingly at the wall for a few seconds, and then shook her head. "I don't think anybody visited the house twice: at least, not that I can remember."

It was a good answer, and left her the option of maintaining that she had been too much in shock to recall minor details. Candace might literally get away with murder if she stuck to her memory lapses, and continued to claim that the car keys had never gone missing. It hinted at the presence of a mastermind able to remove and return the keys without Candace noticing. Then Hannah thought of Nathan, and so did Erith.

"We'll need a list of all the people who were in the house over that weekend: full names and addresses," said Erith.

"But I never ever have that much information about my daughters' friends," Candace protested, laughing: the hapless mother of strong-willed offspring. "You'll have to ask Tiffany and Amber for specifics."

"So you can't identify anyone in the house over the weekend except your daughters," concluded Erith, "and Nathan Wyatt of course."

"Nathan wasn't here," said Candace.

"He wasn't?" Erith attempted to mask surprise, and almost succeeded.

"Though Nathan did phone on Sunday evening, to ask how we were coping, but I don't recall exactly when he rang. How can you expect me to remember anything about that dreadful weekend?" Candace sighed again, and added a nice touch of sorrow to her voice.

"Who's got a key to the house, apart from you and your daughters?" Erith asked, and then added too nonchalantly. "Nathan Wyatt?"

"No. Nathan doesn't live with us now."

"But he could have hung onto the key he once had, and be able to let himself in here at any time without you knowing," said Joel, returning to the fray at mention of the foul lecher who could have seduced and forsaken

Hannah, did Nathan not have the unspeakable gall to find Joel's daughter unattractive.

"We weren't here when Nathan lived with us. I had a really nice house then, handy for Oxford Street and everything, but Owen insisted we move to this shoebox. I didn't know a calculating bimbo had ensnared him." Candace sighed yet again, a wretched victim of cruelty, too frail to fight. "So you see, nobody had my car keys, and your cameras are rubbish."

"Somebody drove your car on Saturday night, and that somebody had the keys." As though an invisible signal had passed between the detectives, Quayle tackled the questioning again, and Erith bent over the notebook he held to catch up with his scribbling. "The car alarm didn't go off."

"You couldn't hear it on CCTV film," scoffed Candace.

"No, but the car headlights didn't start flashing, so it's obvious the alarm system was deactivated."

"Unless I forgot to switch it on." Candace giggled like a schoolgirl, to add to her impersonation of a dizzy blonde. And it had to be an impersonation, Hannah was convinced. Candace now had her strategy fully in place.

"Do you often forget to switch the alarm on?"

"No, never," said Candace, but then the giggle was back: "well, almost never."

"How did somebody manage to deactivate the alarm, open the car door, and drive away if the keys were never missing?" asked Quayle with forced patience. "How do you explain all that?"

"I don't have to, because none of it happened; I keep telling you," replied Candace, apparently confident that she only had to repeat her story often enough for the nonsense to be accepted. She seemed to believe Joel had magical powers that would protect her, no matter what Quayle did or said, and it was the first time that Hannah had ever seen her father regarded as a lucky charm. However, even he knew that the police could not be bamboozled into doubting CCTV evidence, and Joel's already lukewarm support might have become yet more tepid had not the sound of Amber's voice, as the front door opened, entirely altered the situation for him.

"That was the dreariest concert I ever —"Amber paused in mid-sentence at the sight of Quayle in the living-room, but then she saw Joel, smiled and hurried across the room to him. "What's happening?"

"Nothing for you to worry about," declared Joel, at once the authoritative champion of females. "The Inspector's just leaving."

"I still have questions that need answers." Quayle was unimpressed by the attempt to evict him, but Erith, who had glanced up from the notebook, forgot his scribbling, and looked at Amber instead.

"I hope you're not planning to put my daughters, as well as me, through another interrogation," said Candace, resuming her wide-eyed guilelessness.

Tiffany stood in the doorway, her expression wary, but Joel was too busy as Amber's comforter to notice lesser beings. No one was going to console Tiffany, and she probably realized that her instinctive reaction to shield Candace had made matters worse. The presence of security cameras would have been recalled later on, and perhaps even discussed among the Wyatts, because Tiffany seemed to guess what Quayle was going to say to her before he said it. Candace and Amber assumed that men could be easily duped; Tiffany knew better.

"You told me that you drove your mother's car on the Sunday afternoon—"

"Did I?" Tiffany tried to look confused, but was well aware that she had been cornered. "I'm not sure, Inspector. I thought it was Sunday, but—"

"The CCTV footage shows —"

"Inspector Quayle, none of us knew whether we were coming or going that weekend," declared Candace, producing a handkerchief to dab at her eyes. She had no idea that a crying woman was liable to send Joel into rapid retreat, as he associated tears with blame: blame that was usually justified.

"We were stressed out of our minds," said Amber, and Joel immediately put a sympathetic arm around her. "I can hardly remember a thing now, and it must be even worse for Tiffany."

"Only to be expected after such a trauma," declared Joel, not bothering to glance in Tiffany's direction. She, like Candace, might become emotional, and demand too much of him. "It's impossible to recall minor details when you're in shock."

"You told me that you drove the car to a chemist's," Quayle reminded Tiffany, "and you were very definite about it being on the Sunday afternoon, yet now you—"

"I don't remember what I told you," claimed Tiffany.

"Exactly," said Joel. "You misunderstood, Inspector."

"I didn't misunderstand."

"Of course you did," insisted Joel. "I was here, and it was perfectly obvious to me that the whole family were in shock. Why are you hassling them like this? You should be out looking for criminals, not persecuting innocent women."

"Did you drive your mother's car?" Quayle's eyes had never left Tiffany, but Hannah reckoned that he probably suspected her of nothing worse than trying to protect Candace. He had seen Tiffany, alone and frightened, at Owen Wyatt's house on the Sunday morning, and first impressions counted.

"I'm not sure about anything now," maintained Tiffany. "What did I say?"

Quayle took a notebook out of his coat pocket, and began to flip through the pages so slowly that Hannah guessed he had decided to create a little suspense in order to rattle Tiffany's nerves. The Inspector knew exactly how tense she was, and seemed quite prepared to use that vulnerability to his advantage.

"It can't matter what was said at such a time." As Hannah spoke, Erith transferred his gaze from Amber, but only for a second. Hannah could not compete.

"I don't recall Tiffany saying a word about driving my car, or anyone else's car," declared Candace. "We were all far too shocked to gad around."

"It was a trip to the chemist's for aspirin," said Quayle, after consulting his notebook as though in need of a reminder.

"I certainly wouldn't have allowed Tiffany to drive to this mythical chemist, or drive anywhere, after the ordeal she'd been through," stated Candace. "What sort of mother do you think I am?"

"All three of you agreed that there was a journey to the chemist's."

"We must have been thinking about another day, Inspector," said Amber. "Monday or Tuesday, perhaps, but don't ask me what happened when. Like Tiffany and Mum, I'm completely muddled."

"Of course you are," Joel agreed tenderly.

Aware that Joel's attention now centred on Amber, Candace gripped his free arm even more tightly to remind him of her plight. "I bet I'll be accused of speeding next, when I was taking mysterious midnight journeys in baggy track suits."

"What mysterious midnight journeys?" asked Amber.

"According to Inspector Quayle, somebody stole your mother's car that Saturday night," explained Joel, his voice so gentle, he might have been talking to a fragile Victorian lady, about to faint clean away at the news.

"The Inspector must be as confused as we are," said Amber. "How can those forensic people have done tests on Mum's car if it was stolen?"

"Because there's a very kind-hearted thief in this area," Joel informed Amber, pleased to see her smile at him. "Minutes after the joyrider whizzed off, he saw the error of his ways, and returned the car to the very spot he found it in."

"The car wasn't brought back within minutes, but more than three hours later, and parked in a different space," said Quayle. "The CCTV footage —"

"Oh, not those dud cameras again!" wailed Candace.

For all her claims of being a scatterbrain, Candace would surely not leave her car by a CCTV camera had she planned driving it into Surrey with the intention of killing an ex-husband, and a journey in the early hours of Sunday morning hardly indicated a social visit. Whoever took the car had been confident that he or she would not get caught, and such arrogance brought Nathan to mind. Hannah tried to ignore the thought, but it refused to be dismissed so easily. If Nathan had sneaked out of her flat, travelled across London with the car keys he had somehow acquired or copied — but then commonsense came to Hannah's rescue. Nathan would not have had time for a cross-city journey to get to Candace's car, drive out to the Surrey countryside, return the car, and then make his way back to Hannah. There was also the baggy track suit to explain, and going to his own flat to change would take up even more time. Hiring a car for the night or taking a taxi could be ruled out as too risky, because of the future police investigation, and the cameras in the tube system and on buses would also tell tales. The only possible way for Nathan to have done everything was with the help of an accomplice, who left some sort of transport near Hannah's flat, or who took Candace's car, and drove it to a rendezvous where Nathan was waiting. A third possibility had the accomplice alone in Surrey killing Owen Wyatt, while Nathan stayed with Hannah to establish an alibi shaky enough not to seem pre-planned. Three elaborate conspiracies, that relied on Nathan having to trust someone who was prepared to dabble in murder, an indication that the co-conspirator would hardly be the most trustworthy of people. It also meant that Nathan would leave himself open to a lifetime of blackmail, and he was unlikely to be such a fool, especially as he failed to benefit from the death, and had found out on Saturday that his father intended to divorce Flora and presumably make a new will.

Nathan was safely in the clear, and Quayle should be able to reason his way to the same conclusion as Hannah. The investigation would now centre on Candace, despite her continuing performance as a self-absorbed airhead, more concerned with the insult to her fashion sense than the traces of blood detected inside her car.

"I wouldn't allow myself to be filmed in a baggy track suit," Candace was saying, in highly offended tones. "I was a model, and a very successful one, before my marriage. You can look at every single photo of me that there is, and you won't see anything so — so — well, you won't see me in a track suit."

"It's not the clothes, it's the girl inside them," Joel murmured to Amber who giggled, apparently more interested in him than in the police questioning of her mother. She was certainly Candace's daughter.

"I don't have a track suit either." Tiffany might have hoped to sound relaxed, but she spoke too quickly, her nervousness plain.

"And if I had a track suit, I'd have to lie about it, or Mum would disown me," said Amber, unable to take Quayle seriously while Joel smiled at her.

"Whoever was wearing the track suit, he or she walked in the direction of this house after leaving the car park." Quayle presented the statement almost as evidence, but Joel was ready and eager to stun Amber with his quick wits.

"There's obviously no film of the 'he or she' going into the house, or you'd have told us long ago," said Joel, with a glance at Amber to make sure that she appreciated his skilful handling of the situation. Reassured, he continued, "The fact that the baggy track suit walked toward this house simply indicates that someone's trying to frame Candace. Nobody who'd just committed a crime would be fool enough to lead the police straight to their own address."

Candace gasped in admiration, her eyes round with awe. "Joel, how clever you are! I never thought of being framed. It explains everything."

"Why would somebody want to frame you?" asked Quayle, unimpressed by Joel's amateur insight.

"Because she's always been jealous of me," retorted Candace. "I knew she was a scheming bitch, but even I didn't realize exactly how evil she could be. And violent too, as she's the one who killed poor Owen. If Joel hadn't been so brilliant, she'd have got away with it, the murderess!"

"She?" Quayle asked impassively.

"Flora, of course. She hated me from the start, and destroyed my marriage out of sheer spite. I warned Owen about her, and how right I was."

"Flora?" said Quayle. "You mean Mrs Wyatt?"

"Mrs Wyatt!" fumed Candace. "The nerve of the woman! She even stole my name."

"It became hers when she married Dad," Tiffany pointed out.

"Oh yes, Flora made very sure that she married Owen," snapped Candace, "or to be more accurate, married his money."

"Mrs Wyatt was in Switzerland when your car was taken," said Quayle.

"How very convenient." For once, Candace's laugh sounded genuine, perhaps because it was not a laugh of amusement. "So like Flora to have a forged passport. She got in and out of England, and nobody suspected a thing."

"Mrs Wyatt was definitely in Switzerland on the Saturday," said Quayle. "She went to a friend's wedding."

"If the friend's female, she'd better watch her husband when Flora's around," declared Candace.

"Obviously Flora hired a thug to kill Owen, or she seduced some fool like Hugo Portham, and persuaded him to do her dirty work."

Hannah felt embarrassed for Candace, and wished neither Tiffany nor Amber were there to hear the rant, but Tiffany was more resilient than Hannah imagined, and saw her mother's outburst as an opportunity. "Flora gets every penny of Dad's money, and Mum's left practically destitute."

"And what's really infuriating, Owen would have divorced the bitch, if he'd lived just a few more weeks," lamented Candace, and overwhelmed by recollection of a lost fortune, she hid her face on Joel's shoulder.

Joel had long since perfected his ability to ignore awkward facts, but even he was forced to make a special effort to seem unaware of the weeping woman who clung to him. However, if anyone could manage it, that person was Joel, and he continued to smile at Amber. "You mustn't bother about money. Your job is to have a good time, and leave the worrying to someone else."

It was advice that Joel constantly gave to himself, and if he had caught his daughter's glance, they would have shared the joke, but Hannah was forgotten, and the rest of the room faded from Joel's consciousness because, while Amber looked admiringly at him, she was his whole world. Future moments of togetherness were unlikely, as Amber still lived at home, and all of Joel's girlfriends were expected to provide him with free board and lodging, but for a few seconds, he was perfectly happy, and Hannah wished that he could stay in the fantasy. His encounters with reality were slowly destroying him, and Joel needed dreams in the same way that he needed air to breathe.

Quayle was as determined as Joel to ignore the sobbing Candace, and his attention shifted back to Tiffany. "Who could get hold of your mother's car keys?"

"Anybody who comes to the house, I suppose," replied Tiffany. "Mum leaves them in here on the mantelpiece."

"Not in her handbag?"

"I've got more than one bag," Candace said indignantly, emerging from Joel's coat at the slur. "And, besides, the keys have never gone missing, as I keep telling you."

"Do you have a spare set?"

"Of course I do. They're in the green vase on the dining-room table. Not that it's much of a dining-room. I could entertain dozens of people in our other house, but there's barely space enough for one guest here. Owen just wouldn't listen."

Candace was either extremely clever or extremely stupid, because it was possible that somebody had attempted to implicate her in a murder, but also possible that she might be attempting an elaborate bluff. Flora had not seemed foolish to Hannah, and it would be the act of a fool to try and frame Candace for a murder that in no way enriched her. Flora was the sole beneficiary, and still chief suspect in Hannah's mind, no matter how unshakable those Swiss alibis were.

Erith escorted Tiffany into the dining-room, his presence doubtless intended to prevent the addition or subtraction of car keys, and they returned with a bulbous green vase that Erith tipped over a small table. Among a litter of pins, buttons and nail files, a set of keys jangled as they slid across the wooden surface.

"I told you my keys were never missing," Candace announced in triumph, perhaps not realizing that it would be considerably better for her had the keys been absent, or perhaps continuing to act out a bluff. "And my *Sunrise Glow* lipstick too! I wondered where it'd gone."

"When was the last time you saw the spare keys?" asked Erith.

"I haven't a clue," replied Candace. "But I was looking for that lipstick all last week."

"So anybody could have borrowed the keys, had them copied, and returned them," persisted Erith.

"You're right. That's exactly what Flora must have done," decided Candace. "She was in the house the Christmas before last, and obviously came here with the deliberate intention of seducing Owen, then getting him to marry her, so that she'd be a rich widow."

"How many times did she visit you?" asked Quayle.

"Once. You don't think I'd be dim enough to let her inside my house again?"

"So how did she manage to return the car keys to the vase?"

"She must have stolen a front door key too," replied Candace. "Poor Owen never had a chance."

"Who knew that there were spare car keys in the vase?" Quayle asked, unmoved by Candace's flight of fancy.

"Flora knew. How else could she have nicked my car?"

But Quayle was angling for another name, presumably Nathan's. "Did you keep the keys in this vase at your previous address?"

"Of course not. I wouldn't continually decorate around green," declared Candace. "I had a blue vase in the other house."

"But the keys were always in a vase."

"No, I don't keep everything in vases," said Candace, annoyed to be thought so lacking in spontaneity. "I once kept my keys in a china basket."

"Until I dropped it," Amber informed Joel, and the two smiled at each other.

"You see, Inspector, anybody could have taken Mum's keys," said Tiffany.

"Anybody? Flora stole every key there is," declared Candace. "And it's Owen's fault that Flora was able to kill him, because she couldn't have used those keys if he'd bought me a new car last summer. I bet she persuaded him not to shell out, to make sure that she could frame me."

"Has Nathan Wyatt ever driven your car?" asked Quayle, ignoring Candace's tirade.

"He got tickets for a ballet on Amber's birthday, and drove us to the theatre in Mum's car because his own was off the road," Tiffany replied, eager to shift attention away from Candace.

"When was this?"

"January 31st," said Amber. "Now Joel's got no excuse not to send me a card next year."

"I'll put the date into my diary this very night," declared Joel.

"My birthday's next month: the 5th," Candace said immediately. "You must have dinner with me, Joel. I can't think of a nicer way to —"

"What was wrong with Nathan Wyatt's car?" asked Quayle.

"Something to do with the exhaust," replied Tiffany. "It was in a garage, and the repairs cost a fortune, according to Nathan."

"Which garage?"

"You'll have to ask Nathan."

Something Quayle apparently intended to do without delay, because he started towards the door, pausing only to say, "Let us know if you plan to go abroad, Mrs Wyatt."

"That's something you should tell Flora, rather than me," retorted Candace. "She's the one who went tearing off to Switzerland to make sure she had an alibi."

As he followed Quayle out of the room, Erith closed his notebook, but he lingered in the hall, perhaps to do a little eavesdropping. Joel heaved a sigh of exasperation, left Amber's side with reluctance, and hurried after Erith to send him on his way.

"Oh, Hannah, Joel's amazing," declared Candace.

"Yes, he's totally awesome," agreed Amber. "I wish he'd been my Dad."

Hannah felt sorry for Joel. Amber might see him as a father figure, but Joel had no wish for Amber to become a second daughter. "Let's hope that Nathan kept the bill for his car repairs," said Hannah, to change the subject. "I think the Inspector's a bit suspicious of him."

"That's because Quayle's an imbecile. Flora's the person he ought to be questioning, instead of accusing me of driving all over the country in baggy track suits," griped Candace. "If Joel hadn't come to my rescue yet again, I'd have been behind bars by now. He makes miracles happen."

But unfortunately, not for himself. Joel's life was a mess, and miracles were too rare for Hannah to count on.

****

Candace did her best to prolong the leave-taking with Joel, but eventually he disentangled himself from her clutches, and the Thirlbecks were free to re-cross the city, although another family's problem travelled with them.

"Who are they shielding? Nathan Wyatt, no doubt, and the reason they'd bother is the real mystery," said Joel, while the bus trundled out of Central London as if unwilling to leave the elegance for less stylish addresses. "All that rubbish about keys being stolen a year last Christmas. Is Candace really a half-wit, or just doing a very good impression of one?"

"I can't decide," said Hannah. "Silliness works to her advantage though, because she's probably convinced Quayle that such an airhead couldn't possibly manage the bluff of framing herself."

"She hasn't convinced you or me. Why should she convince Quayle?"

Hannah shrugged. "I sometimes think that Candace is doing a caricature of the stereotype dumb-blonde, and secretly laughing at everybody, although her daughters aren't fooled. Tiffany's worried sick."

Perhaps with good reason, but she seems a miserable sort of girl to start with. Now Amber is —"

"Perfection personified."

"Well, you've got to admit that she's lovely, and not just in appearance," said Joel, still able to laugh at the defensiveness of his tone. "I've never met a girl like Amber. She's special, very special."

Joel had met many girls like Amber, and fallen for most of them before the inevitable disillusion set in. Amber was merely one in a series, all of whom had been considered special until they objected to picking up the tab for Joel's life. However, for the moment, he was happy, and even forgot to talk wistfully of cabs, despite the tediously long bus ride.

"It's like we've been away for weeks," commented Hannah, when they eventually arrived at the street that had become hers. Throughout the journey, she had longed to get home, and as they turned the corner, her footsteps quickened, only to come to an abrupt stop.

"What's the matter?" asked Joel, but then he saw exactly what was wrong: his ex-wife Judith, waiting for them.

"Mum!" Hannah exclaimed, hurrying forward in the pretence that she was delighted to see her mother. "How long have you been here? You must be frozen. Why didn't you let me know you were coming to London?"

"Because you and Joel would have gone into hiding," replied Judith. She was an older version of Hannah, but with so much more sense and determination that she made her daughter conscious of being a helpless ditherer. Judith had succeeded in distancing herself from Joel, and seemed unable to understand that it was easier to divorce a husband than a father. "Hello, Joel. Still following your vocation as the Great Sponger, I see."

"The firm went bankrupt," protested Joel, adopting his most desolate air, complete with drooped shoulders and bent back. "Hannah's been wonderful. You can be proud of rearing such a caring and generous girl, Judy."

"Don't call me Judy."

"It was my nickname for you right from the start. We were The Two Jays, remember," said Joel, attempting sentimental nostalgia, although he should have known better. "I've always called you Judy."

"That's why I hate the name," snapped Judith.

"I don't blame you in the least," declared Joel, wilting further into abject meekness. "I made life a nightmare for all three of us."

"Oh, it wasn't that bad," Hannah claimed bracingly.

"Your memory isn't as good as mine," remarked Judith. "What's the current plan, Joel? To live off your daughter until you find the next gullible girlfriend?"

Joel tried to laugh, but if Candace had appeared right then, even in the shortest of juvenile skirts and shrieking at the top of her piercing voice, she would only have had to tell Joel that he was brilliant, for his heart to be mashed into a pulp of gratitude. Judith's acerbity was going to send Joel straight to the comfort of alcohol amnesia unless Hannah could somehow distract her mother, never the easiest of tasks. "It's too cold to stand out here, Mum, and you must have a bit of supper before you go home. What time's your train?"

"8:10," replied Judith, "8:10 tomorrow morning."

Dreading the answer, Hannah willed herself to smile as she asked, "Where are you staying tonight?"

"Here."

"Oh good, we can have a real chat," said Hannah, appalled at the thought of her parents in close proximity for so long. "It'll be lovely having both of you with me. I'll be able to imagine I'm a child again, but to prove that I'm not the complete spoiled brat, you can have the bed, Mum, while I doss on the floor."

"If anyone's on a floor, it'll be me." Joel managed to sound cheerfully magnanimous, despite being even more horrified than his daughter at the prospect of whole hours spent in Judith's company. "Hannah's got the sofa."

"That's so nice of you, Dad." The words were spoken quickly, as Hannah tried to silence whatever comment her mother was about to make, but some things were unstoppable.

"Yes, so considerate of your father to leech off you."

"Well, I'm not planning to present you with a bill for board and lodging either," said Hannah, pretending that Judith had made a joke. The forced laughter was an effort, and Hannah's facial muscles ached, but she went on smiling. "Either parent is welcome to stay with me at any time, for as long as they want."

"Hannah's the best daughter in the world," announced Joel.

"Especially as she's always been a sucker where you're concerned," said Judith.

"You'll be glad that I'm on the scene when you hear about the charlatan who's trying to con her," Joel declared.

"I already know about you," said Judith.

"Pay no attention to Dad and his forebodings," urged Hannah, but she was grateful for the sidetrack. Talk of a disreputable boyfriend would be an excellent way to distract Judith from her daughter's weakness with regard to Joel. "Nathan isn't a gambler: at least, I don't think so. He's never mentioned horses or cards."

"He's a gambler," insisted Joel. "I can sense one a mile off. Judy, he's using Hannah for some devious scheme that she's too honest and straightforward to spot."

"Apparently, I'm Nathan's ringer," said Hannah, "and Dad's going to have a lovely time telling you about the evil con artist."

"Who is this Nathan?" asked Judith, unable to prevent herself from chasing Joel's misinformation, even though she ought to have recognized the tactic.

****

Over supper, an unexpectedly easy meal, Nathan's sly expression, beady eyes and hidden leer were fully described by Joel in graphic detail. It was one of the rare occasions when he succeeded in deflecting the ex-wife's wrath, and he determined to make the most of his godsend, playing on every fear Judith might have that her daughter was destined to make the same mistakes she had.

"How do you know that Nathan's leering if he hides it?" inquired Hannah.

"I know everything about him," declared Joel. "The moment I saw him, I knew he'd gamble away his last pound."

"How much money have you given him, Hannah?" demanded Judith, only too able to picture the swindler of Joel's imagination.

"Nathan hasn't asked me for so much as a penny." Hannah had never before seen a parental alliance, and she was prepared to listen to any amount of slander, if a veneer of harmony could get them through the night. It was cruel to worry her mother, but crueller to allow Judith to shove Joel further along his path to destruction. A Chisholm was strong enough to survive any revelation, but Joel had to be guarded.

"Ever since Hannah's known Wyatt, she's been involved in murders and police interrogations," continued Joel.

"Murders?" repeated Judith in astonishment.

"Singular, not plural," said Hannah. "Nathan's father was killed in a robbery gone wrong."

"Nonsense," maintained Joel. "Wyatt planned the whole thing. It's the reason the police are hanging around him all the time. You won't believe this, Judy, but Wyatt deliberately attempted to incriminate Hannah by pretending he slept here the night his father died, and a stupid detective actually thought that our Hannah might be part of the plot. Sheer luck I was on hand to put him right."

"Dad was amazing," agreed Hannah. "I'd have been terrified on my own."

"I ordered the thick-headed bully to leave," Joel claimed, eager for Judith's admiration, something long absent from his life. "Nobody speaks to my daughter like that."

The story was taking on epic proportions in Joel's mind, and had already become a battle between goodness and malevolence, with him rescuing Hannah from the threats and abuse of the infamous Quayle. Judith deserved better than to be fobbed off with one of Joel's wilder tales, and even though she knew that he was talking to bamboozle her, Hannah's involvement with the melodramatic bunkum altered everything. Some truth lay behind the subterfuge, and mention of a gambler and the police was enough to bring back unpleasant memories for Judith of her marriage. "Hannah, you've got to drop this Nathan Wyatt," ordered Judith. "I don't like the sound of him, even allowing for Joel's usual exaggeration."

"It's not exaggeration," protested Joel. "Wyatt killed his father to grab an inheritance."

"But Nathan didn't actually inherit anything," Hannah pointed out.

"He thought he would," insisted Joel.

"Is he one of your cronies?" demanded Judith.

The question angered Joel, and he glared indignantly at his ex-wife. "Do you think I'd introduce Hannah to a gambler?"

"No, I don't," admitted Judith. "You're quite prepared to freeload off her, but you wouldn't let any other wastrel wreck her life."

"Dad isn't wrecking my life," objected Hannah.

"Not for want of trying," retorted Judith. "Exactly how much has he contributed towards your rent and food bills?"

"Dad's given me his bank card and PIN number, so that I can pick up his unemployment pay," said Hannah, who could only hope that the astounded expression crossing Joel's face went unnoticed by her mother.

"That's precisely what we've arranged," declared Joel, always quick-witted when it came to covering his tracks. "Hannah's going to manage my money from now on. I know what my problems are, Judy; I've never denied them."

"And never bothered to do a thing about them either," commented Judith.

"He is now," maintained Hannah, although the words came more from a need to boost her own morale than to persuade Judith that change was possible. "Dad won't be able to gamble or drink without money. He's determined to make a new start."

"I've heard that before," said Judith.

"This time it's different."

"I've heard that too."

"It is different," declared Joel. "If I let Hannah down again, I'll kill myself."

"You don't think that another of your phoney suicide attempts would be letting Hannah down big time?" demanded Judith. "But emotional blackmail's your speciality, of course."

Bringing Joel face-to-face with reality was never a good strategy. Like a child, he responded best to praise, and Judith's scorn might ruin any chance of Hannah being able to prise the bank card from Joel's grasp. "Dad's never let me down, and isn't going to now. He's hit rock-bottom, so the only way is up. This'll work, because there isn't an alternative."

"Hannah's right," declared Joel. "I've nowhere left to hide."

"You're hiding here," scoffed Judith.

"Dad's my guest," said Hannah. "If I've got a home, then he has as well, and so have you, Mum. It's the way you brought me up."

"I didn't bring you up to be a soft touch for gamblers."

"I'm not," insisted Hannah, although she knew that Joel's presence in the flat was hardly supporting evidence.

"Then what about this Nathan Wyatt?"

"He's my worst nightmare," said Joel, seizing his opportunity to redirect the flak. "I'm so worried about Hannah, Judy: frantic with worry. I can't tell you how worried I am."

But he could, and did.

7

It had not seemed possible that any man on earth could replace Joel as chief swindler in Judith's mind, but she had found a brand new reason for anxiety, and when she left the next morning, Joel was still triumphantly in situ, promising to keep a close eye on the ruses and stratagems of the conniving Nathan Wyatt.

"I can't believe I've survived the night." Joel was gloating rather than marvelling, and Hannah felt miserable to have upset the mother who had tried to give her a secure childhood, despite Joel's activities. "When Judith announced that she was staying, I thought I'd be hurled out into the street before five minutes had passed."

"You know I wouldn't let that happen," said Hannah, "and Mum knew it too."

"Judith only came to make trouble." But Joel was wrong. Hannah guessed that sheer frustration brought Judith to London, because sitting at home, doing nothing, had become too difficult to bear. There were times when even running around in useless circles was better than inaction.

"It's a good idea about giving me your bank card though," Hannah remarked casually. "I'm so glad that you suggested it."

"I didn't," said Joel, amused at the attempt to manipulate him.

"It's still a good idea, whoever mentioned it. If I handle all your money from now on, you can't drink or gamble, and Mum won't have the slightest cause for complaint."

"Oh, won't she?" Long experience of his ex-wife added cynicism to Joel's laugh.

"But don't you think that giving me your bank card would be a really sensible move?" pleaded Hannah.

"Yes, and that's why I don't want to do it."

"But you will, won't you?"

"I know I should."

"Then you will."

"It isn't that easy."

"Yes, it is. Hand the card over, tell me your PIN number, and the problem's solved."

"The problem's never solved." Joel was right, and Hannah knew it, but accepting reality would be admitting defeat, and she had to have some hope.

"When do you get your money?"

"When I'm processed. That's what they call it, processed, just like a tinned vegetable. You wouldn't think I had a brain cell in my head. Losing a job's bad enough, without the indignity of being regarded as a layabout moron." Joel's umbrage was genuine, but it was also a ploy to distract Hannah from the subject of his bank account. He wanted her sympathy, her support, but not a drastic intervention that might actually curb the behaviour ruining his life. "It's one insult after another when you sign on unemployed."

"You don't have to put up with the hassle," said Hannah. "This is your home now, and we'll manage, whether or not the government condescends to offer you a pittance, so if you give me your bank card —"

"I'd have died years ago, but for you," claimed Joel, to switch the topic yet again. "You're my lifeline, my lifesaver, my —"

"Dad, I want your bank card, and I'm not going to throw in the towel." Hannah laughed to sound light-hearted, but the thought of Joel with access to money was no joke. "You might as well hand the card over, because I'm quite prepared to nag until you do. I'm half Chisholm, remember."

"And that's the part you should listen to. It's sane and sensible and terribly depressing for me, because it means I can't fool you." Joel looked rueful, and it was probably a real regret, although he would have despised himself had he hoodwinked his daughter. "I know I should give you the bank card, and I will, but not right now. This evening, maybe."

"You'll feel really proud of yourself: a gigantic step forward. Why put it off?"

"I'm a coward, that's why. I'd have to face the prospect of being me, without any possibility of forgetting who I am and what I am. Take away the money, and you take away my chance of escape."

But should Joel get that temporary release, he would end up as dejected as if he had been controlled. The pattern never varied. "Perhaps your actual problem's depression," Hannah suggested.

"My actual problem is me." Joel shrugged helplessly, submissive to what he regarded as the inevitability of fate. He was a mere pawn in life's imitation of chess, and his air of being defeated before he started made Hannah long to deliver a morale-boosting speech on the necessity of effort. However, the predicament was Joel's, only hers by proxy, and she could not leave him to brood all day on his inadequacies. Better, much better, to go on pretending.

"I think it's wonderful, the way you never lie to yourself, and that honesty's going to give you the strength to tackle a new beginning. There'll be another job, because you're a brilliant architect, and this free time might be exactly what you need to sort things out. Don't let some stupid clerks in an office knock your confidence simply because they're jealous of your qualifications."

"I've no intention of kow-towing to them," declared Joel. To him, praise was more nourishing than food, and he began to lose something of his resignation to cruel destiny. "They're our servants, not our masters."

"You're their bread and butter: the reason they've got a job."

"Precisely," agreed Joel, storing up Hannah's words for use during his next brush with petty bureaucracy. "It's about time someone stood up to their despotism."

"That someone is you," said Hannah, hoping that her father would be banned from the unemployment office and denied the money that was bound to cause trouble, one way or another. "I've got to dash, so we'll resume negotiations about custody of your bank account this evening."

"And the dolts need a lesson in good manners too," declared Joel, slickly ignoring all mention of his credit cards.

****

Lionel usually offered the explanation for his late arrival as soon as he crossed the Farrenton office threshold, but that morning he was preoccupied, and perched on a corner of Hannah's desk without saying a word.

"What's wrong?"

"Wrong?" repeated Lionel, apparently surprised that Hannah had been able to spot any difference in his behaviour.

"Yes, wrong. But you're the boss's son, so feel free to tell me to mind my own business."

"Nothing's wrong. I just don't like the person I am."

It was the sort of thing said by Joel, not uncomplicated Lionel, and Hannah smiled. "I didn't think you went in for self-analysis."

"I don't. I'm straightforward, easy-going Lionel; or rather, I thought I was until I saw behind the image. I'm actually vindictive, petty-minded and bitter." Lionel sighed, but a trace of amusement had crept into his voice, and he appeared to be somewhat impressed by his new identity.

"How did you manage to discover your true personality?"

"Flora rang me yesterday evening. I said the usual condolence guff, and she started to cry. Seemed really upset."

Flora was a better actress than Lionel had given her credit for, thought Hannah. Then she felt remorse at being so cynical because, despite the age gap, Owen Wyatt might have attracted Flora. After all, if the penniless Joel could find a string of young airheads to feed and shelter him, everything became possible.

"It was awful, listening to her cry," said Lionel.

"Yes, really embarrassing."

"No, I meant it was awful because I found myself thinking that at least she had Mr Wyatt's money to comfort her," Lionel admitted sheepishly.

"It's a thought that would cross anyone's mind," said Hannah, feeling better about her own suspicions of Flora's motive for marrying a rich man.

"She told me that she was completely alone and isolated," continued Lionel. "All the Wyatts hate her, with Candace particularly unpleasant, and Nathan not far behind. There's nobody on her side, she said."

Apart from wealthy Hugo Portham. Hannah recalled the gathering at the pub, and wondered if Hugo had since abandoned Flora, in spite of his devotion to her at Owen Wyatt's funeral. Even taking Lionel's usually obliging nature into account, a phone call to a ditched boyfriend had to be the phone call of last resort.

"Do you think I'd be a fool to drift back into a relationship with Flora?" asked Lionel.

"Is it in the cards?"

"She suggested that we meet for lunch and a talk. I'm the only friend she has in the world, she said, the only person she's able to rely on. Then she cried a bit more, and wanted to know if I could forgive and forget. Should I?"

"Don't take my advice. I'm warped and resentful, without the slightest generosity about me. You're probably a lot nicer than that."

"No, I don't think so," said Lionel, after a moment's deliberation.

Good for you, thought Hannah.

"If Flora dumped me a second time —" Lionel shrugged, as resigned to his fate as a defeated Joel. "And she would dump me; I know she would. What happens once goes on happening."

"Yes, it does," agreed Hannah, thinking of her father.

"Would you trust Nathan again if he let you down?"

"I told you, I'm warped and embittered." Could Lionel be dropping a hint that Nathan was about to ditch his ringer? Wounded pride hurt, but never more so than when somebody else knew of the humiliation.

"You wouldn't have anything to do with second chances?" persisted Lionel, apparently needing Hannah's sanction to snub Flora. Either that, or he wanted to be assured of Hannah's unwillingness to cling, should Nathan feel secure enough to discard the ringer. "You wouldn't see him again?"

"I'd look the other way every time Nathan walked into the office."

"So you don't think I'm being too hard on Flora?"

"Nobody would."

But Hannah knew that she was weaker than Lionel. Joel's soft touch and Nathan's camouflage had very little self-respect or dignity. She accepted a supporting rôle in other people's lives, allowing her own choices to wait in the wings. In Joel's case, she feared that he would kill himself, although by neglect rather than suicide; however, with Nathan, Hannah fostered a hope that he would like her more if she allowed his smokescreen to continue. He was probably gay, but until the fact became one hundred per cent established in her mind, Hannah could stick to a childish yearning for the traditional Hollywood ending, when the hero realized that the girl-next-door, who had been his loyal friend throughout the film, was actually the girl he loved.

Hannah needed a very small amount of encouragement to go on hoping, especially as, when

Nathan breezed into the office, he was at his confident best, smiling, handsome and generous.

"Hannah, I've neglected you shamefully. A thousand apologies, and let's have lunch together. I mean proper lunch, incidentally, so don't reach for your sandwiches. And I'm not talking café snack either, but posh restaurant meal in the sort of place I haunt to impress our Mr Moneybags with the wealth that's an everyday part of life when you're in the Farrenton Film Company."

"Romney doesn't pay me enough to impress anyone with restaurants, posh or not," said Hannah, too pleased that Nathan had remembered her existence to wonder why he was determined to make amends with what he imagined would be a treat.

"I'm picking up the tab," declared Nathan. "There are weeks before I have to bother about my overdraft, and it's always a good idea to be seen at the trough where money gathers. Besides, I get withdrawal symptoms when I'm separated from the rich list, so let the phone answer itself for once. Not that anybody interesting will ring. I think Romney's retired from the film business."

"Romney's going to hold out until he finds a script that he really likes," said Hannah, defensive of perfectionism. She wanted her own future films to be made because they deserved to be made, and for no other reason.

"Romney's going to hold out until he finds a script that's got a decent part in it for him. He's still basically an actor, not a producer at all."

There was some truth in Nathan's claim because Romney certainly did cast himself in every Farrenton production, and the lack of a plum rôle, in which he could shine, was considered a flaw in any screenplay he looked at. "Romney's got good taste though," argued Hannah, "and a small company can't afford to produce rubbish."

"A small company can't afford to stagnate, and that's exactly what's happening at Farrenton Films," Nathan declared gloomily.

****

A West End restaurant was less of a treat to Hannah than an ordeal, and she balked at Nathan's choice. "I'm not dressed for a place like that."

"Only pretentious snobs dress for lunch," decreed Nathan. "Aristocrats always look as though they buy their clobber from the nearest jumble sale."

"You're such a comfort."

"Our clothes have a higher pedigree, almost up to charity shop level, so the waiters will assume we're celebs."

"Celebs they don't recognize."

"Not our fault they're behind the times. Anyway, you've got to get used to mixing with the money if you're serious about being a director."

Pricey meals in pricey restaurants might be part of the film industry, but it was a part that Hannah could do without. Deferential waiters belonged in a world that her Chisholm genes maintained was flummery, but Nathan thrived when those around him were obsequious, and Hannah tried to appear equally at home, although she found the atmosphere of needless expense stifling. Food was merely food to a Chisholm, and required no plush or silver to make it taste better, just as a dull film could not be made interesting by a gaudy première. In spite of Nathan's claim, there were no jumble sale aristocrats on display, forcing Hannah to remind herself that she cared only about Nathan's opinion, and he was not ashamed to be seen in public with her. Nonetheless, she felt happier when a waiter guided them to a table in an alcove, which would help foster the illusion that they were alone, and it was an illusion worth having.

"Candace seems greatly smitten," remarked Nathan, after ordering a lunch that he informed Hannah she would enjoy. "Smitten yet again, I should say, as we're talking Candace. She only has to look at a man to start yearning, but your father's made quite an impact with his masterful handling of the police. I wish he'd come to my rescue."

"Are they still hassling you?"

"Not really. I'm luckier than Candace. My car isn't accused of wandering off with an unidentified driver who, for all his or her faults, had the courtesy to repent. No, my car stayed put throughout that Saturday night, and I've never been happier to live in a city teeming with CCTV. Quayle attempted to create a few waves by asking if I had keys to Candace's car, but even he probably realized that the question was a bit pointless. I'd hardly admit to possession of those damning keys if I had been swanning around London in a track suit: an idea I consider as insulting to my sartorial splendour as Candace does to hers."

"Has she seen her solicitor about Quayle?"

"She feels that Joel offers a superior service, but Tiffany will get her back into a lawyer's office, and if there's a man behind the desk, Candace won't mind consulting him."

"Do you think somebody tried to frame her?"

"I think there's a simpler explanation of the vanishing and reappearing car. Amber borrowed it to visit a late-night boyfriend, and doesn't want to admit that she was driving without a licence. She'd hate to get banned before even passing the test."

"Amber struck me as straightforward to a fault. I think she'd tell the truth if Candace was in a jam."

"Oh well, Amber in a track suit is my theory, anyway. She's been something of a sly child from infancy, and might be wary of mentioning a boyfriend in case her competitive mother sprinted out the front door in pursuit of him. Not all families are as uncomplicated as yours."

"Oh yes, we're incredibly uncomplicated," said Hannah, pleased with Nathan's picture of Thirlbeck domestic life. "It must make everything much worse for you, having the police hanging around. You don't get a chance to put what happened into the past."

"My father was practically a stranger, and I can't pretend otherwise. He's probably the least lamented man in history, and that's his own fault." For a moment, Nathan's pretence of skimming across the surface of life disappeared, but then their meal was served, and he regained his usual nonchalance. "The solution is work. I need a prospective film, and I need it now. Come on, Hannah, you want to direct. Reveal a cherished future project, and I'll raise the dough to get it into production."

The waiter drew back from their table, almost bowing, and Hannah suspected that Nathan had deliberately mentioned films and finance to impress the man. Certainly Hannah was impressed: impressed and intimidated. "None of my ideas would make money."

"What Farrenton film ever does? This is about giving me a challenge. Have you got a script?"

"No, but there's a book," Hannah said reluctantly, unwilling to expose a dream to harsh daylight: "an old novel by Edith Olivier."

"Good. I can tell potential backers that they'll get a cut of the publishing profits when the film makes the book a bestseller. I hope it's out of copyright?"

"I'm not sure of that, but I am sure it wouldn't be a bestseller nowadays."

"This sounds more and more like a challenge worthy of my glib talents. What's the book called?"

"*The Love Child*."

Nathan grimaced and sighed. "Not some single mother with a drug problem hiding from her violent boyfriend in a rundown block of flats, I hope."

"It's a period piece: early twentieth century. A comfortable house with servants in a picturesque English village. Big hats, long skirts, trees, lanes, cottages, and so on."

"Thank goodness. It's so dismal trying to sell a slum. What's the plot?"

"Shall I get you a copy of the book?"

"Why?" asked Nathan.

"Don't you want to read it?"

"What for? I don't have to read a book to sell it. Tell me the story line."

"Well, a lonely spinster invents an imaginary little girl, who somehow becomes real," Hannah said even more reluctantly, knowing that Nathan was going to hate the plot. "The child grows into a beautiful young woman, falls in love, and then vanishes because the bond with her creator fades away."

"There's nothing like gritty realism," commented Nathan.

"OK," Hannah conceded, laughing. "It's a definite case of suspending disbelief, but I think I could make an interesting film of the book one day."

"Fair enough. Knock out a treatment, cobble together some sort of script, and leave the rest to me. We'll square it with Romney later on, or start our own film company if he refuses to tag along."

"Nobody's going to part with good money to let me fulfil a dream," objected Hannah.

"Every director has to make a first film sometime."

"Yes, but I don't think —"

"This isn't the time to think, it's the time to do, and I'm totally committed to the project," declared Nathan, before adding somewhat less whole-heartedly, "I don't suppose you'd consider swapping the lonely spinster for a career woman in, say, the fashion world, and have her spook involved with MI6?"

"I still prefer the original story, oddly enough."

"You don't think it'd be improved by a few car chases then?"

"Not really."

"Oh well, I said I wanted a challenge." Nathan shrugged in resignation, and Hannah tried to believe that he admired her perseverance.

"I know it'd be a financial disaster, but you did ask what film I'd like to make."

"And so you will. Cinderella is going to the ball. Talking of Cinderella —" Nathan scowled at something on the other side of the restaurant, and Hannah glanced around to see what had grabbed his attention. "Cinders latches onto another Prince. How lucky there should be such a plentiful supply."

Tastefully dressed in a black suit so fashionable that it had no connection whatsoever with mourning, Flora was half way across the room with an attentive Hugo Portham at her side. The eyes of male diners followed Flora's progress, and Hannah turned back to Nathan, smiling as she remembered Lionel's account of the pathetically weeping widow.

"She phoned Lionel, told him that he was the only friend she had in the world, and suggested lunch together."

"Don't tell me that the nobly long-suffering Lionel had the guts to decline her offer?" demanded Nathan.

"Flora was probably surprised as well," said Hannah, unwilling to admit that she too had underestimated Lionel.

"But, luckily, Flora's got another only friend to comfort her. I wonder why she bothered to phone Lionel, when Hugo Portham's very much in the picture? But I suppose you can't have too many only friends."

If she had not heard Lionel's account of the telephone call, Hannah would have thought that Nathan was speaking with exaggerated cynicism. However, Lionel's tale had been told, and it made a difference. Flora was the sham that the Wyatt family believed her to be, and Hannah felt awkward when Flora saw Nathan, and promptly veered in his direction.

"Here she comes, all ready to do the desolate widow act," muttered Nathan. "I wouldn't mind so much, if I didn't have the feeling that she wants to gloat over her newly acquired riches."

"How lovely to see you again, Hannah," said Flora, a nicely judged wistfulness in her smile. "Though I bet Nathan's going to be totally obnoxious as usual. You wouldn't credit how brutal he is to me, Hugo."

Hugo coughed and shuffled his feet, uncomfortable with Flora's candour. English conditioning always preferred any sort of fudged attempt at civility, and Hannah sympathized with the gaucherie. Everything would have been much easier had Flora simply pretended not to see Nathan.

"Don't worry. I haven't time to hurl insults at anyone. I've got to get back to work," said Nathan. "Some of us have to toil for our pittance, Flora, and the least you can do is pay my lunch tab. People are supposed to be charitable to orphans."

"And to widows," added Flora.

"I don't think we've ever spoken, Hannah," said Hugo, his thin face pink with embarrassment as he endeavoured to ignore the horror of a possible scene in public. "I know all about you though. Congratulations."

"What for?" asked Hannah.

"Your engagement, of course."

"I'm not engaged."

Hugo looked helplessly at Flora for guidance. "But I thought —"

"I thought too," said Flora. "Blame Candace, Hannah. She's told everyone that you and Nathan are engaged."

"She must be thinking of another Hannah and Nathan. We're not the lucky couple." It was the best that Hannah could do, and she wondered why Nathan had been so determined to parade his ringer before Candace, whose opinion he despised. "Perhaps it's just as well. My father would disown me."

"Yes, the charm of my personality entirely escapes Joel for some reason," said Nathan. "But you'll understand his point of view. Flora."

"If you spoke to him the way you speak to me, it's no surprise the pair of you didn't hit it off."

"But I'm sure everything's going to work out, whether you're engaged or not," Hugo assured Hannah, to cover what seemed a horrifying gaffe to him, and he laughed nervously in his effort to turn the conversation into mere social chit-chat. "Let me pay for your lunch, Nathan, and Hannah's too, of course. My treat."

"No, it must be Flora who pays," Nathan insisted. "Poetic justice."

"OK, OK." Flora sighed, feigning an exhaustion brought on by long and tedious argument. "If nothing else will please you, —"

"You could always give me, Tiffany and Amber the inheritance you've cheated us out of," suggested Nathan. "That'd please me all right. Just an idle thought, naturally, but it would be such a nice gesture."

"I hear that you work for the Farrenton Company, like Nathan," Hugo said to Hannah, in another attempt to ignore what he found impossible to ignore. "It must be very interesting and — and — yes, very interesting."

"I'm currently raising finance for a film that Hannah's going to direct," announced Nathan. "It might be a good investment for your ill-gotten gains, Flora. There's a perfect rôle in it for you: a beautiful vision of a young girl who isn't actually real. Surely it'd be worth putting a couple of quid into the production in return for a starring rôle."

The thought of the impeccably coiffured and manicured Flora as an ethereal product of imagination appalled Hannah, and she knew that she would prefer never to make the film than be forced to accept an earthbound woman, with limited acting ability, in a difficult leading part. "Actually, I don't think —"

"It's a rôle tailor-made for you, Flora," claimed Nathan, speaking over Hannah's objection. "I hate to say it, Hugo, but the camera loves Flora. She looks better on screen than she does in real life."

"Impossible!" said Hugo, spurred into gallantry by a remark that might possibly have been true, because Nathan's tone was grudgingly matter-of-fact.

"It's so sweet of Hannah to consider me for a starring rôle, but I haven't got the sort of money that'd finance a film," said Flora, reprising her wistful sadness as she smiled at Hugo. "I'll have to be hired on my talents, or not at all."

Not at all, thought Hannah.

"It won't be an expensive film to make," declared Nathan: "a handful of actors, and hardly any location shooting. Three million at the most, so it'd be in profit days after release."

"Three million!" Hugo said in astonishment. "That's your idea of cheap?"

"It's virtually nothing for a film," replied Flora. "But to me, it's a fortune. Even if I sold the house, scraped together every penny —"

"Think of the profits," urged Nathan.

"It sounds a bit of a risk to me," ventured Hugo. "What if the film isn't a success? I'm sure Hannah's a brilliant director, but —"

"Don't expect me to be sensible, Hugo," said Flora. "It's my dream, and I need something to get me through this dreadful time."

"You can't throw everything you have into a dicey enterprise." Hugo tried to sound masterful, but could only manage apologetic. Anybody with a little determination would be able to overrule him, even when he knew that he was right.

"I don't expect Flora to finance the entire production," said Nathan. "There'll be other backers: companies wanting the prestige of their name linked to a project part-funded by the Arts Council and the BFI."

"Then you won't require a contribution from Flora," Hugo pointed out.

"I'll expect one, if she wants that leading rôle."

"And it's such a marvellous rôle too," added Flora.

"You don't know that yet," Hugo reminded her, with a diffident glance at Hannah to assess how hurt she might be by his opposition. "We haven't heard much about it."

"It's a starring rôle. What could be better?" asked Flora, surprised that an explanation was necessary. "I have to be seen to get anywhere, Hugo. The actual film doesn't matter."

"But, in fact, it's an incredible script," declared Nathan. "I've never read a better one: an adaptation from a runaway bestseller."

An imaginary script for an imaginary child. Most likely the film would be equally imaginary, and Hannah need not anguish about a treasured dream being ruined by a non-actress prancing around in a charade of childishness. "It's an unusual book," conceded Hannah, "a book you remember."

"If only I knew somebody with a company that would support the Arts," Flora said longingly: too longingly, with the heir to the Portham business empire standing at her side. Lionel was right, and so was Hannah's instinct; Flora would never be a convincing actor.

"Hugo's about to be vamped," remarked Nathan.

"Hugo! Of course!" Wide eyes turned in his direction as, somewhat unsuccessfully, Flora feigned astonishment. "I'd completely forgotten about your father. Is he interested in culture?"

"Not really," admitted Hugo, loath to disappoint Flora.

"Your father might be interested in good publicity though," said Nathan. "There are knighthoods for patrons of the Arts, and Hannah's film is clearly destined to be a classic of British cinema."

"Oh, Hugo darling, could you — would you talk to your father?" Flora clasped her hands together in an imitation of prayer, and looked beseechingly at Hugo. She was certainly beautiful, and undoubtedly persuaded that she could seduce any man into doing what she wanted; but she was a manipulative adult, not the naïve innocent she attempted to portray. Hugo would be fooled though, and Hannah felt sorry for him. "You will ask, won't you, darling?"

"Yes, I'll ask Dad." However, Hugo did not appear confident of the result, and probably had enough business sense to know that a film was hardly the most secure of investments. The Porthams had not become rich by listening to conmen like Nathan.

"Oh, Hugo, you're an angel." Flora hugged and kissed him as if the money were already available. "You've changed my whole world. I thought I'd never smile again, but you've given me a reason to go on living. I can actually believe that there's a future for me now. How will I ever be able to thank you?"

"Dad might not be interested in a film."

But Hugo's warning was said half-heartedly, because Flora's gratitude overwhelmed whatever commonsense he had, and Hannah marvelled at how much easier life was for an attractive woman. Hugo saw a face and figure, and entirely missed the calculating falseness. The artificial show of youth was more polished than Candace's, but still a performance, and Flora had yet to reach the nemesis of anybody who put too much faith in appearance: growing old.

"I only wish that I had time to order champagne at Flora's expense," said Nathan, "but Hannah and I have to get back to the office. You owe us a magnum at least, Flora."

"Whatever." Flora waved a hand to dismiss Nathan. She was ready to concentrate on Hugo, and anyone else would be a distraction from her task.

"A fly caught in a spider's web, that's Hugo," Nathan murmured to Hannah, as he led the way out of the restaurant. "We can leave the fundraising to Flora."

"She couldn't possibly be in any film of *The Love Child*," declared Hannah, prepared to risk Nathan's disapproval to protect her vision. "She's totally wrong."

"Flora's beautiful, and that's what audiences are interested in," said Nathan. "But don't worry. Today's exercise is just to put feelers out for money. Flora doesn't even know what rôle she's talking about. Invent a second girl, while you're bashing out a script, and bung the character in enough scenes for Flora to think it's a good part, and if she does end up in the film, we can leave her efforts on the cutting room floor. Besides, if I can't wrench any funding from Colin Portham, Flora's out of the production anyway."

"Hugo's father would have to be a real sucker to put money into a film directed by somebody so unknown, she's practically anonymous," said Hannah, relieved that Nathan had not been offended. "No one with the Portham riches could be that much of a fool."

"But I have inside information on Colin Portham. He yearns for a title, even to the extent of backing some of the opera he sleeps through, so if I play up the cultural aspect of the film and mention the Arts Council enough times, there's a fair chance he can be persuaded to cough up something."

"Not if he's got any sense, and Hugo won't be much of an advocate."

"Hugo's only purpose is to introduce Flora to his father, when it'll be 'Goodbye, Hugo angel; hello, Colin darling.' An object is only as strong as its weakest point, and women are the chink in Colin Portham's armour. According to rumour, he even had a fling with Candace years ago, despite being a business associate, whatever that means, of my father's. If screeching Candace is able to seduce the allegedly astute Mr Portham, then he hasn't a hope of resisting Flora. When she wants something, she gets it, and she wants to be a star."

An imaginary girl given a form of reality, a bit like a film itself, could never be understood or portrayed by a woman whose only interest was in fame without achievement. To Nathan, the venture represented a challenge for his money raising skills, and he saw nothing special in *The Love Child*. Such indifference ought not to matter, but it did to Hannah, and a minuscule hope of making her film fizzled out as they faced the coldness of the street, more noisy and crowded than before after the hushed grandeur of the restaurant. She was back in the real world. "Even if Colin Portham handed you a cheque for five million, you'd never get a distributor interested in the film, and you've said often enough that, without a cinema chain or television, no film has a chance."

"Oh, we'll stick it in a festival or two: Cannes, for example. That'll impress the distributors. Don't be so defeatist. Farrenton Films are due a smash hit."

Nathan knew the realities of independent film making even better than Hannah did, but he believed in his own ability to outsmart the world. Joel was right; Nathan had all the characteristics of a gambler. "Romney wouldn't let a mere production assistant direct an advert, never mind a feature. Besides, he won't have a thing to do with any project that included Flora, after the way she treated Lionel."

"Oh, Lionel!" muttered Nathan, a touch of scorn added to the usual disdain that was in his voice whenever he spoke of either Farrenton, "Don't you think that this purported distance between Lionel and Flora seems a tad contrived?"

"No," said Hannah, surprised at the question. "She dumped him,"

"You don't think there's something fishy going on?" inquired Nathan, amused by Hannah's slowness. "If Flora ditched Lionel, why did she phone to whine on about him being her only friend, when Hugo's very much around? That call doesn't make sense."

"Perhaps, at the time she rang, she hadn't heard from Hugo, and couldn't face the prospect of a day on her own."

"A woman who looks like Flora is the least alone person in London," said Nathan. "Anyway, she could have phoned Hugo to claim that he was the only friend. Why select no-hoper Lionel for the honour?"

"Your guess is bound to be better than mine. I hardly know Flora." But the mystery could easily be explained in Hannah's opinion. Lionel's film producer father was enough to make an ambitious would-be actress cling to such a contact with show business.

"Lionel went out of his way to tell you he'd sent Flora packing. Why?"

"You don't think that my kind and sympathetic nature encouraged him to speak freely?" asked Hannah, smiling at Nathan's scepticism on so trivial a point. "Or are we speaking of a dastardly plot to hoodwink me?"

"My hatred of Flora gives me an insight denied less vindictive people." Nathan pulled a rueful face, but he was comfortable with his faults, and more than a little proud to be aware of them. "Flora might be using Lionel, the way she uses everybody, but if you ask me, he's a co-conspirator."

"No one would conspire with Lionel. He'd give the game away at the first police question." Hannah wanted to protest that they were talking nonsense, but she knew that Nathan was brooding on his father's death and hoping to blame it on Flora.

"You're probably right," admitted Nathan. "Lionel's rôle in life is to be the dupe. But he still made sure that someone could back up his story of the phone call. Don't you think that's odd?"

"No."

"I suppose I don't either," Nathan conceded. "Lionel isn't clever enough to cover his tracks."

"No problem, if he doesn't have tracks to cover."

"That's because Flora did the planning," declared Nathan, but he laughed as he spoke, and shook his head. "All right, I'm concocting the sort of melodramatic script that would delight Romney's heart, especially if he could play the villain. Take no notice of me."

"I never do," said Hannah, but Nathan would know that she was lying.

****

Despite being entitled to a lunch hour, Hannah felt guilty to have abandoned the office for so long, particularly when she saw a man studying the sign informing him that the Farrenton Company conducted its business on the other side of a locked door. However, the visitor was no eager young writer, with script in hand, trying to storm the film world. The reality was far worse because, as he turned to look at Hannah, she recognized Detective Sergeant Erith, and had to force herself to smile.

"If it isn't me you want to talk to, then you're out of luck. The Farrentons are still at lunch, and Nathan Wyatt's gone to cajole some money out of a potential backer."

"When will Lionel Farrenton reappear?"

"Your guess is as good as mine," replied Hannah, instinct adamant that to part with any information at all would be akin to betrayal. "Lionel mightn't bother with the office again today. Lunch can go on forever when deals are discussed."

"Where would he be discussing these deals?"

"That's something you'll have to ask the Farrentons. Production assistants don't get invited." Hannah opened the door, assuming that she had managed to discourage Erith, but he followed her into the office.

"How long have you known Lionel Farrenton?" Erith made an attempt to sound casual, but he was waiting for a detailed answer.

"I met Lionel when I came to work here. He's an associate producer."

"Impressive title. What does it mean?"

That Lionel was the boss's son. However, a long and boring account of an associate producer's hypothetical duties should be enough to send Erith on his way, and Hannah launched into a lengthy description of a film company's hierarchy, but Erith listened with an attention that her dull explanation hardly merited. It was talking for the sake of talking, and Hannah wished that the phone would buzz, or a jobless friend of Romney's drop by: anything to help her escape from a situation that felt never-ending.

"I have to start work now," Hannah said abruptly, certain that she would be unable to stop chattering unless she silenced herself. "Why don't you try calling at Lionel's flat? He might be there."

"Do you know Flora Wyatt?" asked Erith, doubtless aware of what Hannah's answer would be.

"We were introduced at Mr Wyatt's funeral, but I can't say that I know her."

"Did Lionel Farrenton ever mention her to you?"

"He told me that she was once his girlfriend," admitted Hannah. "But I don't think he's seen her in ages."

"Does he have another girlfriend now?"

"Ask Lionel. I don't know."

"Yet he was at school with Nathan Wyatt."

The implication seemed to be that Hannah and Nathan were so devoted, they knew everything about each other's friends: an assumption that Hannah wished could be true, and was reluctant to deny. "Nathan and Lionel aren't especially close," she said, as a compromise.

"Did it cause trouble between them when Owen Wyatt appropriated Farrenton's girlfriend?"

"Flora was never Lionel's property, so she couldn't be appropriated by anyone," Hannah pointed out, only to be irritated by Erith's smirk of amusement. Clearly, in his mind, Flora was a possession that Owen Wyatt had stolen from Lionel without Flora having any say in the matter. She could very well have been bought, but it was Flora's decision to put herself up for sale, and although such a choice might not be exactly to Flora's credit, Hannah felt prepared to defend the right to make it. Lionel's rejection was his failure, rather than Owen Wyatt's victory.

"When the girlfriend made her momentous decision, did it cause trouble between the Farrenton and Wyatt families?" asked Erith, pandering to somebody else's absurd views. "Is that why Nathan and Lionel aren't very pally?"

"Obviously not, or Nathan wouldn't still be working here." Hannah sat down at her desk, and picked up a letter to indicate that she was too busy to waste further time, but Erith had a job to do as well, and no intention of having his questions curtailed by the person with the lowest rank in the film industry.

"Don't you think it'd be natural for Lionel to resent losing his girlfriend to a rich old man?"

"Was Mr Wyatt all that old?" queried Hannah, uncertain whether or not she had helped Lionel. "Anyway, Flora wasn't a big deal in Lionel's life, I gather: just one of a string of girlfriends passing through. The only difference is that Flora went on to marry Nathan's father. If that hadn't happened, I expect Lionel wouldn't even remember her name."

"So he has had other girlfriends since Mrs Wyatt's departure."

"I don't attempt to keep track of his social life." Hannah smiled, to imply that Lionel flitted from affair to affair with butterfly grace, even though Erith was unlikely to be fooled.

"Has there been any contact between Lionel and Flora since they split up?"

"Lionel said something about her ringing him," Hannah disclosed, remembering her duty as corroborator of the phone call. "Flora suggested they had lunch, but Lionel turned her down."

"When?"

"Yesterday evening, I think. He mentioned it this morning, anyway. But Nathan and I saw Flora a little while ago with another man in a restaurant."

"Do you know who he is?"

"Colin Portham's son." Poor Hugo would always be a son, never a person in his own right.

Erith digested the imposing name, and Hannah trusted it had given him a more complete picture of Flora: one that might free the Farrenton Company from police attention. Whatever the truth behind the relationship between Flora and Lionel, Hannah could only imagine him as a pushover at worst. Malevolence and Lionel simply did not go together. "Are you sure it wasn't a man who resembled Portham's son?" asked Erith.

"I've met Hugo a couple of times," replied Hannah, as casually as if multi-millionaire's sons were in plentiful supply among her acquaintances. It was information that Erith ought to be left to mull over at his leisure, but Hannah could not resist adding, "Flora won't be short of a friend while Hugo's around."

"Then why did she ring Lionel Farrenton yesterday?"

It seemed to be a rhetorical question, and Hannah remained discreetly silent. In any plot involving Flora, Hugo's rôle, like Lionel's, would be that of patsy, and if Hannah had Erith's right to demand answers, she would demand them of Flora. Nathan's prejudice was now Hannah's prejudice, and Lionel's appearance at the door announced the arrival of one of Flora's victims.

"Hello, Sergeant. Do you want to speak to me again?" asked Lionel, unfazed by the sight of a detective stationed in front of the reception desk.

"There are one or two details —" said Erith, with a glance at Hannah that made her feel she had been caught eavesdropping. "Is there anywhere more private?"

185

Lionel led the way into Romney's office, and Erith closed the door behind them with a firmness that intimated he thought Hannah would be tempted to listen at the keyhole, if there had been one, but her actual instinct was to get help for Lionel, despite being uncertain what form that help ought to take, and she dithered over whether or not to dial Romney's mobile number, until the problem solved itself.

"Any messages?" asked Romney, with the usual urgency that always suggested Hannah must have been swamped by callers during his absence.

"No messages, but Sergeant Erith's in your office interviewing Lionel."

"Why on earth —?" Romney, in hero-to-the-rescue mode, hurried past the reception desk.

"Erith wanted to talk privately to Lionel," warned Hannah.

"Nonsense!" Romney flung the office door open and marched inside with an arrogance worthy of Joel at his most haughty. A five-year-old Lionel, alone and facing the school bully, would have required such speedy intervention, but there was no reason to assume that Erith routinely browbeat the people he questioned, or that Lionel could be infatuated enough by any woman to collude in the murder of a husband; yet Hannah sensed that things had come to a head. Of course Lionel was completely innocent, but establishing that innocence would be a drawn-out process, unpleasant for everybody, and heralded the end of an era. Time was about to divide itself in two and, from then on, Hannah would think of events as happening before or after Erith's interrogation of Lionel.

However, as so often, life had no intention of mimicking the dénouement of a film, and Erith emerged from the office, chatting amiably to Romney about *The Pirates of Penzance*, perhaps the most unlikely topic that Hannah could imagine them discussing.

"I saw it on television as a kid," Erith was saying. "I'd never heard such brilliant tunes, and got hooked right from the start."

"We did a production of *The Mikado* at school, and that was it for me. I've been obsessed with the words and music ever since." Romney spoke with an enthusiasm that sounded genuine to Hannah, but he was an experienced actor who could make himself seem an expert with only a modicum of knowledge at his disposal, and he had never previously mentioned either Gilbert or Sullivan. "I can't think of a better way to learn how to enunciate clearly than by performing the patter songs."

"They're incredible," declared Erith, his face alive with a fanatic's ardour, and Hannah was surprised that a detective sergeant should have so innocuous a passion. "I always think the *Nightmare Song* is my favourite, but then I hear the *Heavy Dragoon* or the *Modern Major General*, and change my mind."

"Ah, yes, the *Nightmare Song*. Absolute brilliance," said Romney so smoothly that it confirmed Hannah's suspicion, and she knew that he had come to the end of his knowledge concerning Savoy Opera, especially as he glanced about for further inspiration. "But I don't suppose Hannah will have the slightest idea what we're discussing."

"You're wrong. My mother's in our local Gilbert and Sullivan Society back home, and I was roped in from earliest childhood to sweep the stage and prompt, so I've known both words and music practically my whole life."

Erith looked at Hannah as though he had never before seen her. She was no longer a mere figure in the background of an investigation; she had become a person. "That must have been an ideal introduction."

"Ideal," agreed Hannah, and all due to a father whose drinking had often meant that she could not be entrusted to his care. If Judith wanted to go out in the evening, the child Hannah went too. "My mother designs the costumes, and often makes them as well. She works in local government, so Gilbert and Sullivan are as good as a holiday for her. The next production's going to be *Utopia Limited*."

"I've never seen that one performed," said Erith, with the regret of a collector short of one final piece.

"Visit East Anglia next summer, and you can."

"That's a really good idea, Hannah," declared Romney, faithfully mirroring Erith's enthusiasm. "I've never seen *Utopia Limited* either."

"Nor have I." Lionel, a free man, ambled out of Romney's office apparently regarding policemen on the premises as a normal part of the working day.

"We'll make a special journey," announced Romney. "It's an excellent opportunity that mightn't occur again in a hurry."

"What are the performance dates?" Erith asked Hannah, and she hoped that he did not count on seeing either Farrenton in *Utopia*'s audience.

"I'd have to get the details from my mother," said Hannah. "She'll be very pleased if I manage to sell tickets as far away as London."

"Three sold already," declared Romney.

"You should put up a poster somewhere, Hannah." Lionel's thespian skill lacked Romney's finesse, but he did what he could. "Do a spot of advertising."

"Why didn't you tell us that we could see *Utopia Limited* this summer?" asked Romney, to cover the woodenness of Lionel's acting.

"It slipped my mind, and I can't think why," replied Hannah. "Nobody could work here half an hour without realizing how keen you are on Gilbert and Sullivan."

There was a danger that Erith would guess they were joking, but although a detective ought to be the last person anyone could hoodwink, he saw no reason to doubt the commitment of other worshippers at the same shrine. Owen Wyatt's death seemed to have been temporarily forgotten because *Utopia Limited* dominated the rest of Erith's visit, and when he left, both Farrentons slumped into a post-performance lethargy.

"Thank goodness I can wipe the infatuated grin off my face," said Romney. "Good work, Hannah, inventing all that guff. Making your mother design costumes instead of singing, as anybody would expect, was a particularly smart touch."

"It's the truth, rather than quick thinking. There actually is a production of *Utopia Limited* in rehearsal, and Mum's doing the costumes."

"Then we'll leave all dealings with the Sergeant to you in future." Romney pulled a sour face, presumably in imitation of Erith, and the resonant voice became clipped and reedy. "What time exactly did the telephone ring, Mr Farrenton? Precise to the second now: none of this 'give or take five minutes' vagueness."

"Why didn't Erith just check the phone company records, if he really wanted to know?" asked Hannah, exasperated on Lionel's behalf.

"Luckily, Gilbert and Sullivan fanatics are above suspicion in word and deed," said Lionel. "Dad brought the interrogation to an end without Erith spotting a thing."

"I once played a TV cop, and I asked the series adviser about conducting interviews to help me get into character," Romney disclosed, proud of having turned police information against its source. "If you can establish a link, like a shared interest or worry, it makes the other person less defensive, because he or she begins to imagine you're on the same side, and it's easier to fool them."

"But I wasn't trying to fool Erith," Lionel pointed out. "I told him the truth."

"How unimaginative," commented Nathan, pushing open the street door. "I thought that was Erith beating a retreat. What did he want?"

"Me to confess, but I didn't oblige," replied Lionel, too lightly for Nathan to take him seriously. Because Romney's death would be a great sorrow for Lionel, he shied away from talk of Owen Wyatt, supposing Nathan to be equally sensitive. "Anything more interesting happen to you this afternoon?"

"Yes, of course. I've been raising finance for the next Farrenton Film Company's grand production."

"I've no idea what it'll be yet, so how can you raise even a quid?" asked Romney, as glad as Lionel to move onto safer ground.

"Hannah's got a brilliant script —"

"No, I haven't," objected Hannah. "There isn't a word on paper."

"A detail we can ignore for the moment," said Nathan. "There's a rôle in it tailor-made for you, Romney, and a mere handful of other characters. The screenplay's based on a book written by Laurence Olivier's aunt —"

"I don't think she was actually his aunt —"

"Hannah, stop interrupting when I'm in full creative flow," ordered Nathan. "You'll love the treatment, Romney."

"So a treatment exists?"

"Practically," replied Nathan, brushing aside a minor point. "The story's got everything: drama, pathos, humour, mystery, and even challenges our very concept of reality."

"Before you challenge mine, have you read this book?" inquired Romney, immune to Nathan's sales pitch.

"Reading is Hannah's department," said Nathan, with another airy wave of a hand. "She's told me the plot, and I've more or less got the finance in the bag."

"Though 'rather less than more,' as Sergeant Erith would quote at you," commented Hannah.

"Erith? What would he know about film finance?" demanded Nathan. "I've told my contact at Four that the Beeb's interested, and my Beeb contact that I'm negotiating with Four, and told them both that the Portham Corporation's involved."

"Although, in fact, you haven't got anybody signed up." Romney shook his head at Nathan's deceit, but would offer no objection if the money were ever forthcoming.

"Making the film is all that matters," declared Nathan, "and the dosh is out there. We just have to get it heading in our direction."

"By giving Farrenton Films a reputation for double-dealing?"

"I'm simply juggling with time," argued Nathan, "and everybody knows that time's a state of mind. When Jules Verne wrote about space travel, it wasn't true, but it became the truth, unless you're a conspiracy buff and believe that the moon landings were filmed on a back lot at MGM. A lie isn't a lie when it eventually becomes real, and Hannah's film will."

"So what's the book, not written by Larry Olivier's aunt, that even a conspiracy theorist might fork out good money to see?" asked Romney.

"It's called *The Love Child*," Hannah said reluctantly, knowing that Romney would recoil in horror before she managed to get half-way through the plot.

"That was one of Imogen's favourite books," remarked Romney, to Hannah's surprise. She had expected to flounder on about the vivid imagination of lonely spinsters until both Farrentons were dazed with boredom.

"All women adore the book," declared Nathan. "The film's going to be part of TV's Christmas schedule right from the start: perfect family viewing."

"Too expensive a production for us, with the costumes and location shooting." Romney had no interest in the proposal, Hannah could tell, but he was kind enough to dismiss her idea gently, still unaware that his lowly production assistant was the proposed director.

"It'd be nice to do a film that Mum would have liked," said Lionel, but he too sensed Romney's indifference, and glanced apologetically at Hannah.

"We could dedicate *The Love Child* to Imogen's memory," Nathan suggested, alert to any angle. He was throwing himself into the project with an eagerness that Hannah guessed had nothing to do with a potential film. Nathan was trying not to think of his father, and her own inconsistent feelings about Joel meant that, although she dreaded his death, she was conscious of the fact that bereavement would set her free, and self-knowledge brought miserable guilt with it. Should Joel die before her, she would need all the distraction she could get from that guilt, just as Nathan did.

"It could be an interesting film," conceded Romney. "A lot would depend on the script."

It was true of any film whatsoever, but Hannah's expectation of Farrenton Films producing *The Love Child*, and allowing her to be its director, had not been high, and so Romney's cool reaction barely registered as a disappointment. However Nathan was not prepared to give up.

"Wait until Hannah finishes the script."

"*Hannah*'s doing the script?" Romney struggled to sound graciously encouraging, but his astonishment was only too plain.

"There's no need to be polite," said Hannah.

"If you're committed to adapting *The Love Child*, I'm sure a film's going to happen one day." But that day was very far in the future, Romney's tone implied.

"Of course it'll happen," declared Nathan. "When I get the finance sorted out, I'll start my own film company, and its first production will be *The Love Child*. You'll be sorry when it's a smash hit, Romney, and you're stuck making documentaries. Americans always go for cottages with roses around the front door in English villages."

"Sounds like it could be a success," remarked Lionel, who probably had no idea of the book's plot, but hated to crush somebody's hopes. "I wish it'd been suggested years ago. Is there a part that Mum would have wanted to play in it?"

"The leading rôle," Nathan said immediately. "She'd have been perfect. I can't imagine anyone who'd be better than her. You should have made this film with Imogen, Romney. It's got everything: drama, humour —"

"— pathos, mystery. Yes, you mentioned all that before." Romney laughed, shielded his head with both hands as though warding off a barrage of blows, and went into his office to escape a renewal of Nathan's patter. Equally unwilling to stay for a lecture on the glories of *The Love Child*, Lionel hurried after his father, and the door closed firmly behind them.

"End of Round One," said Nathan.

"Not end of contest?"

"No, Hannah, the beginning. Now that I've got the idea of filming *The Love Child* into Romney's head, it's a simple matter of talking about the production as an established fact. When I get backers, he won't be able to resist the prospect of a full-length feature film, especially if I keep playing the Imogen card."

Hannah was repulsed by the thought of using the memory of a wife and mother to manipulate Romney, but Nathan appeared to regard such a manoeuvre as both legitimate and natural, and he made Hannah feel like an amateur to be so squeamish. Clearly, she had to cultivate some professional callousness if her ambitions were ever to be fulfilled.

"Get that treatment on paper, knock a script together, and leave the rest to me," said Nathan, with undaunted self-confidence.

****

Joel was still stretched out on the sofa watching television, but something seemed different about the flat, although Hannah had no idea what it could be, until she walked inside and detected a lingering trace of perfume in the air.

"Who was your visitor?"

"Visitor?" repeated Joel, pretending to be so absorbed in a toothpaste advert that he barely noted Hannah's arrival.

"Yes, visitor. The one who wears expensive perfume."

"Oh, visitor," said Joel, as if he finally registered Hannah's words. "Amber Wyatt dropped by to see you. Both she and Tiffany are frightened that Candace might have had something to do with their father's death. They're quite right, of course."

"I thought Nathan was the villain," commented Hannah, not fooled by Joel's casualness. Amber had stormed the flat to see him, whether by invitation or on impulse. "How did she know where I live?"

"You must have told her."

"No. Did she phone you?"

"That Nathan Wyatt's a villain all right," declared Joel, ignoring the question. He was usually proud of his seductive powers, but Amber would be the first of his conquests who was younger than his daughter, and he feared criticism from Hannah more than from anybody else. "Candace is probably childish enough to kill in a toddler-like tantrum, but she hasn't got the brain to work out a plot, and there's a definite plot going on. If you ask me, Candace and Nathan Wyatt are allies, and they're both guilty of murder."

"Why would they bother taking such a risk, when neither benefits from the death?"

"They benefit somehow," declared Joel. "Perhaps they were stealing money from Owen Wyatt, and he found out."

"How could they possibly get access to his bank account?"

"It's amazing what a wife can discover about your finances."

As Joel rarely had any finance worth mentioning, he hardly spoke from experience, and Hannah smiled at his theory. "Oh well, I think we can leave all detecting to the experts. Sergeant Erith was at the office today, and it turns out that he's a Gilbert and Sullivan fanatic."

"Introduce him to your mother. That'll serve him right," said Joel. "And tell him that if this police harassment doesn't stop, I'll make a formal complaint. Typical of them to hassle you when I'm not there. It's downright bullying, and I won't allow it to continue."

"Erith turned up to see Lionel, not me, but Gilbert and Sullivan saved the day, and I've been instructed to ask Mum when *Utopia Limited* hits the Town Hall stage. Erith seems to be planning to go there, just to see the production. That's dedication for you."

"Why did he want to talk to Lionel?" asked Joel, suspicious of possible hidden agendas. "Did Erith question him about you?"

"No, about Flora, but the police are clutching at straws. She's gone in for more impressive company than Lionel. I saw her at lunchtime with Colin Portham's son." There was no point in discussing *The Love Child*. Joel would only start another tirade against Nathan, and even if the film were ever made, it was unlikely to be in the near future. Hannah Thirlbeck's directorial début remained illusive, like the girl Flora would never masquerade as, if Hannah had any say in the matter. "I'd better phone Mum now. Erith might tear around to the office first thing tomorrow, and expect me to have the *Utopia* dates to hand."

"If you're ringing Judith, I'm not here," said Joel.

"Don't you want to give her the latest on the dastardly alliance between Candace and Nathan?"

"You won't find it such a joke when both of them get charged with murder."

"Flora's the only person with a motive," said Hannah, picking up the telephone to stop Joel's slanders against Nathan. There must have been an alliance, if Flora were responsible for her husband's death, and Hugo might be Flora's personal ringer, because nobody would believe that Lionel Farrenton was in the picture when

Colin Portham's son happened to be the competition. But Lionel as killer? It was a scenario worthy of Joel at his most vitriolic, or one rooted in the scripts Hannah read at work: scripts that were clearly going to her head. However, nagging at the back of her mind was Nathan's suggestion that Lionel had wanted to establish his distance from Flora by telling Hannah about the phone call, and roping her in as a sort of witness, but the thought felt uncomfortably close to accusing Lionel of murder, and it was a welcome distraction to hear Judith's voice.

"Hello, Mum. When's *Utopia Limited* on?"

"That's a strange opening question," commented Judith. "And this is the first time you've voluntarily rung me since your father reappeared to sponge off you yet again. What's going on?"

"Nothing. I mentioned *Utopia Limited* to somebody, and he wants to see it."

"He? The gambler?"

"Nathan isn't a gambler." Hannah frowned at Joel, but he had no intention of contradicting her, and alerting Judith to his whereabouts. "You know how Dad gets a bit overprotective at times."

"I know he usually manages to con you."

"Perhaps," Hannah admitted reluctantly.

"There's no 'perhaps' about it, but I suppose I shouldn't blame you. After all, I was so conned, I married the wastrel, and ended up supporting him for years." Judith's laugh turned into a sigh, as it always did when she tried to speak lightly of her marriage.

"So when is *Utopia Limited* on??" asked Hannah, although the question would merely postpone Judith's attempt to talk some sense into her daughter.

"Who in London wants to know about an amateur production in the provinces?" It was a Chisholm tendency to respond to a question by asking another question before parting with information, even information that seemed innocuous, and Hannah steeled herself for a lengthy cross-examination.

"A man came to the office today, and he got talking about *The Pirates of Penzance* with Romney."

"What man?"

"Somebody called Erith. I don't know his first name. He's never seen *Utopia Limited*, so when I mentioned it, he wanted to know the dates."

"Is he a friend of Nathan Wyatt's?"

"No." Absolutely not. Definitely not. At least Judith had been given one answer that was unequivocally true. "What's so suspicious about somebody liking Gilbert and Sullivan? You're a fan yourself."

"After life with Joel, everything's suspicious. Does he know about this Erith? Tell your father I want to speak to him."

"Dad's out at the moment."

"He isn't. That's what he told you to say."

"No, he didn't." The protest was automatic and unconvincing. Far better to switch the subject back to Gilbert and Sullivan, even though Judith would recognize the tactic, because it was one of Joel's. "When are the performances, Mum? If you treat the details as top secret, you're not going to get much of an audience."

"Are you sure this Erith hasn't made up a story about wanting to see *Utopia Limited* so that he could arrange a second meeting with you?"

"You missed your vocation, Mum. Scotland Yard could have done with your deductive skills."

"I'm only wondering," Judith protested. "How old is he?"

"I suppose he's in his thirties, at a guess."

"He's too old for you."

"Then that's that," declared Hannah. "The affair ends before it starts."

"What affair?" demanded Judith.

"Let's go back to the beginning. When can Erith get his heart's desire, and see a production of *Utopia Limited*?"

Something was wrong. Judith knew that something was wrong. Every instinct informed her that Hannah had done a little editing around the saga of the Gilbert and Sullivan fan, and when Hannah prevaricated, Joel was involved. "I want to talk to your father."

"I told you, he isn't here."

"Yes, he is."

"No. He met a girl —"

"Not another simpleton! What on earth do they see in him?"

"What you once did, perhaps," suggested Hannah.

"Oh yes, how well I know the vulnerable look, the misted eyes, the claim that nobody understands him. The next move is to maintain that she's the only true friend he has in all the world. No half-wit can resist."

Then it was a compliment to Lionel's intelligence that he could see through Flora's artifice: assuming he had, of course. However, to picture Flora as a female version of Joel acquitted her of cold-blooded murder. Joel could be a petty thief, but was too much of a coward to risk anything that might be officially investigated. The accomplice, if an accomplice existed, had been the ruthless one, and ruthless and Lionel were not ideas that went together. Feeling happier, Hannah finally extracted the *Utopia Limited* performance dates, and put the phone down, leaving Judith to brood at her leisure on the nefarious intentions of the mysterious Erith.

"Dad, no woman could talk you into murdering her husband, could she?"

"How can you even ask such a question?" demanded Joel, haughtily offended. "I know I've got my faults, but I'm nothing like Nathan Wyatt. Besides, he'll have talked Candace into it, not the other way round."

"I just meant, could you imagine ever being persuaded into doing something you wouldn't otherwise do."

"You're asking me if I've got integrity." Joel, always on the lookout for insults, leapt on his chance to be the victim, overacting to get Hannah's reassurance. "But I don't blame you for doubting me. I never gave you the slightest reason to trust my word from the moment you were born. In fact —"

"In fact, you're talking rubbish," said Hannah, and she could only hope that her laughter sounded genuine. "I wasn't querying your integrity. I just wanted you to imagine something, or rather somebody."

"A woman who'd be able to turn me into a murderer? There's no such female."

"She'd have to be incredibly strong-minded and beautiful, a real Hollywood temptress. But could you —"

"You think I'm so weak-willed, I can be talked into anything."

"Dad, you know I don't."

"Then why say any woman could persuade me to bump off her husband?"

"I didn't," protested Hannah, forcing herself to smile. "I asked if you could picture a woman able to talk a man into becoming a murderer. As you can't, she clearly doesn't exist, and your integrity's above reproach, exactly as I thought all along."

"You really think that?" Joel yearned for as many compliments as he could get, and Hannah was his only reliable source of them. He knew before he asked what her answer would be. "You really believe that I'm not some gullible fool?"

"Of course you're not," Hannah assured him, knowing that Joel would fail to spot any over-egging of his cake. "You do get silly ideas into your head at times."

"Glenda always jumped to the wrong conclusions about me," Joel complained, with his usual eagerness to share whatever blame was going around. "She never gave me any support or encouragement."

"Forget her."

"How can I? Glenda did nothing but knock my confidence. It's no wonder that I'm paranoid. She'd say I was capable of murder. She'd say I was capable of any crime. I know she would." Joel sounded hurt, his mind hearing the accusations he imagined, and soon he would convince himself that Glenda had actually said the words. She might not have helped, but Joel's paranoia dated much further back than Glenda. "It's a slur on my intelligence as well. My luck's lousy, so I'd never get away with murder, even if I was stupid enough to try it."

"That's probably what Lionel would think," remarked Hannah.

"What's he got to do with it?"

"Well, Erith's been questioning him."

"But not about Lionel Farrenton's secret life as a master criminal. I know I've only met him once, but I can't imagine Lionel having the nerve to drop a chewing gum wrapper on a pavement," said Joel, more disdainful than approving. "I reckon Erith questioned him because Nathan Wyatt deliberately left something at the crime scene that implicates Lionel."

"I'm Nathan's alibi," Hannah reminded her father. "If there's a conspiracy between Candace and Nathan, then I've got to be part of it too. Are you saying that my integrity isn't all it should be?"

"Certainly not. You inherited it from me. I'd be insulting myself." However, Joel had no intention of being talked out of a pet hate, and he continued undaunted, "I told you, Wyatt's a gambler, and he gambled you wouldn't notice he left the flat. It's the only explanation of him not even trying to seduce you."

"Unless Nathan's integrity happens to be as admirable as yours and mine," said Hannah, amused that the suspicious Joel had yet to realize the probable reason for Nathan's overnight indifference to her. "Anyway, how could he get to Candace's, borrow her car, drive into Surrey, kill his father, return Candace's car, and get back here all in a few hours? He couldn't risk public transport, and didn't use his own car."

"Candace drove him," replied Joel, as if speaking of an established fact. "She picked him up here. It's easy to work out what they did."

"The driver might have been Amber," Hannah suggested teasingly. "She seems a determined young lady who gets what she wants."

"Slander!" said Joel, but he smiled as he spoke.

****

"*The Love Child* money's practically in the bag," Nathan announced, too busy to waste time on a conventional hello or good morning, as he hurried into the Farrenton office. "I've got an appointment to see Colin Portham."

"And he's meekly going to hand you a cheque for the odd million or two?" queried Romney, unimpressed.

"When I get the dough, you'll be sorry you were so dismissive of *The Love Child*, but it might be too late by then. There's no reason why I can't produce the film myself."

"Except that you don't know enough about film production."

"Nor did you, before tackling your first one."

"True," conceded Romney. "But I'm not prepared to discuss *The Love Child* until I've seen a script, or at least a treatment."

"Hannah's working on both," declared Nathan, his look commanding her to agree.

"The treatment's almost ready," said Hannah, as a compromise. "With the right actresses, the film could be quite —"

"Let's get our hands on some money before we worry about casting," said Nathan. "But this film's got to have a female director, hasn't it, Romney?"

"Not necessarily."

"Well, I think it's an absolute necessity."

Hannah wondered if Nathan had decided to use the unlikely prospect of her directorial début as an inducement to keep his ringer on message. They would appear to be an ambitious young couple, eager to turn their dreams into reality, and should Nathan actually succeed in raising the money for her film, Hannah was prepared to go along with any pretence he chose.

"If you're the producer, Nathan, have any director you like." Romney was humouring Nathan without the slightest faith in the possibilities of *The Love Child* and, for a moment, Hannah began to doubt her belief that she could make an intriguing film out of the book. If an experienced producer/actor like Romney saw nothing of interest in the project, perhaps she had made a fool of herself by telling Nathan about a daydream. Then stubbornness came to Hannah's rescue, and informed her that films were created by those who believed in them, not critics, and Romney's opinion was merely one opinion, and might be wrong.

"I'm telling Colin Portham that we'll have a woman director," declared Nathan.

"Then go tell him, but don't forget you also work for Farrenton Films, if there's any finance on offer," said Romney, smiling at Nathan's overconfidence as the street door slammed shut behind the treasure seeker. "It must be terrific never to doubt yourself, but Nathan's going to get an awful shock sooner or later, when somebody says no to him, and refuses to budge. Are you the female director so essential to the film?"

"I told you at my job interview that I hoped to direct," Hannah replied defensively, although Romney's tone had not been scornful. "But Nathan won't get backing for *The Love Child*. He's just filling in time until you decide on the next Farrenton project."

"It's not as simple as Nathan thinks to produce a film, yet it's not impossible either. If you really want to direct *The Love Child*, there's a sporting chance that you will one day."

"But you don't think it'll be in the near future, and you're right," said Hannah, willing herself not to feel discouraged. "I need to learn more, a whole lot more. I've only directed once, and that was a thirty-minute short at college, a film so intense and brooding that if it ever resurfaces, I'll die of embarrassment."

"If you can visualize *The Love Child* as a film, go with your instinct, and don't listen to whiners like me." Romney was just being kind, but he spoke to Hannah as a colleague, because he had once travelled along the same road. "Give me the script when you finish it, and don't do a rush job, no matter what Nathan says. No promises, but if I can see what you see in the story, I'll consider it. Incidentally, should there be a decent rôle for me in your script, that'll certainly grab my attention."

Hannah laughed, but she knew enough about the practicalities of film-making to say, "Raising the money would still be the biggest hurdle for my script to jump."

"Why does Nathan think he can play Colin Portham like a violin?" asked Romney. "Even for Nathan, he seemed amazingly sure of himself."

"It's because of Flora Wyatt," Hannah explained, reluctant to mention the vamp who had discarded Lionel for greener pastures, yet aware that Romney would be pleased to think even more badly of Flora. "She's keeping company with Hugo Portham, and Nathan promised her a lead part in *The Love Child*, but if I ever get to direct it, she'd have to be the last actress alive on earth before I'd allow her anywhere near the shoot."

"She's made a quick recovery from the loss of a husband," commented Romney: "astonishingly quick when you consider the circumstances."

With a rebound conveniently in the direction of another rich man, thought Hannah. Money made life easier, offered choices, meant there was less likelihood of getting trapped, and it also brought opportunities denied to the unfortunate. Nobody should scorn wealth, but there was still something distasteful about pursuing money as an end in itself. "Perhaps Flora had a poverty-stricken childhood, and swore never to be broke again," suggested Hannah.

"Or perhaps she's got a mother who needs expensive medical treatment only obtainable in Switzerland. That was the standard reason for a Hollywood heroine marrying money."

"Yes, I'm trying to make excuses for Flora," admitted Hannah. "But she might not be the type to wear her heart on her sleeve."

Romney laughed, the cynical man of the world: the sort of rôle he thoroughly enjoyed. "Yes, Flora could be hiding profound grief behind a façade of merriment, as she gads about town with Colin Portham's son."

"She was only having lunch with him, and that's not exactly gadding."

"It's near enough, especially when she's prepared to ease Nathan into the Portham office to kick-start her career as a celebrity."

Romney was quite right. Excuses were not exoneration, and it should have been too soon for Flora to listen to Nathan's flannel about starring rôles. If she had had any fondness at all for her husband, Flora would be in shock, unable to make sense of the world, as she wandered through it with the frightened bewilderment of someone caught up in a nightmare. Nathan had said that his father was on the verge of divorcing her, and it seemed Owen Wyatt had made a shrewd decision, perhaps his first since encountering Flora.

"Even if Nathan did succeed in wrenching money out of the Portham empire, which he won't, he wouldn't let Flora benefit in any way. She never fooled him for a second. He warned Lionel about her — but that's history now, gone if not forgotten." The street door opened as Romney spoke, and he glanced around. "Amber! What a surprise. A welcome surprise, naturally. Why the visit?"

"I've brought sandwiches for you all, so I'm not just here to get in Hannah's way."

"You're never in the way, Amber," declared Romney, "especially if you're running the Farrenton Company's catering service. Have you written a script you want me to turn into a smash hit? Of course, I've got a loftily artistic soul that recoils from the taint of commercialism, but the rest of me has no objection whatsoever to making millions."

"Then I'll dash off a blockbuster for you the instant I've got a few minutes to spare, but actually I came to talk to Hannah. Mum said you always have sandwiches for lunch, Hannah, and eat them at your desk."

"Usually." But not always. However, a meal in a West End restaurant with Nathan could be counted as the exception that proved the rule.

"I'd better make myself scarce if you two have secrets to share," said Romney, his tone implying that he spoke to a pair of giggling schoolgirls. "I'll retreat to my office on condition that you bribe me with Lionel's sandwiches as well as my own, because he isn't here and I'm hungry."

Romney assumed that Hannah and Nathan's half-sister were close enough to exchange confidences, yet Joel was the only topic they had in common, and he seemed an unlikely subject for Amber to discuss with his daughter. "What do you want to talk to me about?"

"I'm bothered —"

"Wait! Wait! I'm still among those present, and able to hear every word." Romney, balancing sandwiches on a coffee mug, closed the door of his office with exaggerated carefulness, and Amber sighed.

"Is he always so tedious?"

"I like him," said Hannah, struggling to keep her voice free of truculence. Romney was part of her second family, her work family, while Amber remained an outsider. "I'm learning a lot about film-making from

Romney. He doesn't shut me out because I'm only here to answer the telephone."

"Nathan says the Farrentons haven't a clue how to get their hands on money, but that's Nathan. He's the most conceited, arrogant, bumptious —" Amber stopped abruptly and pulled a rueful face. "Sorry. I shouldn't talk like that to you, but Nathan drives me mad. I'm just the nuisance kid half-sister, and he will insist on saying *half*-sister, as if there's only fifty per cent of me in existence. Still, you're practically one of the family, so you ought to know about the resentment surging around."

"I wouldn't describe myself as practically one of the family," said Hannah, noting yet again the determination to exploit a ringer.

"Nathan told us that you don't rush headlong into things, and that he relies on your caution to keep his craziness in check. He's not normally level-headed about women, or even a good judge of character, but you've changed all that."

"You're painting a very drab picture of me," commented Hannah. Nathan was a better judge of character than Amber imagined. He knew that Hannah would support his cover-story, especially with a chance, no matter how slight, of *The Love Child* being filmed.

"I'm actually giving you a compliment, because commonsense is rare in my family, and I need somebody sensible to tell me that there aren't any ghosts."

"You've picked the wrong person. I've been terrified of ghosts from earliest childhood, and it'd be such a waste of fear if they don't exist."

"Then I suppose I'll have to face my ghosts." Amber grimaced and tried to sound light-hearted, but there was still anxiety behind the words. "I went to your flat to see you, but —"

"You went to see *me*?" Hannah queried in surprise.

"Did Joel forget to tell you? I rang up first, and he wasn't sure exactly when you'd be home but thought it'd be soon, so I went around on chance. Your Dad's lovely, and I'm totally jealous of you for having such a wonderful father, but I couldn't talk to him somehow. He's so cheerful and positive that I didn't like to upset him by being miserable."

It sounded plausible, although for Joel to answer a telephone voluntarily was suspicious in itself, and indicated that he knew exactly who the caller would be. Hannah's memory of Joel's caginess added to her doubts, as did the feeling that Amber's visit would have gone unmentioned but for the telltale hint of perfume in the air. However, any relationship was Joel and Amber's business, not Hannah's. "What couldn't you talk to my father about?"

"Tiffany."

"Tiffany?" repeated Hannah, after waiting in vain for clarification.

"I think she was the baggy track suit who drove Mum's car that night. Talk me out of it."

"Well, to start with, does Tiffany own a baggy track suit?" asked Hannah, wondering why Amber had chosen a comparative stranger to be her confidante. "If there's no baggy track suit in her wardrobe, case closed."

"She could have bought one in a charity shop or somewhere, and got rid of it after — afterwards."

"Why would you even think that?"

"Well, it had to be one of us — me, Mum, or Tiffany — and I know it wasn't me and couldn't have been Mum, not in a track suit. That leaves Tiffany." Amber looked proud of her reasoned train of thought, and glanced at Hannah, apparently expecting praise for the logic.

"The car might be nothing to do with what happened, and any visitor to your house could have taken and returned the keys. Why single out Tiffany?"

"She's been acting weird lately. Really weird, like she's scared of something."

"She might be frightened that you were the baggy track suit. Have you talked to her about it?"

207

"I tried to, but she practically snapped my head off, and then wouldn't speak at all. Anyway, I've flunked my driving test twice, so she knows the track suit can't have been me."

Someone contemplating murder would hardly be daunted by a detail like driving a car illegally, but Amber failed to spot the flaw, and because Candace had been so entirely dismissed as the track suit wearer, Hannah began to suspect Amber of attempting to map out a false trail, in the hope that it would be reported to the police and sidetrack them from Candace. The idea was borrowed from Nathan's suspicions of Lionel and Flora's telephone call, but, although second-hand, the same theory could be applied to Amber.

"Tiffany said that Dad wanted to see her on the Sunday morning, but it could have been the night before," added Amber. "There's no proof that anything happened the way she claims it did."

"Your father arranged to see Nathan on the Sunday morning too," Hannah pointed out. "It was probably intended to be a family conference, perhaps about the divorce."

"The divorce! I'd forgotten the divorce. Tiffany wouldn't do anything that'd benefit Flora." The words were spoken with such exaggerated relief that Hannah again wondered what was going on, because Amber could have worked her way to the same conclusion without any input from Hannah. "Flora must have planned the whole thing. Nobody else collects; in fact, Mum's at her wits' end, and hasn't a clue how we'll manage if Flora cops Dad's loot."

It had all been said before, and Candace's lament over her lost income was loud and continuing, as Amber would know only too well. However, Candace complained of her ex-husband's tight-fistedness with equal rancour, and had she gone to his house to demand more money, a bitter row might have turned violent. Joel had said that Candace was childish enough to kill in a tantrum, and

Tiffany must have believed the same thing when she lied to the police. Amber was doubtless just as eager to shield Candace, because both sisters would know that their mother's limited intelligence would not enable her to outwit Quayle, and Hannah's part was presumably to relay Amber's conjectures to him.

"Could I venture out for a second cup of coffee, or are secrets still flying around?" asked Romney, opening his office door with unnecessary noise to announce himself.

"We've finished," said Amber, jumping briskly to her feet, "and I've got to dash. Bye."

"What was that all about?" inquired Romney, as the street door crashed in Amber's wake. "I wouldn't have thought that you and young Miss Wyatt had much in common."

"Amber gave me a message she wants delivered," said Hannah.

"Ah, Candace still has her sights on Joel." It appeared to be explanation enough for Romney, and he laughed with booming theatricality. "But, unfortunately for her, Candace isn't exactly in Joel's league."

Hannah was pleased with the compliment to her father, but even more pleased that a veteran actor had been unable to see through the impersonation of a successful architect whose life was under control. If the bluff could be maintained, there seemed a better chance of Joel making his image a reality one day, although Hannah knew that she was fooling herself as much as her father had hoodwinked Romney. "Dad's a tremendous ladies' man," said Hannah, smiling at what she trusted Romney would dismiss as a minor foible on Joel's part. "He flirts like mad with every female who crosses his path."

"Candace thinks she's irresistible, so doesn't need any encouragement to get her hopes up. The sight of Joel was all she required, but the Wyatts aren't your sort of family, any more than they're Joel's," said Romney, and

209

Hannah suspected that she had been given a warning about the danger of allowing herself to care too deeply for Nathan: the warning that Lionel received from Nathan concerning Flora. "Owen Wyatt was solely interested in money, and he attracted women with the same obsession, and they reared their children to aim at being rich. Not that I despise money. I only wish I had more of it in the bank, but as a means to an end, not the end in itself. Nathan still has to understand what I'm trying to do here."

"I don't think he'll ever work it out. Nathan's convinced that the script doesn't matter, if you can people a film with enough beautiful celebs."

"He's his father's son, and would be happy for Farrenton Films to churn out one trashy pot-boiler after another. Art is supposed to enhance life, not grovel in the mud." Romney was overacting the high-minded producer, but he knew it and laughed at himself. "I hope you paid attention to my lofty thought for the day."

"I'll remind you of it when I present a life-enhancing script of *The Love Child*, guaranteed not to boil a single pot or make any money whatsoever."

"I'm glad Nathan hasn't converted you to his commercial outlook, though a little crass commercialism might ensure that the Farrenton Film Company stays afloat."

It was a roundabout warning, but Romney had not told Hannah anything novel. He failed to guess that the ringer knew exactly what part she played in Nathan's life, because Romney merely saw somebody who might repeat Lionel's mistake of trusting the untrustworthy. "I'd sooner make one good film than a string of them rehashing the same formula," said Hannah.

"Yes, there are nothing like principles for keeping you on the breadline, but at least you can comfort yourself with the thought that you didn't sell out."

"I'm far too stupid to do something so financially astute. If I had any sense, I'd have gone in for a job with a pension at the end."

"All gamblers together," declared Romney.

"Absolutely," agreed Hannah, uncertain whether or not Romney had subconsciously picked up the fact that Joel's life was lived closer to the breadline than Romney would ever approach, despite his frequent claim that Farrenton Films tottered on the brink of ruin. "No need to go to a betting shop when you work in the British film industry."

"Or don't work, as the case may be," added Romney, with automatic professional gloom. "Any interesting scripts arrive today, or are we stuck with the homicidal MP?"

****

Hannah envied Lionel more than anyone else she had ever known, because his background was rooted in show business. With both parents jobbing actors, and film production added to the family CV, Lionel had grown up surrounded by contacts and opportunities that Hannah could only acquire in daydreams, yet he stuck with the Farrenton Company simply because he had no particular ambition to do anything else. Romney could have run a shop or a café, and Lionel would have been equally content to work in either; but nothing seemed to affect him deeply. Perhaps he had had an overdose of melodrama, with a father who enjoyed wringing every possible drop of emotion from the most mundane of situations, but Lionel gave no sign of reining himself in. He was just Lionel, who avoided conflict by agreeing with everybody, and taking a stand was so unlike him, that even he appeared surprised when it happened.

"Flora rang me again," reported Lionel, warming his hands around a mug of coffee, as he sat on Hannah's desk. "I felt guilty."

"Why?"

"Flora was depressed, and said she had to talk to someone, but I told her it wouldn't be a good idea for us to meet. Do you think I'm being hard-hearted?"

"Of course not," replied Hannah, unsure what Lionel hoped to achieve by asking her opinion. Nathan's theory began to seem more and more credible.

"Flora got upset, and said that everybody was against her. Apparently, you suggested her for a part in the next Farrenton film —"

"No, I didn't," stated Hannah.

"I thought it was odd, because Dad hasn't mentioned finding a script. Besides, I don't think he'd cast her, even if Flora was perfect for the rôle but she's got it into her head that Nathan's going to stymie the whole thing."

"He probably would, if he could, but the situation exists only in Flora's imagination," declared Hannah. "Nathan's still pretending to raise money for *The Love Child*, but it's to force Romney into deciding on his next project."

"Oh, *The Love Child*. I didn't realize." Lionel made an attempt not to sound dismissive, and failed. "Flora seemed to think there was a film up and running, with Dad as director, and Nathan the sole obstacle in her way."

"No, Nathan's just using *The Love Child* to galvanize Romney into action." Hannah was speaking to Lionel, but really telling herself again that Nathan had no chance of persuading potential investors to back an unknown director. Even Flora knew that, should *The Love Child* ever be a Farrenton production, Romney would direct.

"Flora's under the impression that she's a cert for the lead rôle, and even talked of selling the Surrey house, to get money to put into the film. I had to point out that it costs a lot more than that to finance a picture."

Quite clearly, Flora expected Lionel to talk Romney into producing *The Love Child*. Like many attractive people, she placed too much trust in appearance, and thought that, if she met Lionel again, she could seduce him into doing whatever she wanted. Hannah knew that it was a mean-spirited conclusion to draw, but Flora's past actions did not suggest a sensitive woman desperate to find something to live for, after the death of a husband.

"Are you going to see her?" asked Hannah.

"No, but she assumed we'd be working together, if I got Nathan sacked. I should have said something about Dad being unlikely to oblige, but she'll be in for a disappointment soon enough." Lionel's tone implied that he had weighed the options and then made a decision not to bring Flora down to earth, but he had kept quiet out of cowardice, and must have known it, because he added, "Flora needs all the hope she can latch onto, at the moment."

"Everybody needs all the hope they can get," said Hannah.

****

The telephone started to ring as Hannah opened the door of her flat, and she was surprised to see Joel hurry to answer it. He must have expected to hear Amber's voice, because he looked decidedly taken aback by the identity of the actual caller. "Hello, Judy. Hannah's just this minute arrived. I'll put her on." An insistent buzzing from the phone indicated that Judith wanted a word or two with her ex-husband, but Joel ignored the sound, and dropped the receiver as though it might contaminate him.

"Answering the phone twice in the same week?" remarked Hannah. "Wonders never cease, but get even more miraculous."

"I'm growing forgetful in my old age." Joel grimaced, but was less troubled than normal by the contact with Judith. He had gambled on the caller being Amber, and Joel was accustomed to losing.

"Hello, Mum. What's happening?"

"Why has your father taken to answering a phone?" asked Judith. "I suppose he thought it was the deluded new girlfriend."

"Probably. Is everything all right?"

"All wrong, when he's freeloading off you. I wish he'd move in with the latest airhead. At least you'd be rid of him for a bit."

Not while Amber continued to preoccupy Joel. She lived at home, had no money of her own to support him, and so was a sidetrack, rather than a destination. "How's *Utopia Limited* coming along?"

"Don't try to distract me. I want to talk to your father."

"You know that isn't going to happen."

"I know." Judith sighed in frustration, and then resigned herself to using Hannah as the go-between. "You can't be saddled with Joel for the next year, or however long it takes him to leech off his next victim, so tell him to come home."

"Home?" The word made no sense in connection with Joel, because the nearest he could come to having a home was with Hannah. No other option existed.

"He can stay in your room, and I'll feed him until he gets a job, or another half-wit falls for his sob story, and that's the likelier of the two alternatives."

"You mean, home with you?" Hannah demanded, startled. "It's impossible. It wouldn't work out."

"Of course not, but it'd remove him from your place."

"He wouldn't leave."

"He'd have no choice if you threw him out."

"I couldn't. I won't."

"You've got to."

"No."

"You'll never be free of him otherwise."

"If I don't mind, why should you?"

"Because I'm your mother."

"That's the only part I can't argue with," said Hannah, trying to laugh. "We'll have to agree to differ on the rest. Don't worry. I know what I'm doing."

"And that's the worst bit of all," lamented Judith. "He's quite prepared to sponge off you forever and a day, but you won't do a thing about it."

"There's nothing I can do."

Joel would grasp that he was the subject of the dispute, but he also knew that Hannah had no intention of deserting him, and, looking purposeful, he strode into the kitchen. His culinary skills were somewhat limited, but Joel switched on the electric kettle, and rummaged inside a cupboard, presumably searching for a tin to open.

"I'll have to go, Mum. Dad's got dinner on the table."

"Dinner! Is it tinned soup or tinned beans?"

"Dad's progressed beyond that these days," claimed Hannah, although Judith would refuse to believe anything good about Joel. "He's done the cooking ever since he got here, and it's a real treat to have a meal waiting for me."

"You're not fooling either of us." Judith's voice suddenly constricted, making it plain that she was on the verge of crying, and remorse sent Hannah close to tears herself. She had to upset one of her parents, whatever she did, and the situation was not going to alter.

"Oh, I must tell you about the most amazing thing at work," said Hannah, fighting emotion by launching into a tale that was worthy of Joel, who needed no more than an iota of truth to create a convoluted epic. "Romney's asked me to do a script based on Edith Olivier's *The Love Child*. I chanced to say that I've always thought the book would make an interesting film, and he wants to see my ideas written down. Not that a film is definite. In fact, it might never happen, because it wouldn't be commercial enough to pull in backers, but doing a script is good experience, especially if Romney tells me how I can improve it."

"At least you're willing to listen to somebody," commented Judith.

"Romney's able to look at a script from an actor's point of view, as well as producer and director," Hannah continued, ignoring the bitterness in her mother's voice. "I'm learning such a lot at Farrenton Films."

"What about that gambler who needs an alibi? Is he mixed up in this?"

"Nathan doesn't work on scripts," replied Hannah, grateful that Judith had been diverted from Joel, although the thought of Nathan was unlikely to bring much comfort with it. "I haven't seen him lately. He's very busy, and so am I."

"But he's still around?" Judith's question was a statement, because she saw her daughter as the perennial dupe of gamblers; but a dupe remained unaware of being used, and Hannah knew that she was Joel's soft touch and Nathan's ringer.

"I really do have to go, Mum. Dad's been labouring at the stove for hours, and I don't want my dinner to go cold."

"Tell him what I said about coming home. He's got to think of you for once. It's the only way out."

"I'll tell him. Bye." Hannah put the phone down before she could get trapped in another round of the bout that never came to an end for Judith, because there could be no end while Joel needed his daughter, whether he deserved to be helped or not.

"What are you supposed to tell me?" Joel asked warily.

"Mum wants you to go home."

"What?" Joel looked staggered, and abandoned his half-hearted search for tinned soup. "Judy wants me to go back to her?"

"She'll look after you until a job comes along."

"But she threw me out. She divorced me," Joel protested, automatically shielding himself from any blame that might be revived, even though the original episode had long gone. "Judith said she never wanted to see me in the house again. She said that I was the most useless —"

"I imagine a lot of things were said, but circumstances change."

"What circumstances?" demanded Joel, convinced that there had to be a plot against him.

"It doesn't matter, because you're not going back, are you?"

"It's too late. I couldn't have refused, if Judith had asked me when you were still at home. I'd have done anything your mother said, anything to stay with you, but now —"

But now Hannah could provide free accommodation for her father, therefore Joel saw no reason to face his ex-wife again, and he was right to dismiss the idea. Judith's plan came out of desperation, not her usual good sense. "I promised Mum I'd tell you, but I think it'd be a disaster, and would make both of you miserable."

"Exactly," declared Joel, as surprised as he was pleased to be considered more realistic than Judith. "I can't think what brought this on, unless Judy's finding the loneliness too much to bear, now that you're gone. I suppose it's difficult for her to keep relationships going, because she's always been such a strong person, and men find that threatening."

"If Mum's so intimidating, why did you marry her instead of retreating rapidly in the opposite direction?" asked Hannah, reminded of the gently obliging females Joel had since encountered, all of whom were transformed into screeching harridans when life with him turned sour.

"It was Judy's strength that attracted me to her. She seemed strong enough to solve every problem I had, and it never occurred to me that I'd simply drag her down to my level."

"All in the past now," Hannah said briskly, before Joel could talk himself into despondency. "Mum will be OK. She copes with everything."

"Yes, she does," agreed Joel, making his words a criticism.

****

Romney and Lionel were together when they eventually arrived at the office, and both seemed agitated, although passive Lionel hid it better than volatile Romney.

"What's wrong?" asked Hannah.

"Nothing's wrong," declared Romney, so emphatically that the invisible audience he constantly entertained would know that something was very wrong indeed. "The world's completely mad, but apart from that, we're fine."

"The police are testing my DNA," explained Lionel, "and Dad's certain that they're going to plant it at the crime scene to frame me. The exact same thing happened to him, twenty years ago, in an episode of *Yard Shout*."

"And it took practically the whole hour before I was released with spotless character," said Romney, but he had to force himself to sound unruffled. "The police are just being ridiculous, utterly ridiculous. Lionel's got more sense than to oblige an ex-girlfriend by eliminating her husband, which is doubtless the scenario currently playing in whatever passes for Inspector Quayle's brain."

"A DNA test will put an end to his stupidity." It felt oddly like a holiday to Hannah, hearing of problems that had no connection with Joel.

"They keep DNA on file forever." Not to be cheated out of any available drama, Romney spoke so gloomily that Lionel smiled.

"Then I'd better renounce all thought of a life of crime, because the cops would be on to me before I had a chance to flee the country."

"Of course Flora Wyatt had an accomplice, but that doesn't mean Quayle has to be absurd," declared Romney, sounding extraordinarily like Joel in one of his rants.

"Flora wouldn't kill anybody: at least I hope not. I don't care for the idea of having dated a murderess." Lionel was doing his best to turn the morning into a comedy, but a man had died and someone had killed him. The unmourned Owen Wyatt seemed to be the forgotten bit of the investigation surrounding his death.

"Candace!" announced Romney. "She and Flora are in league. It explains the car, everything."

"Except the fact that Candace would be more inclined to murder Flora than remove the alimony provider. There's no conspiracy, Dad. Mr Wyatt was simply in the wrong place at the wrong time." Lionel should have been more cynical about Flora than anybody else, but still he was charitable, or determined to appear charitable; Hannah could not decide which.

"Both Flora and Candace would do anything to get their hands on money. They agreed to split the dosh between them." Romney's mind had already jumped ahead to the end of act three — Quayle humiliated, Lionel's good name restored, Candace and Flora in custody, final curtain. "Mr Wyatt was hoist with his own petard: greed. He should have tried to produce a British film, and then he'd never have had so much as a penny to make the vultures circle."

Lionel shook his head and continued to smile, but Romney was pleased with the intricacy of the plot he had outlined. It appealed to his sense of justice, as well as his sense of theatre, and gave meaning to a death that might merely have been the result of a random act. A murderer ought not to appear for a few minutes, and then vanish to take no further part in a film, despite the Scottish play's precedent. Therefore, a petty thief who ran off into the night, and anonymity, was out of the question. "Flora's the mastermind, obviously. Candace would have done nothing but gripe about Wyatt's stinginess otherwise."

"Not much of a mastermind if you can see through the evil scheme with an ease denied to Inspector Quayle," commented Lionel. "Flora should learn to cover her tracks better."

"She didn't leave any tracks," Romney pointed out. "She's managed to implicate Candace, but keep herself in the clear. When Candace tries to wriggle off the hook by spilling the beans, it'll be dismissed as vindictiveness."

"Flora's no actress. She isn't skilled enough to fool the police." Lionel stated a fact, rather than objected to his father's imagination, and Romney paused.

"You're right. It'd take real theatrical flair to bring in Candace's own car as a double-bluff," conceded Romney. "I'm crediting Flora with too much intelligence."

To Hannah, there seemed more spite than intelligence behind the use of Candace's car, unless Amber had simply chosen an unfortunate night to borrow some transport for a discreet visit to an unauthorized boyfriend. Candace hardly appeared to be the sort of mother who scrutinized her daughters' activities, but few parents would tolerate either a junkie or a drunk, and reluctance to confess might explain Amber's attempt to move the spotlight onto Tiffany, especially as commitment to family was not a Wyatt strong point.

Abandoning the puzzle, Hannah tried to do some work, but her mind fixed on *The Love Child*'s unwritten script. She had an outline of most of the scenes, but a gripping first one, vital to capture and hold an audience's attention, eluded her. Uncertain whether an unearthly atmosphere ought to be established from the first shot, or if the supernatural should be a surprising later addition, Hannah was torn between a camera tour of a story book hamlet or spookily empty lanes on a windy night. It was not a decision in need of being made that day, or even that month, but Nathan's arrival in the office added a little urgency to the question.

"Colin Portham's practically in the bag," declared Nathan. "Hugo showed his father some pictures of Flora, and Colin Portham suddenly recalled that he's a patron of the Arts. Flora's to be introduced to our Mr Culture this very evening. Of course, Hugo will be there as well, but the other two aren't going to notice, so he shouldn't get in the way."

"I told you, Flora's all wrong for *The Love Child*," groused Hannah, exasperated with Nathan's casual attitude toward the most important thing in her life.

"And I told you that this bit's about finance, not the actual film. A few shots of a fetchingly dressed Flora, or better yet, an undressed Flora, will be the sole artistic compromise I'll expect of you."

"There are no naked bodies in *The Love Child*, not even to entice a backer," stated Hannah. She knew that Nathan was simply being realistic when it came to easing money from reluctant hands, but still his methods jarred.

"A highly-principled director makes my job even more difficult," complained Nathan. "You'll have to accept the fact that money prefers to wing its way to self-important men, who see no reason why luscious-looking youth shouldn't be enthralled by their limited charms. It's often the only vulnerable spot, and I bet it was exactly the same in Shakespeare's day, if you want an artistic precedent."

"I don't suppose it matters anyhow," said Hannah. "The film will never be made with me as director."

"You're depressingly defeatist, as bad as Lionel. You know how long it takes to get a film up and running. We're talking years, not next week. It isn't very tactful of me to point it out, but you'll be a lot older on the first day of shooting, and so the CV I'm inventing for you should seem more believable then. We'll have backers queuing to throw money at *The Love Child* — that extravaganza of tears and laughter, triumph and tragedy, passion and whatever else I come up with."

"This is my dream you're trampling on," Hannah protested.

"No, I'm forcing the dream to come true, because things don't happen if they're left to their own devices. You have to give fate a shove now and then, or it'll never produce the goods. And talking of producing —" Nathan glanced at the door to Romney's office, and then looked questioningly at Hannah.

"I don't think today's the best time to approach either Farrenton with anything but unadulterated good news and Colin Portham's signature on a contract. The police wanted a DNA sample from Lionel." Nathan was going to hear the news sooner or later, but Hannah would have preferred not to be the messenger. Nathan, however, seemed more startled than subdued by the reminder of his father's death.

"Lionel! What evidence have they got against him?"

"There can't be any."

"There must be something to make them demand DNA."

"I imagine it's just to clear him out of the way."

"Let's hope it does." But Nathan shrugged, as though the hope might be a vain one.

"Lionel would never hurt anybody," declared Hannah.

"He was besotted with Flora."

"And then she dumped him."

"But did she?" murmured Nathan.

"Flora married another man. That's dumping, and how."

"Then why is she phoning Lionel, claiming he's her only friend in the world when she's got Hugo Portham obediently at heel? There's something odd going on here, and I'm not surprised that the police have picked up on it."

"We're talking about Lionel Farrenton. There won't be anything to pick up."

"You don't know Lionel very well, but I do. He puts on an act of bumbling niceness, because he wants to be liked. He'd do absolutely anything to please someone."

"Not anything," objected Hannah.

"Anything," stated Nathan. "I've known Lionel most of my life, and he's always been desperate for approval."

"Not that desperate," said Hannah, unwilling to oppose Nathan, but ill at ease with his arrogance. He saw Lionel's amiability as weakness, and weaknesses, in Nathan's opinion, were meant to be hidden; therefore Lionel had to have a devious agenda behind a façade of benevolence.

"He'd do anything to keep Flora. She's the most spectacular girlfriend he ever had: a real trophy to parade around London." As usual, Nathan was judging by appearance, and to his way of thinking, Flora and Lionel's story had an inevitable end. Beautiful women gravitated toward rich men, just as men aimed at money. Character was of little importance in Nathan's world, and there seemed no place at all for love.

"I don't think Lionel would want Flora back," said Hannah.

"You're crediting Lionel with sense, a quality distinctly lacking in the Farrenton DNA, as Inspector Quayle's probably learnt by now. Lionel's putty in the hands of a woman like Flora."

Whereas a woman like Hannah was nothing more than a ringer. "Your Lionel's a stranger to me. Easy-going doesn't mean thick as a plank."

"No one could be as easy-going as Lionel pretends he is."

"I'm not sure it's a pretence."

"I am. Sometimes he doesn't seem to have a mind of his own, and that's got to be phoney at Lionel's age, because it'd be phoney in a seven-year-old."

Nathan had a point, but Hannah shook her head. "Lionel prefers to avoid a quarrel. That isn't phoney."

"It is when somebody agrees with everything other people say. In fact, it's downright unnatural."

"You only think that because you enjoy a good argument," said Hannah, loath to give ground and admit that Lionel could raise compliance to a superhuman level at times. "Besides, when Flora whined about him being her one friend in all the world, he told her to take a running jump."

"According to Lionel. Just two individuals know what was actually said during that phone call."

"Lionel's account is good enough for me."

"But apparently not for Inspector Quayle."

"The man's as cynical as you, if he thinks a peaceful nature means that DNA testing ought to be done."

Nathan laughed, but he must have understood how very compliant some people were, or he would not have selected Hannah to be his ringer. Without knowing anything of Joel, Nathan had realized that Hannah would accept the rôle he intended her to play, exactly as Joel was confident that she would never let him down, and Hannah's inability to refuse help was worse than Lionel's agreeableness because, while she backed them up, neither Joel nor Nathan would tackle whatever problems made them rely on her to maintain their own particular charade.

"I suppose I'd better go and do a powerful bit of acting to express my horror at Lionel's devastating DNA ordeal," said Nathan.

"You won't be convincing if you use that tone of voice."

"Oh, I'll stay totally in character, then switch the conversation to Colin Portham. Romney will be pleased to hear of a potential backer."

"Leave Flora out of it though," urged Hannah. "The third Mrs Wyatt won't be the most tactful of subjects today for the Farrentons."

"Do you think I'm insensitive? That's a rhetorical question, incidentally. No reason to lie merely because you feel my ego needs boosting." Nathan glanced again at the door to Romney's office, but was in no hurry to go inside and do his duty. "Perhaps after lunch —"

The more time Nathan gave Lionel to get used to the idea of being a police suspect, the better. Hannah knew that Nathan believed he could fool anybody, but his attitude would imply that getting caught, rather than a false accusation, deserved the sympathy, and there was a chance that both Lionel and Romney might sense Nathan's less than whole-hearted support.

"Yes, this afternoon would be easier," agreed Hannah, trusting that Nathan was too self-centred to detect the real reason why she reckoned the Farrentons ought to be left undisturbed for as long as possible.

"OK, I'll offer the condolences after a fortifying spot of lunch," Nathan was saying when the street door opened, and Candace appeared, defying the chill of the day in clothes more suitable for Mediterranean warmth. "No, on second thoughts, I'll see Lionel right now, and get it over and done with. Anything's better than facing Candace."

"Hannah's going to think you absolutely hate me," said Candace, her childish giggle very much present.

"Hannah would be quite accurate," Nathan retorted, hurrying into the sanctuary of Romney's office.

"Nathan's a dreadful tease, Hannah. He likes to pretend I'm the wicked stepmother, so you mustn't take any notice of him," said Candace, positive that she was universally admired. "I've brought sandwiches for another of our girl-talk lunches, but perhaps I should fetch more grub, if I'm catering for the Farrentons, and Nathan as well."

"Nobody expects you to feed them." Hannah's heart sank at the prospect of lunch with Candace, but feigned gratitude insisted on grovelling its way out. "I'll be glad to have some company again. Is Amber sharing the sandwiches?"

"Amber?"

"She's a fellow luncher here. Didn't she tell you?" There was no reason for Amber's visit to be classified information, but Hannah felt that she had betrayed a secret.

"My daughters never tell me a thing," said Candace, her helpless sigh accompanied by the rueful smile of an oppressed mother with strong-mined offspring. "But I'm thrilled to discover that you and Amber have become such friends. It's not surprising though. I felt close to both you and Joel from the very first moment we met. It's like destiny brought us all together."

Destinies could be bad as well as good, and Hannah wished that the cosmos had minded its own business. Amber would distract Joel from his woes for a few weeks, even months, but it was going to end disastrously, the way all his relationships did, and Hannah herself could have done without the disappointment of being a mere ringer in Nathan's life. The Wyatts were more drawback than bonus to Thirlbeck peace of mind.

"There's something about Joel," Candace was saying, an adolescent crush behind every word. "He's so sensitive, he understands me like nobody else ever has. Of course, he's suffered too, and known the agony of loneliness. I can't get over how much we have in common. It's amazing."

"Tea or coffee?" asked Hannah, to avoid commenting on the extent of the amazingness.

"When he told me how he gave up his Mayfair flat because he was so worried about you being alone in a strange city, I knew then that I'd found an exceptional man. It must have been such a comfort when he moved in with you."

The logical question for Candace to ask herself would be why Hannah had not simply moved into Joel's flat on arrival in London, but Candace and logic were rather distant acquaintances. "Dad always thinks I'll be targeted by drunks and gamblers who'll leech off me."

"He must be so happy that you've met Nathan. You're lucky to have a Dad who cares about you. How I wish Tiffany and Amber could have been as lucky, but they hardly realized that they had a father."

"I'm very aware of mine," said Hannah.

"Yes, Joel couldn't be more perfect if he tried," declared Candace, gazing wistfully at nothing, where she presumably saw an image of her flawless man. "I feel I've known him all my life, but it's like that with special people."

Candace could have been any of the girlfriends Joel managed to attract so regularly, although she was older than the rest and should have had more sense than to be fooled by a glib tongue, but Hannah was pleased she need not apologize for her father, during that lunchtime at least. Joel made friends very easily, but lost them with equal rapidity.

"You must come to dinner again. And bring Joel with you." Candace appeared to have made a decision, because her voice became suddenly brisk, and the wistful gaze was replaced by a hunter's eye. "This evening OK?"

"Dad said something about a business meeting with a client," replied Hannah. "I wish he didn't work so hard, but that's Dad."

"Some men are born high-flyers." Joel might once have had the potential to live up to Candace's delusion, but his failings were now too entrenched, and would always drag him down from any pedestal. Candace ought to be given a gentle warning, but Hannah preferred the fantasy.

"Dad's one of the best architects around. He never forgets that people have to live and work in the buildings he designs."

"That's so like Joel: totally considerate. I'll expect to see both of you tomorrow evening then."

"I'll have to check with Dad."

"Yes, yes, of course." Candace's attention was beginning to drift from the paragon's daughter, now that the dinner invitation had been delivered, and the thought of a less intriguing but more immediately available man took over. "Doesn't Romney bother with lunch? He should look after himself better. Are they having one of those tedious conferences that go on forever? I think I'll interrupt."

"I'm not sure that's a good idea —"

Candace ignored the advice, hurried across the room, and flung the office door open without the formality of a knock. "Why the gloomy faces? You all need cheering up, to say nothing of a meal."

The faces were more startled than gloomy at the intrusion, but Romney stood up, prepared as always to give a performance. "Candace! What a delightful surprise. Lunch is an excellent plan."

"Food's a luxury when we've got to secure money for the next Farrenton film," said Nathan. "Perhaps Candace would like to contribute a quid or two."

"You know that I'm virtually penniless these days." Candace laughed, but a distinct touch of rancour tightened her voice as she added, "Try Flora. She's the one with the overflowing bank account."

"Flora isn't the most diplomatic of topics right now," remarked Lionel.

"Is she ever?" said Romney. "Let's adjourn to the cheapest café we can find, and feast on bread and water, as we're all paupers together."

"That'll be such fun," declared Candace, entirely forgetting about sandwiches and girl-talk with Hannah. "We can swap hard-luck stories."

"A glorious opportunity that I must decline," said Nathan. "I've got money to chase."

"Then start running." Romney waved Nathan out of the door, summoning all his actor's ability to pretend that everything was normal, and he linked arms with Candace as though the prospect of a meal with her banished every other thought. "Let's storm the town."

"I'd better stay here and do some work for a change," said Lionel. "Order me a pizza or something, Hannah."

"Are you sure you don't want a break?" asked Romney.

"He'll be fine. There are sandwiches." Candace was already dragging Romney outside, eager to be seen lunching with a film producer, especially a male film producer. She was no longer a model, but youthful ambition lingered.

"I'll leave my mobile switched on," Romney told Lionel. "If anything should happen —"

"It won't," Lionel assured his father, but he smiled as the door closed behind Romney and Candace. "Dad doesn't seem to have much faith in my innocence."

"Everybody else does," Hannah declared stoutly, giving Candace's pristinely wrapped sandwiches to Lionel, and then retrieving her own amateur lunch from a desk drawer.

"Nathan said it's Kafkaesque, and the odd thing is that I feel I've been found out. I'm certain the police are going to match my DNA to the stuff at the scene, and yet I know I've never been near Mr Wyatt's house."

"I'm glad the police were called before Nathan and I got there, even though it was awful for Tiffany." If Nathan had found the body, Hannah's DNA would presumably also be tested; but should Quayle have doubts about Nathan's alibi, she might already feature on a list of suspects as conspirator. The idea made her uneasy, and she understood Lionel's irrational feeling of guilt. "I think Candace is the one with the police problem, because of her car."

"Unless Quayle plants my DNA inside it; normal police procedure, according to Dad," Lionel said wryly.

"The police would need to prove a lot of to-ing and fro-ing that night," Hannah pointed out. "You'd have to get from Surrey to London for Candace's car, drive back into Surrey, return the car to London, then it's Surrey again."

"Unless I wasn't at Gideon's house at all. Or Candace and I are in cahoots, and she drove the car to meet up with me," said Lionel. "Those might be the stories running through Quayle's mind."

"Why would Candace want to make her ex-husband's new wife rich?"

"Quayle probably thinks I was eager to turn Flora into a wealthy widow."

"That's rubbish," protested Hannah.

"I'm not sure the police agree with you," said Lionel, but he sounded more resigned than troubled.

"They have to go through the possibilities, I suppose, but Quayle's looking for complexity when a robbery went wrong. Nothing else makes sense."

"Then where does Candace's car fit in?"

"It was borrowed, and the borrower doesn't want to admit the reason why."

"That wouldn't explain the traces of Mr Wyatt's blood."

"They got there via Tiffany somehow, or the police laboratory made a mistake: Quayle's headache, not yours. After all, it isn't illegal to spend a night alone in Surrey, and that's the entire case against you."

"Plus a one-time relationship with Flora."

"Not a hanging offence. Anyway, if you had dispatched her husband, Surrey would be the last place on earth where you'd have spent that particular night."

"I could be trying a bluff," said Lionel, amused at the idea of himself as wily mastermind. "But you're right. If I'd known what was going to happen, I'd have an alibi placing me as far from Surrey and Candace's car as I could get."

Just like Flora, thought Hannah.

****

"How's the suspect?" asked Nathan, leaning against a filing cabinet, his languid grace an imitation of Romney's matinée-idol pose.

"If Lionel's a suspect, Quayle's an idiot," replied Hannah.

"An idiot with the power to order DNA tests, unfortunately for Lionel."

"Not in the long run. It'll prove his innocence."

"You've got a touching faith in Lionel's integrity."

"Haven't you?"

Nathan smiled, unwilling to abandon his sardonic air. "No, I can't really picture Lionel as ruthless villain. He's Flora's patsy."

"The idea's crazy," declared Hannah.

"Lionel was obsessed with Flora. It's odd that she's a duff actor in front of the cameras, because Flora's better than Bernhardt in real life. I suppose you've dismissed her as a harmless phoney, and she's phoney all right, but definitely not harmless. Flora's manipulative and calculating, the sort who'd do anything to get what she wants." Nathan chose words with more care than usual, but then the flippancy was back. "My father met his match in Flora, but he deserved it, if only for being vain enough to think that he was irresistible."

Almost as conceited as Hannah Thirlbeck had been when imagining that Nathan Wyatt could be attracted to her. "Perhaps your father saw too many Hollywood films about true love solving everything," suggested Hannah. "Those wet Sunday afternoons in front of a television influence you more than school and family put together."

"My father wouldn't waste his time with Technicolor mush. He'd have watched business training documentaries from earliest youth, with a spot of cost analysis thrown in for light relief. Flora was purchased, and he thought money was all he needed to control her, because he had no idea who she is or what she's capable of. Underestimating Flora was the biggest mistake he ever made."

"She doesn't seem bright enough to be anyone but the Flora on display," Hannah said tentatively, although Nathan would not object to any disparaging remark about Flora.

"That's part of her cleverness. It'll be fun to watch the third Mrs Wyatt being stymied over *The Love Child*. Between you, Romney and Lionel, Flora hasn't an earthly of starring in any Farrenton production."

"If *The Love Child* gets made, it won't be a Farrenton film. Romney said he'd look at the script, but I could tell he wasn't interested."

"Romney won't be able to resist giving you advice, and that's how he'll get sucked into the project," Nathan declared, with the supreme overconfidence that so amused his employer. "The Farrenton name's going to come in handy, because it's easier to raise funds when you can talk about an established production company, even if its track record doesn't exactly shout meteoric success."

"Colin Portham didn't create a business empire by listening to a conman's spiel, or by investing in British films," said Hannah, preferring pessimism to future disappointment. "You'll never get a penny out of him."

"I won't; Flora will. You're underestimating her as much as my father did."

"I think it might be Colin Portham who's being underestimated."

Nathan shrugged, undaunted. "Then there'll be another mug along, sooner rather than later, because they travel in packs like buses. Concentrate on the script, and leave the double-dealing to me."

"It won't work."

"Nobody has any faith in me," complained Nathan, "yet I managed to raise the money for Romney's biog of George Orwell, and that deserves an Oscar in the *Most Boring Film Made Since The Dawn Of Time* category. If you don't trust me, we might as well end our relationship now." With Romney's flourish of despair, waving hand that was then pressed to brow, Nathan left the office, apparently under the impression that referring to a relationship proved one existed. There was no thought of asking Hannah out again for a meal or a drink, either because Nathan considered it unnecessary, or he feared that Hannah might expect the purported relationship to become a more physical one, and he recoiled from the idea. Presumably he realized that the slight possibility of directing *The Love Child*, no matter how far into the future a film might be, would keep Hannah in line, and it was, perhaps, the sole reason he attempted to string her along. However, with a smooth talker like Nathan raising the finance, there was just a chance that a miracle would happen: the sort of chance Joel believed in.

8

"Your father's pretending not to be in."

Hannah had known that her mother would make a return visit to London or, more accurately, as many return visits as it took to dislodge Joel, but still the sight of Judith in the orange glow of a streetlamp was an unwelcome one. Just as troubling, when the man at her side glanced around, he turned out to be Detective Sergeant Erith.

"Dad mightn't be pretending; he might actually be out," said Hannah. "He does have a life to live."

"At present he'll be living it stretched out on your sofa in front of the television." And as though Joel's lackadaisical habits were a comical trait, Judith smiled, because Erith was to witness Chisholm spin at its most inventive; even his status as fellow Gilbert and Sullivan enthusiast failed to permit him to approach the inner circle.

Feeling unable to cope with the combination of parental encounter and police inquiry, Hannah turned to Erith. "More questions, I suppose."

"Just one or two points." Erith rummaged in his overcoat pocket for a notebook, turned towards a streetlamp, and began to flip through page after page.

"It's cold out here," Judith remarked. "Can't we go inside?"

"Not worth it. I only need to check something," said Erith, but he continued to search his notebook for inspiration.

A detail important enough to have brought Erith to Hannah's doorstep on a winter's evening was unlikely to slip his mind, and Hannah suspected that Judith's presence might be Erith's actual problem, rather than a lapse of memory, but no true Chisholm could be displaced when she was determined to stay. Judith raised her coat collar against the wind, and stood shoulder-to-shoulder with Hannah, as hostile as Joel would have been.

"Did Nathan Wyatt appear in any way different before you got to his father's house that Sunday morning?" Erith asked eventually, his notebook search abandoned. "Did anything seem out of character?"

"No," replied Hannah.

"He wasn't agitated or worried or — or anything?"

"No."

"What about Lionel Farrenton these past few weeks? Any difference in his behaviour?"

"No."

"Nothing at all about either of them changed?"

"No." Apart from Nathan's sudden need of a ringer to double as alibi, and Lionel's executive decision to discuss a telephone call from his ex-girlfriend with the lowly production assistant.

"Well, if you think of anything, even the slightest detail—" Erith reopened his notebook, and started to scribble numbers. "That's the case reference. Quote it, if you phone, and ask to speak to me."

"OK." Hannah took the piece of paper from Erith, and put it into her shoulder bag, wondering what he hoped she would remember. The police had to be desperate if they were counting on her recollections, rather than solid evidence, to solve the case.

Business concluded, Erith returned the notebook to his pocket as a symbolic ending of the interview, and became unexpectedly chatty. "I've put in for leave around the *Utopia Limited* dates. I should hear in plenty of time to book tickets."

"No rush. The box office isn't usually swamped." Judith ought to have been considerably more gracious to a potential audience member, but Erith had offended merely by doing his job, because questions from officialdom brought back vividly unpleasant memories of her marriage.

235

"I'm looking forward to seeing the production. It'll be —"

"Yes," said Judith, to stifle whatever opinion Erith was about to express on the merits or otherwise of amateur opera. "Come on, Hannah, open the door. It's too cold to stand around."

"That was a bit abrupt," commented Hannah, as the dismissed Erith crossed the road to his car.

"Who cares? Why didn't you say that the *Utopia* creep was a policeman, and why is he toadying to me? He hasn't got any interest in a provincial dramatic society."

"Actually, I think he has, if only for one particular production."

"That doesn't entitle him to hound you. He's suspicious because they've seen Joel's record," Judith declared sourly.

"It wouldn't make any difference to this case."

"They're always suspicious when your father's involved."

"But Dad isn't involved."

"That's a first." Judith, always severe on Joel, was being harsher than usual with her daughter caught up in the mire surrounding a stranger's death, even though the police apparently regarded Hannah as audience, rather than actor, and knew that somebody else was director.

"You're overreacting, Mum," said Hannah, as she unlocked the front door, and Judith began to stamp her way up the stairs to the attic.

"Impossible, when your father's in the vicinity."

****

"I knew that you were pretending to be out," Judith announced at the sight of Joel lounging on the sofa.

"I didn't realize you were there, Judy," protested Joel. "I glanced out of the window, saw one of those tiresome so-called detectives, and couldn't be bothered telling him to get lost."

"No problem, Dad," said Hannah. "Erith only wanted complimentary tickets for *Utopia Limited*."

"He didn't have free tickets on his mind, and he didn't intend to talk in front of me either," declared Judith.

"I thought you'd like him, Mum: a Gilbert and Sullivan soul-mate for you."

"It'd take more than Gilbert and Sullivan to make me get conned by another two-faced liar. What's going on, Joel?"

"The police are always trying to bully Hannah, because of that Nathan Wyatt," said Joel, imagining he had an opportunity to ingratiate himself with Judith. "I send them packing."

"Yes, Dad's been incredible," Hannah agreed promptly.

"It's just a matter of firmness," declared Joel, basking in the praise.

"Yes, Dad was really firm."

"It's the way to deal with bullies. Stand up to them, and they can't —"

"Cut the flannel," said Judith. "I've got you a job."

"A job?" repeated Joel, taken aback. "But you don't have any contacts in London."

"A job back home, in the planning department. You could do the work in your sleep, but it's fairly secure, and I'll take charge of your bank account. I've got everything fixed, so you only have to show up for an interview."

"Corruption in local government?" Joel smiled, amused at the thought, and he relaxed a little, perhaps spotting his escape route. "If anyone found out you'd rigged things, Judy, you might lose your job, and I couldn't allow that to happen."

"Nobody's going to be sacked, because you're the best qualified candidate. I've seen the other application forms." With an effort, Judith changed tack, and attempted Hannah's approach to the problem of Joel, although it went sorely against the grain to praise him. "They'll be lucky to get you."

"A planning department sounds a bit on the dull side," ventured Hannah, unable to imagine Joel tolerating boredom for long, even if he could be persuaded to live on pocket money doled out by an ex-wife.

"We're talking employment, not entertainment," Judith declared austerely.

"A more interesting job might turn up," said Hannah.

"And it might not," retorted Judith. "Anyhow, being in one job doesn't stop you applying for another, and everybody knows that you stand a better chance at an interview when you're already in work."

It was plain that Judith had thought of answers to all possible objections, but Hannah felt certain that the plan was doomed, and she intervened again. "Dad's been London-based for years. All his contacts and friends are here."

"And much good they're doing him. It isn't about choice these days. You have to grab any job you can." Judith could not have expected Hannah to be an ally, but was still annoyed at opposition to the plan, just as Joel would be hurt if Hannah seemed to be pushing him out of the flat, and therefore out of her life. There was no neutral ground for a daughter in the parental combat zone.

"What do you think, Dad?"

"I think I'd be risking your mother's career," replied Joel. "I'm not worth it, Judy. You have to put yourself first."

"I'm putting Hannah first, exactly as you ought to do. She's in a badly-paid, dead-end job, and can't afford to support you indefinitely."

"Her job isn't dead-end," Joel protested. "It's an apprenticeship. How else can she learn about professional film-making? You don't want her to get trapped in something she hates, too afraid to try for her dreams."

Joel had always been good at sidetracking, but he failed to allow for Judith's experience of his methods.

"Are you going to make an effort, or are you going to freeload off Hannah for the rest of your life? It's time to stop fooling yourself, Joel. You won't get another opportunity like this at your age."

"I don't think it'd work out," said Hannah, unable to keep her distance from the row. "They say you should never go back, and Dad wouldn't be happy, wasting his skills in a district council office. I know you're worried about me, Mum, but I'm fine."

"One of us ought to be in London, Judy, keeping an eye on that Nathan Wyatt," added Joel. "I couldn't bear to see Hannah making the same mistakes you did."

"Nathan doesn't gamble," declared Hannah.

"He's not only a gambler, he's a killer as well. It worries me sick, Judy, because Hannah's been deliberately targeted."

"If Nathan killed his father, it was the most altruistic murder ever committed, because he won't get a penny out of it," said Hannah.

"There are other motives besides money," declared Joel. "I can't leave Hannah alone at the mercy of a callous double-dealer, Judy."

Joel had overplayed the Nathan card. Judith could be fooled once, but never twice. "I've got more faith in Hannah's judgement than yours, Joel."

"She's being conned," insisted Joel. "Hannah trusts people too much to be suspicious, so I've got to look after her. I'd never forgive myself if that Wyatt wrecked her entire life."

"If anybody's being conned at the moment, it's the mighty Colin Portham, and even Nathan isn't persuasive enough to get him to back a film." It was simple truth, as cold as the February wind, but Hannah must still have had a little hope to be dashed because the earth was suddenly a bleaker place.

"Wyatt's definitely conning somebody," declared Joel. "I recognize myself in him."

"I don't think Hannah's going to make my mistakes." However, Judith spoke with less certainty, fear putting doubt into a mind that had managed to cope with her own difficulties, but would be shattered if a daughter's life became an echo of the mother's. Hannah represented Judith's second chance, a consolation prize for everything the past had thrown up, and perhaps Hannah would vanish from her mother's world, just as *The Love Child* had ceased to exist, if disappointment became too great for Judith to bear.

"You can stay in Hannah's room, Joel, until you find somewhere of your own." Judith often tried the Chisholm strategy of assuming that a suggestion was a fact and, in her imagination, Joel had returned home, started a new job, and was seeking the rented accommodation that would be his when a salary payment went into the bank account that Judith controlled. With the Joel problem solved, perhaps Hannah might then be persuaded to consider a less precarious career than one in the British film industry. Occasionally, a touch of Joel's baseless optimism seemed to have rubbed off on Judith's practical nature.

******

"Judith's right of course," Joel admitted. "She probably is offering me my last chance, and I suppose it could work out, if I let her handle the money. The only cash around in a planning department would be when somebody attempted a spot of bribery to get an extension built."

"You'd never be able to cope with the boredom," said Hannah, "and it would be the most boring place on earth to work in."

"But it'd get me out of your way. I hate sponging off you, but I go on doing it, time after time. I should put you first, exactly as Judith's done. She doesn't want me back home, reminding her of everything she'd rather forget, but she's prepared to sacrifice herself for you, and that's what I ought to do as well."

"I'm not worth it. Nobody deserves to be sentenced to a job in a provincial planning office, and definitely not because of a daughter who won't listen to either of her parents."

"I suppose we all have to make our own mistakes," Joel conceded, "but watching you get conned is the hardest thing I've ever done in my life."

"And it's just as bad for Mum to know that I haven't got a secure job with a pension at the end. Yet you think I made the right decision to take my chances in a film company, don't you?"

"Being targeted by a gambling psychopath is another matter entirely. He's already got you in a mess with the law —"

"That wasn't Nathan's fault."

"— and you'll be dragged down even further if you don't get away from him."

"Nathan hasn't asked me out again. I think his encounter with my ferocious father had an effect."

"Oh, Wyatt will be back, especially when he needs another alibi."

"Then perhaps I can look forward to a livelier social life each time Nathan murders somebody."

"It isn't a joke," declared Joel. "Candace will be next, you'll see. She must have been in it with Wyatt, that's obvious, so he's got to silence her before she gives the game away."

"Your theory doesn't explain why Candace would plot to enrich her ex-husband's third wife."

"How can I explain what goes on in a killer's mind?" asked Joel, to avoid the vicinity of logic. "I know what happened, and the police are bound to think you're somehow involved."

"It's their job to be suspicious of everybody. Anyway, Nathan's a good excuse to keep you from the horrors of a planning department, so you ought to be grateful to him. Even Mum can't disapprove of you trying to protect me from a psychopathic associate producer."

"You won't find it so funny when Candace gets her comeuppance."

"Nathan might be in more danger from her," suggested Hannah, amused by Joel's fraught tone. "She must have done the actual killing, as I'm Nathan's alibi, so she's the one I'd give a wide berth to."

"It's her daughter I feel sorry for," said Joel, sighing with tender sympathy.

"Daughters. There are two."

"Tiffany's the cold sort, well able to look after herself. But Amber's —"

"— the embodiment of gentle vulnerability, with just a hint of patience on a monument."

"Well, I like her," Joel said smiling, but with a certain defensiveness in his voice. "Amber doesn't belong in that family. There's no hypocrisy about her, no pretence at all. She's a hundred per cent genuine, and how Amber managed it among those Wyatts is a mystery to me."

Hannah was not quite as sure as Joel about the authenticity of the frankness on show, but his attraction to Amber would be another reason for him to stay in London and avoid Judith's petty bureaucratic world, where he would have time to brood on his cruel fate. "You won't listen to Mum, will you? Her plan's all wrong for you in just about every way."

"You don't think I'm capable of building a life for myself," Joel declared, in need of yet more reassurance.

"I think you're too intelligent to stand the narrow-mindedness back home after escaping it once."

"Intelligent is the last thing I am," Joel said ruefully. "I had everything, family, career, future, and threw it all away."

"You've still got family," Hannah reminded him, "and another job will turn up, so you mustn't accept one that's going to make you feel worse than before."

Joel held up his hands in surrender. "If I lounge around unemployed for months, you won't despise me?"

"I'd think that you'd made a sensible decision to protect yourself from depression. Everything's going to work out, especially after you give me those bank cards of yours. You really should hand them over right now, or you'll have to face the prospect of being nagged at for the next hour, to say nothing of the next week."

Joel laughed and shrugged, but then he stood up, suddenly decisive, and held out his wallet to Hannah. "Quick, take it."

"You're sure?" Hannah asked in astonishment, but she grabbed the wallet before Joel's willpower had a chance to crumble.

"I'm positive at this second, but can't guarantee that I won't try and persuade you to give the cards back in a minute or so. Don't listen to me, whatever I say."

"Agreed." Hannah opened the wallet and took out three credit cards, marvelling at the banks' fecklessness in supplying them to somebody with Joel's history. "You won't report the cards stolen, I hope, and get then replaced?"

"You're clued up to all my dodges," said Joel, regretful but also ashamed. "I won't let you down again, I promise."

"I know," declared Hannah, aware of how many promises Joel had made and then ignored.

"I mean it this time."

"I can tell that you do." Joel always meant what he said at the time he said it; the future of any promise was more problematic. To change the subject, Hannah glanced at a piece of paper caught between two of the credit cards, and asked, "Is this Amber's mobile number, or your PIN cunningly disguised?"

"Neither. It's the number of Nathan Wyatt's accomplice, or else the girlfriend he can't introduce to his family. I found it on the floor, the time you went tearing after him to return his wallet."

"You shouldn't have kept it," protested Hannah. "It might be important: one of Nathan's business contacts."

"Then why isn't the number stored inside his mobile? Wyatt plainly didn't want it recorded on anything the police could get at."

"I'm surprised you haven't dialled it, to discover exactly what Nathan's guilty secret is," said Hannah, sighing at the melodrama behind Joel's suspicions. "How on earth did you resist the temptation?"

"Somebody's got to look after you, especially when you won't listen to a word against that charlatan."

"You have dialled the number," Hannah declared, recognizing evasiveness when she heard it. "Dad, how could you?"

"Where's the crime in dialling a number? But don't worry; I used a public call box in case the police are tapping your phone."

"That's total paranoia, and I pity anyone ever forced to eavesdrop on the trivia of my life. I gather you weren't connected to Assassins Anonymous, as you didn't pass the number onto Inspector Quayle."

"The mobile was switched off both times I tried," Joel complained. "Why bother with a phone, if it's never used?"

"I'm confiscating this piece of paper, as well as your bank cards. I'll drop it somewhere in the office and, when the number's found, hope that Nathan thinks it was there the whole time. Leave snooping to the police, Dad. It's what they're paid to do."

"Quayle doesn't realize what he's up against," Joel declared. "Wyatt's cunning, very cunning."

"A mere detective can't expect to be as shrewd as you," said Hannah, exasperated by her father's obstinacy about Nathan, but unwilling to contradict Joel when he was prepared to make yet another attempt to tackle his weaknesses. "I'm so proud of you, Dad, giving me your credit cards, and if you ask for them back, I'll threaten you with that planning office. This is the start of your new life."

"I've had more new starts than you probably get with reincarnation, but this one's different; this one's permanent."

"Absolutely," agreed Hannah, too readily and too emphatically. "Besides, you only have to get through one day at a time."

"One minute at a time is about all I can manage," said Joel, with a regret that was genuine for once.

****

"You look happy," commented Romney, as he arrived in the Farrenton Film Company's office, employing the brisk stride of his successful-producer impersonation.

"Do I usually look miserable?" asked Hannah, but the relief of knowing that Joel's bank cards were safely out of his reach was enough to keep her smiling.

"Nathan's always convinced that he can raise the finance for any project whatsoever," said Romney: a warning that was unnecessary. "I hope you won't be too disappointed if it doesn't work out for your film."

"I take Nathan's schemes with a pinch of salt," Hannah assured Romney. "I know the chances of *The Love Child* being made are non-existent."

"I wouldn't go as far as that, but don't put too much faith in Nathan's spiel. Keep working on the script though. It's amazing what stubbornness can achieve, given time."

"I've got the stubbornness all right. You only have to ask my mother."

"If you don't believe in yourself, nobody else will. I don't think Nathan's going to prise open Colin Portham's coffers, but all sorts of films do get made. Eventually. Why not yours?"

"I won't hold my breath while I'm waiting," Hannah promised, touched by Romney's struggle between realism and encouragement.

"Besides, I need you here a bit longer before you go waltzing off to put my artistic efforts in the shade. A friend of mine at Four — well, actually I loathe the bloke, but business is business. Anyway, I had a drink with him yesterday, and chanced to mention the Victorian theatre. He imagined I was talking shop, and said it might be an interesting commission."

"A documentary?"

"No, I was utterly inspired, and promptly claimed to be working on an idea for a series of over-the-top melodramas, to be filmed on stage. I was thinking on my feet, so I had to gloss over details, but the man's a commissioner and he was listening. I'm not sure that the plays have novelty appeal as he seemed to believe, and no doubt he'll be less enthusiastic when he sobers up, but the series would be different, and indoor shooting will keep the costs down."

"No need to convince me. It'd be fun to work on, but they don't often commission fun."

"They prefer urban misery, so I'll play up the contrast. I'm not losing a glorious opportunity to rant on stage as a moustache-twirling villain, if I can help it. Probably too good a commission to be true, but these chance conversations sometimes have better results than months of planning."

"It's an idea no one else will submit."

"That's for sure. I'll work on a presentation but, like you, I won't be holding my breath while I'm waiting for this particular commission to materialize." However, Romney's attempt at cold-blooded reason was less convincing as he added, "I've always longed to stamp around in one of those old melodramas."

"You could claim that the plays were the earliest form of soap opera."

"While talking up the historic and educational aspects at the same time to cover all bases." Then Romney laughed, and admitted, "That *Love Child* of yours is looking more and more commercial. At least a quaint English village might interest the Americans."

"What about including the play that Abraham Lincoln saw in Ford's Theatre the night he was assassinated?" suggested Hannah. "The series might sell to the States on the back of that one production."

"Life imitating melodrama. Not a bad idea. Assuming the play was a melodrama, of course. Are there any other American events linked to a theatre? What was playing when Chicago went up in flames?"

"I'll have to get back to you on that one," said Hannah, enjoying the ebullient mood that seemed to pervade the whole day. Anything was possible when Joel allowed her to control his money. "Perhaps each of the plays could be connected to a historical event: like whichever melodrama William Terriss was starring in, when he got murdered at the Adelphi stage door."

"We could throw in a half-hour documentary, to be shown before or after the play. Is this what used to be called a brain-storming session?"

Hannah laughed with Romney, pleased to be sharing his ideas, no matter how unlikely they were to result in actual film. Lionel would normally be the privileged confidant, and the fact that Romney was cheerful meant the DNA test had been relegated to the background, less important than a commission he would relish; but a worry could only be postponed, not ignored completely.

"Has Lionel phoned?" Romney paused on the way into his office, even though he knew that Hannah would already have passed on any messages from a Lionel under arrest. "What about police bloodhounds in here, hot on the trail?"

"Nobody's phoned or dropped in," replied Hannah. "Actually, I saw Sergeant Erith yesterday evening. He was hanging around when I went home."

"To ask you about Lionel?"

"Nathan. But Mum got rid of him."

"Mum? Are both your parents the nemesis of policemen?"

"Mum and Dad act as one, in those situations."

"What was Erith hoping to learn about Nathan?"

"I've no idea. I couldn't help him, anyway."

"Did he mention Lionel?"

"Not a word," lied Hannah.

"The police seem to be drifting aimlessly like jellyfish," complained Romney. "Quayle doesn't have an earthly of his memoirs being turned into a TV mini series."

"Perhaps he and Erith just want to grab some overtime pay."

"Perhaps. What did Erith ask about Nathan?"

"If he appeared in any way different on that Sunday morning."

"His father died suddenly and violently. Of course Nathan's different," Romney said irritably. "What does that fool Erith expect?"

It was unfortunate that Detective Sergeant Erith should choose to walk into the Farrenton Film Company offices at that precise moment, forcing both Hannah and Romney to struggle against embarrassed laughter

"Good morning, Sergeant — Sergeant — I'm terribly sorry, but I can't recall your surname; a sign of impending senility, I fear," said Romney, with a presence of mind that left Hannah awed at such aplomb. "What can we do for you? My son isn't here just now, so if you've come to apologize to him, it'll have to wait. The DNA test proved his absolute innocence, naturally."

"The results aren't back yet," reported Erith, betraying no wonder at the remarkable coincidence of Hannah and Romney discussing one Erith as another arrived. "I'm here to ask Miss Thirlbeck a question or two."

Presumably the questions that Erith had been reluctant to broach in front of Judith, and Hannah immediately felt guilty without anything specific to feel guilty about. Talking to a policeman, particularly one who doubted her word, was an unpleasant reminder of powerlessness against acerbic teachers, and Erith's authority was even greater, but Hannah strived to look relaxed, while Romney sat on a corner of the reception desk, plainly intending to stay exactly where he was throughout the interview.

"I'd like to talk to Miss Thirlbeck alone," said Erith.

"Why?" demanded Romney, the haughty producer unaccustomed to being told where he could or could not sit. He was acting out a hero versus villain scenario, and since Lionel's DNA test, Erith had definitely been cast as a villain.

"It's OK," said Hannah.

"You're sure?" asked Romney, evidently believing that Hannah might be putting herself in dire peril if left unprotected with Erith.

"Yes, it's fine."

"I'll be in my office," Romney said to Hannah, his tone informing Erith that the Farrenton Film Company would not tolerate any more police harassment of employees. "Call out if you need me, Hannah."

"Thanks." It occurred to Hannah that, as Romney had clearly hoped to monitor the questioning, Erith might assume she had information about Lionel that the Farrentons preferred to keep hidden, and Hannah leaned back in her chair, trying to look unperturbed, but then decided that treating a police interview as a routine part of the day would seem odder than a show of apprehension.

"I always imagined that a film company would look more — well, more show biz," remarked Erith, presumably to reassure Romney that the visit was so unimportant, it verged on the social side.

"Glamour belongs in Hollywood, not the British film industry," Romney declared frostily, reacting to what he plainly perceived as an insult. "We don't do tinsel."

"I've never understood why tinsel gets so bad a press. I think it's lovely," said Hannah, to show Romney how at ease she felt. "I like sparklers too."

"Then you should direct some very popular films one day." Romney went into his office, and gave such a performance of carefully closing the door behind him, that Hannah was certain he planned to stay very close to it, eavesdropping.

"Are you from a religious family?" asked Erith, taking Hannah aback with the unexpectedness of his question.

"Religious? Not particularly. Why?"

"I thought that, if you had strict parents, it'd be understandable to protect them from anything they'd find distressing," said Erith, and he picked his way through the words with a delicacy that amused Hannah.

"Nathan and I didn't share a Saturday night bed. He's not that close a friend."

Erith stared at Hannah for a few seconds, apparently convinced that he was a human lie-detector, and then demanded, "Is Wyatt gay?"

"You'll have to ask Nathan," replied Hannah, pleased with Erith's inadvertent compliment that implied only a gay man could resist her.

"Did he ever spend a night at your place before that Saturday?"

"No, and it only happened then because he'd had a glass or two of wine, and wouldn't risk driving." Even to Hannah, the story was beginning to sound more and more like a tale concocted to give Nathan an alibi, although one that meant he could have left the flat at some time during the night: a possibility perhaps intended to add the appearance of truth. Life was so rarely clear-cut, the pair of them might have thought the police would be less inclined to suspect a conspiracy if Hannah claimed that she and Nathan spent the night in separate rooms. However, Erith continued to look at Hannah as though hoping she would wilt before his gaze, and add a detail that incriminated both herself and Nathan

"So you can't be sure that Wyatt was in your flat the whole night." Erith studied Hannah's reaction, but his words were not as momentous as he seemed to think.

"That's what Inspector Quayle said, but Nathan would have been taking a bit of a risk."

"Is he a risk-taker?"

"He doesn't strike me as a gambler," replied Hannah, unwilling to be more emphatic for fear of protesting too much.

"What do you imagine a gambler would be like?"

It needed no imagination to picture Joel, and Hannah wondered if Erith had picked up something of her family history. He might be issuing a challenge to see exactly how straightforward Hannah Thirlbeck was, and weighing the rest of her answers by the response to that one question. A compromise had to be found between helping Nathan and instinctive Chisholm spin. "Somebody in my family has a problem with gambling, and Nathan isn't anything like him."

Erith was silent for a minute or two, scribbling in his notebook, and making Hannah feel more uneasy than at any other time during the interview, nervous that he would demand the identity of her gambling relative: information she preferred to keep from a listening Romney. However, Erith appeared to accept that she was not going to add anything useful, and he closed the notebook, although he looked thwarted rather than convinced. "I gather Nathan Wyatt isn't here at the moment. Where can I find him?"

"I don't know." Hannah was tempted to mention Colin Portham's imposing name as evidence of the Farrenton Film Company's influential connections, but sending the police around to the Portham office would hardly improve Hannah's chance of directing *The Love Child*, and so she added, less impressively, "Nathan organizes his own timetable, and he's often out at meetings or lunches."

"Does Lionel Farrenton have —"

As Erith began his question, the telephone rang and Hannah snatched up the receiver, grateful for an excuse to avoid his gaze, and even the shrill voice of the caller was a respite, one that made Hannah speak with a warmth not usually there when talking to Candace. "Hello. Everything all right?"

"What's Joel's mobile number? I've simply got to contact him."

"He doesn't have a mobile," said Hannah, relieved to see Erith wave a hand, and then open the street door. Romney would be happy to discover that questions about Lionel were not deemed urgent enough to justify waiting for a telephone call to end. "Dad says he'd never do any work, if clients could get hold of him whenever they felt like a chat."

"I know how he feels. I'm being persecuted, absolutely persecuted, by that ridiculous Inspector. He was here again a few minutes ago, but I simply didn't answer the door. Sometimes you have to be ruthless."

Then Joel was very ruthless indeed, because he rarely answered a front door in case he encountered a vengeful creditor on the other side. "Would you like me to pass on a message to Dad?"

"Oh, Hannah, that's so kind. You're a real life-saver; there's no other word for it. I don't know how I'd have got through these awful days without you and Joel. Give me his office number, and then I won't have to take advantage of your generosity all the time."

"Dad isn't in the office today," said Hannah. It was a perfectly true statement that still sounded as if it had been hastily invented, and so there seemed no reason not to add a little embellishment. "He's away on a business trip. Exeter."

"Joel works far too much. I can see that I'll have to be very firm with him," declared Candace, and mock severity combined with her juvenile giggle. "What hotel is he staying in?"

"He's at a friend's house actually."

"A friend?"

"Yes. Clarissa Bodenham."

"Clarissa Bodenham," repeated Candace, and a hint of steel crept into the previously ingenuous chatter. "Is she a close friend of his?"

"They hit it off right from the start," replied Hannah, attempting her own version of guilelessness. "He often goes to stay with her, and Clarissa's in London most weekends."

"How old is she?" Candace demanded, affronted at the thought of a rival who had the power to draw Joel halfway across England with such ease.

"Twenty-ish, but Clarissa's the ageless sort."

"Any woman can be ageless if she goes in for cosmetic surgery," Candace remarked sourly. "I'll tell Joel to bring her to dinner the next time she's in London. I want to meet her." However, Candace's tone indicated that she was thinking less of a new acquaintance than sizing up the opposition. Joel was going to approve of the Clarissa strategy, and enjoy manufacturing his own details of the mirage should Candace track him down again. Just like Nathan, Joel could always find a use for some camouflage.

****

Romney emerged from behind his office door with overacted caution, and mimed heartfelt relief to see Hannah alone in reception. "I wondered why our favourite Sergeant had gone oddly quiet. I thought he couldn't still be brooding on his interrupted question about Lionel."

"Erith must have realized that I can't tell them anything they don't already know, but he seems very suspicious of poor Nathan."

"What a waste of taxpayers' money. I suppose every possibility has to be investigated, but the flights of fancy are getting ludicrous."

"Especially as it's obvious what must have happened to Mr Wyatt."

"Precisely," Romney declared, apparently in the belief that his ruling closed the case, because the ponderous jocularity made a sudden return. "By the way, I must get Joel to introduce me to the ageless Clarissa."

"I was trying to let Candace down gently. Dad just isn't interested, and she'll only be hurt if she doesn't get the message soon," said Hannah, embarrassed to be caught lying, although she had told plenty of fibs on Romney's behalf, and knew that he was prepared to invent any fiction that would benefit Farrenton Films. "It's quite easy for you to meet Clarissa though. All you have to do is produce *The Love Child*, and you can pick the actress who plays her."

"You're learning a lot from Nathan," Romney commented.

"It's not his fault. I was born with a one-track mind: films or nothing," said Hannah. "Life must be so much easier if you settle for an ambition that's within your grasp."

"Easier perhaps, but not as interesting or worthwhile."

"You're right. I wouldn't swap."

"Nor would I. Absolutely no security, but the life I'd choose every time, if we were offered retakes. Though I'm not sure that Lionel would have made a deliberate choice to work here, if his surname hadn't been Farrenton, but Lionel's the sort who'd be happy in any job, and he knew I'd support him whatever he did."

"My father once claimed that he'd disown me if I became a tax collector, lawyer or banker. I think you're a very liberal parent."

"Three actors in one house would have been altogether too much. Not that Imogen went in for artistic temperament, and Lionel takes after her, luckily for me. I never like to share the limelight," admitted Romney, laughing at his own vanity. "The advantage of working with Lionel is that he stops me making too many rash decisions simply by looking doubtful. It's a technique he learned from his mother, who'd let me ramble on about my brilliant schemes without once pointing out the flaw in whichever idea I was convinced would take the world by storm."

Imogen sounded too impossibly perfect ever to have been mortal woman, but Hannah smiled sympathetically. "I wish I'd known her."

"You'd have adored Imogen; everyone did." Romney doubtless meant what he said, but it was such a powerful portrayal of a man trying to come to terms with the loss of a beloved wife that Hannah found herself admiring the skill of the acting before she remembered that Imogen had actually existed. "If she could have played the Agatha Bodenham character, I'd be a lot more supportive of *The Love Child* project. I know Imogen was never a star name —"

"She would have been, after the film's release," declared Hannah. "She was perfect for the rôle."

"Yes, Agatha would have suited her down to the ground. Imogen managed to say more with a glance than I do ranting and raving and throwing myself around a stage. Her Agatha would have been perfectly judged: understated yet intense."

"That's exactly how Agatha should be played: an absolute contrast to Clarissa."

"I can see Imogen so clearly in the part. Why on earth didn't I think of filming the book years ago?" Romney gave a regretful sigh, before moving onto practical producer mode. "Getting the money would have been a job though, even in good times. Not that there are many good times when it comes to finance and film."

"No warning required," said Hannah. "If I've learnt anything here, it's that backers are an endangered species on the verge of extinction."

"They're so greedy," complained Romney, immediately switching to high-minded artiste. "How much money does somebody need? They've already got more than could be spent in a lifetime, but they're determined to hoard a gigantic fortune that their kids will probably squander on drugs and drink, yet a film offers everybody involved the chance of immortality: a lasting legacy that the entire world can share."

"Yes," Hannah said dutifully, conscious of certain Farrenton productions that the world had chosen to ignore.

"After all, businesses come and go, but art is the sole thing that gets passed down through the generations. We can only know the Elizabethans and Victorians through their literature and music and paintings. The moneymen of those days have completely vanished, apart from the books and buildings they commissioned."

"Perhaps you, rather than Nathan, should be tackling Colin Portham."

"I couldn't keep the sycophantic smirk going long enough to ingratiate myself. I despise grasping money-chasers like Portham, and their empty lives." Romney stood tall and proud: a hero facing the scaffold for the sake of lofty principle, an emperor defying power-hungry ministers, a poet scorning a job in advertising. He was a bastion of integrity, unable to compromise, and despite the pose, Romney meant what he said, even though his dramatic stand against the taint of commercialism seemed too overblown to be genuine. "Luckily, I won't have to kow-tow to the Porthams of this world, because they're not interested in the work I want to do."

"No, there won't be any Portham millions sloshing around here," agreed Hannah. "And it doesn't matter how persuasive Nathan is."

"He hasn't managed to persuade the police," Romney commented.

"It's me who can't persuade them. I'm Nathan's alibi, but they doubt every word I say, and make me feel like a total liar."

"They know you're telling the truth all right. If you and Nathan were in league, a night spent in the throes of passion would be the story, and nobody could prove otherwise."

"I suppose so."

"I suppose nothing," declared Romney, before adding rather less emphatically, "Assuming you're not bluffing, of course."

"I'm glad you've got faith in my honesty. Such a comfort."

"I'm giving you credit for enough brainpower to bamboozle the police force. It's the least I expect from my staff."

As Romney had overheard details of the chaste Saturday night in Hannah's flat, he was also aware of Erith's other questions. Should Nathan ever realize that his camouflage no longer protected him, he would presumably find it disturbing, after having gone to such lengths to hide what was no one's business but his own. Romney would not think less of Nathan for being gay; nor would anybody connected with Farrenton Films. It was Nathan who valued the secrecy; the rest of London would pass by untroubled.

****

"Never say I don't do anything for you, Hannah. I'm covered in dog hair, and had to endure a hound, who weighed approximately five tons, balancing himself on my lap while he slobbered over my face," said Nathan, one hand sweeping furiously at his jacket. "Colin Portham's devoted to a half-witted pooch, so of course I had to be devoted as well. Still, at least I'm through the office door, and next time I'll take some dog biscuits with me to ingratiate myself even further."

"Unless pooch has something of a weight problem. Check before you feed him," advised Hannah.

"OK, but why anyone would take the Hound of the Baskervilles to work is beyond me."

"Portham might judge people by how his dog reacts to them."

"Then I'm plainly on a winner because the mutt adored me." Nathan made another attempt to clear away the débris of his visit, and then sighed in defeat. "I'll have to go out and buy a clothes brush, or the world will assume that I'm a country hick who thinks movies are still silent. If anybody phones me, patch them through to my mobile."

"No problem," said Hannah, reminded of the scrap of paper that had been appropriated by Joel: a scrap of paper that Nathan had to find by chance. As he left, Hannah glanced around the office in search of a strategic spot to deposit the evidence; between two filing cabinets seemed the best choice, offering a hope that Nathan would think the phone number had been there for days, and that no sleight of hand was behind its reappearance. Hannah reached into her shoulder bag, only to jump nervously and drop the paper beside some letters on her desk when the street door opened. However, it was not Nathan making an unexpected return, but Lionel, who wandered inside, too abstracted to notice anything.

"Quayle popped in for another of his little chats," reported Lionel. "A detail he needed to check, he said, before proceeding to ask every question he's already asked."

"Erith was here earlier, but he didn't want to know about you," said Hannah. "Nathan was his target. Anyway, they'll leave you alone when the DNA results come through."

"Unless they're busily fabricating evidence to frame me, like Dad's convinced they are," suggested Lionel, trying to joke about something that would be no joke should it come true.

"Think of the screenplay you'd be able to commission about your harrowing treatment at the hands of a corrupt police force. Your only problem would be deciding which superstar most resembles you."

"I could play me in that film." Flora stood by the doorway, posing like a celebrity who expected to be caught on camera as she entered a room. "Oh, Lionel, I feel dreadful about everything, and won't be truly happy ever again." But for somebody wretched with misery, Flora looked good, hair perfectly styled, clothes perfectly judged, and it would take a great actress to carry off devastated widowhood when dressed with the style of a fashion model.

"What do you want?" asked Lionel, awkwardly abrupt.

"I came to have a word with Hannah about our film." Flora smiled as she spoke, confident that beauty removed all obstacles from her path.

"There isn't a film," said Hannah. "There isn't even a script."

"But there will be. I know this is going to happen, because it's exactly the chance I've been waiting for all my life." Flora's smile widened, and she seemed incapable of understanding that to want something did not automatically guarantee getting it.

"Even if Nathan succeeds in raising a bit of money, *The Love Child* won't be produced by Farrenton Films," said Lionel, attempting a decisiveness that tailed off into an apology as he glanced at Hannah, uncertain whether or not he had just destroyed her hopes.

"Romney won't consider it," agreed Hannah. "There's no real commercial potential."

The words sounded impressively like professional jargon, but Flora shook her head. "I had dinner with Colin Portham last night, and he's interested."

"In you, perhaps, but not in throwing money away."

"Oh, Lionel, you can be so funny at times." Flora tried to laugh, but sighed instead. "I'd like you to be involved, but if your father won't do the film, somebody else will. It should be a fairly cheap production: a few million at most. We're not talking Hollywood extravaganza."

"A bargain-basement film," said Hannah, amused at the airy dismissal of millions. Nathan himself could not have been more casual.

"A million's chicken feed to Colin Portham," declared Flora. "He wouldn't even miss ten million."

"That doesn't mean he'd hand it over to you," warned Lionel. "You're going to be disappointed."

"If I worried about that, I'd never do anything." The artificial Flora suddenly spoke with genuine feeling, and Hannah caught a glimpse of the strength of mind beneath a pretence of naïveté. Flora and Candace should have appreciated each other more, as they were very alike. "You ought to work on that script, Hannah, because I'll get the money for our film somehow."

Flora underestimated Hannah's determination to find the right actor for each rôle, and therefore the willingness or otherwise of Colin Portham to shower the film with money was irrelevant. "Something modern would suit you better, not last century provincial."

"But, Hannah, I love old-fashioned costumes," said Flora. "I can swish around in a long skirt with the best of them, and those hats were a dream."

"They wouldn't be fashion plates in the provinces."

"It won't be a documentary," Flora pointed out.

"No, but it has to look authentic, and the characters seem believable."

"Flora, Dad isn't going to produce this film," said Lionel.

"Then Nathan will," announced Flora.

"He wouldn't let you within a mile of the set. You know that better than I do." Lionel managed to keep all trace of *schadenfreude* out of his voice, but he was human, and probably felt that Flora deserved a taste of the medicine she had dished out to him. "Nathan's stringing you along because he wants to get money for Hannah's film."

"Colin Portham will only finance it if I'm the star," Flora declared complacently. "Nathan's going to have to do what he's told for once, especially as Hannah herself suggested me for the rôle."

"No, I didn't," stated Hannah.

"But you can see that I'm the only one able to play the part." Flora crumpled her face like a sulky child about to cry, and then giggled animatedly to display the range of her abilities. "I can do comedy and tragedy; I just haven't had an opportunity before. That's the reason I want to get away from modern stuff, and do some real acting. I know you'll give me my chance, Hannah, for all you're pretending to be so cool. Why else would you have my mobile number on your desk?"

"But I haven't."

Flora pointed at a piece of paper: the piece of paper that Hannah had confiscated from Joel. "Did you think I wouldn't recognize my own number?" Flora asked in triumph.

"It can't be yours," said Hannah.

"Dial it and see." Flora laughed, not expecting the suggestion to be taken seriously, but Hannah picked up the telephone on her desk and began to dial. Seconds later, a metallic version of *Greensleeves* was jangling shrilly from the mobile that Flora held up in triumph. "Why pretend not to know my number when it's right in front of you?"

"Perhaps Nathan put it there," said Hannah.

"Nathan? Nathan doesn't have my phone number, and wouldn't pass it on to you if he did," declared Flora, smiling at the absurdity of the idea. "It was you, darling Lionel; I know it was. You put my number on Hannah's desk to make sure that she could contact me, didn't you?"

"No."

"You're a dreadful tease, Lionel. Who else around here would have my mobile number? I knew we'd always be great friends, and this proves it." Flora beamed, her smugness so reminiscent of Candace that it seemed Owen Wyatt had merely traded in one flawed status symbol for a newer version. "You and I were destined to be close, Lionel, and it's wonderful to know that I have a true friend after all these days of feeling completely alone."

Flora's smiling façade suddenly froze into a garish Halloween mask of darkly accentuated eyes and crimson slash of lipstick. For a split-second, Hannah saw with the insight of imagination, and to learn that beauty could be repulsive was a revelation.

"I didn't leave your phone number on anyone's desk," Lionel stated.

"Oh, all right. Be my anonymous benefactor if that's what you want." Flora laughed again, a ringing crescendo that grated harshly in Hannah's mind, but was perfectly suited to the tawdry deceit of the figure before her. "I came to beg Hannah for some scenes from *The Love Child* script, so that I could begin studying my rôle. But as there's no script yet, what shall I do?"

"Read the book," suggested Lionel.

"Brilliant idea!" exclaimed Flora, as if Lionel had demonstrated the inspiration of genius. "Where can I get a copy?"

"Try a bookshop," said Hannah, willing Flora to leave. The perfume that had been a pleasant addition to the office was now cloying in its sweetness, and represented an ideal choice of fragrance for the saccharine Flora to have made.

"I'll dash off then, and read, read, read. Bye, darlings."

"Who is the fairy godfather, leaving Flora Wyatt's mobile number on film production company desks?" asked Romney, venturing out of his office as the street door closed behind the would-be star.

"You're getting to be quite an eavesdropper, Dad, but you haven't discovered anything. I'm not the sponsor promoting Flora's career."

"The number fell out of Nathan's wallet," said Hannah. A problem shared was supposed to be a problem solved, and it seemed that the old saying had come true when Romney smiled.

"Nathan's even prepared to endure Flora in his desperation to get hold of a million or two? He ought to know by now that there are plenty of wannabe actresses who'd happily volunteer as bait for Colin Portham."

"Nathan left his wallet in my flat long before Portham or *The Love Child* were on the scene," Hannah explained, hoping that Romney would be able to smile away another fact. "I forgot to bring in the piece of paper until today."

"Nathan would never have Flora's mobile number," said Lionel. "He hated her even before she went off with his father."

"A meeting engineered by Nathan himself," Romney pointed out.

"What exactly are you hinting at?" asked Lionel. "A conspiracy?"

"I'm on the track of a devious plot here," declared Romney. "Don't try and restrain me with commonsense. Perhaps the distance between Flora and Nathan isn't quite as far-flung as they pretend."

"The police must have given him the number," said Lionel. "Someone had to break the news about her husband to Flora."

"Yes, that's what must have happened," agreed Hannah, reassured. "He put the number in his wallet, and simply forgot it was there."

"Why would he put it into his wallet?" asked Romney. "If the police told him to ring Flora, they'd want it done straightaway, not at Nathan's leisure."

"Well, whatever happened, Nathan and Flora aren't in a murder conspiracy together, in spite of your dark suspicions" declared Lionel. "She was in Switzerland, while Nathan spent that Saturday night with Hannah."

"They were in separate rooms," said Romney, still playing the detective. "And Hannah was a last-minute substitute, after Nathan shunned both you and Surrey."

"Only because he's allergic to dogs."

"Not when a multi-millionaire's the owner" said Hannah, uneasily. "Nathan was covered in dog hair when he dropped by earlier, after an encounter with Colin Portham's cherished mutt. No mention of an allergic reaction, and no sign of one."

"Nathan told me that he'd be wheezing for days, with blotches all over his face, if he so much as went near a dog. I know he exaggerates, but —" Lionel paused, searching for a reason that exonerated Nathan, then added, "Perhaps he invented an allergy because he couldn't face an evening in my company."

"Why did he ask to stay at your flat in the first place, if you're so horrific a prospect?" inquired Romney. "Nathan was quite prepared to tolerate your failings until he realized that you were in Surrey: too near his father's house and too far away from Candace's car."

"Are you seriously claiming that he cold-bloodedly planned a murder?" Lionel said, marvelling at the very idea. "Dad, I've known Nathan since my first day at school. At worst, he and Flora were having an affair, and pretending to hate each other so that nobody suspected."

"It doesn't explain why Nathan lied to avoid being in Surrey with you that Saturday night," commented Romney.

"Desperately seeking drama, that's you," Lionel declared. "How did Nathan manage to spend so much time out of Hannah's flat without her noticing?"

"He plied the inexperienced country girl with strong liquor so that she'd sleep throughout the night," decided Romney. "Standard procedure for a villain."

"We have tasted alcohol in the provinces: cheap superstore plonk, admittedly, but still fairly potent. You'll be telling me next that Nathan doped my wine," said Hannah, recalling Joel's theory of the ploy that would have been stymied by Hannah's strategic use of a wastepaper bin.

"You're young, so drugged or not, you sleep soundly every night, and Nathan figured he could count on it," declared Romney, enjoying the challenge of solving Quayle's case for him. "Anyway, Nathan must have borrowed or stolen a car, and left it waiting by Hannah's flat. Then he drove to Candace's —"

"Why?" demanded Lionel.

"So that the police investigation would centre on her, of course." But Romney's elaborate plot reminded him of his beloved melodrama, and he smiled as he spoke. "Nathan couldn't mention losing Flora's number, so he gambled that Hannah wouldn't associate the piece of paper with him when it was found."

"Gambled?" repeated Hannah, alert as always to that particular word.

"Nathan overestimates his luck," said Romney, "like all gamblers."

"He's never talked about horses or cards," objected Hannah.

"Gambling's a character trait, rather than a penchant for raffles."

"Yes," said Hannah, not in need of a lecture on the subject. "But gamblers aren't automatically murderers."

"Don't spoil my theory," ordered Romney. "I'm on a roll here, with the case practically solved. I played

Inspector Marston in two episodes of *Thames Valley*, remember, and it's really paying off now."

"We're talking about Nathan," protested Lionel. "Even if you proved he and Flora had an affair, and that he absconded from Hannah's flat, I still couldn't believe he'd kill his own father."

"I don't believe it either," said Hannah, although she only knew the surface Nathan, the official Nathan, the Nathan he wanted the world to see, and she had no idea whether or not he was capable of murder.

"Why did he bother driving into Surrey on the Sunday morning to see the father he claimed to hate?" asked Romney, so addicted to the sensational that he apparently relished the thought of having employed a patricide. "Why did Nathan take his alibi with him?"

"He told me that he needed a peacekeeper present," said Hannah.

"Unfortunately, his father neglected to mention ordering Tiffany to visit him that day as well, assuming there was an invite for Nathan. I bet he wanted to be on record as having discovered the crime scene, so that he had a reason for any inconveniently placed DNA," declared Romney, ignoring Lionel's exasperated sigh. "Why else would Nathan go there?"

"Because Mr Wyatt was about to divorce Flora," said Lionel. "You know how addicted Nathan is to money. He probably had hopes of an inheritance if he played his cards right, but he doesn't get a penny now."

"He's in league with Flora, and they'll split the loot between them," decreed Romney. "The plan is to start a film company, make Flora a star, then sit back while the millions roll in."

"Hannah, ask Nathan for Flora's mobile number," Lionel said wearily.

"Good idea," declared Romney. "Tell him you had the number, Hannah, but can't find it now, in case Flora's already told Nathan what happened. No reason to let him know we're on to them."

"Dad!" exclaimed Lionel, shaking his head incredulously.

"You want Nathan to have every opportunity of making me ashamed of my suspicious mind," said Romney. "Besides, Hannah ought to know if he's two-timing her."

"Nathan owes me no loyalty." A ringer who knew that she was a ringer expected nothing, but Hannah would feel swamped by humiliation if she learnt that Nathan and Flora had been laughing behind her back. It was probably better not to find out, but Romney and Lionel were waiting.

"Hannah, I can't talk," Nathan said urgently, answering his mobile on the second ring. "I followed Colin Portham from his office, and I'm just going into a restaurant to meet him entirely by chance." The restaurant meeting with Flora and Hugo had been entirely by chance as well. Nathan asked Hannah for a film project, Flora turned up to claim the lead rôle, and start the Portham treasure hunt with Hugo: all entirely by chance.

"Have you got Flora's mobile number?" said Hannah, certain that Nathan would be able to sense a trap. "She wants a scene from *The Love Child* script, and I thought she could show it to Colin Portham. Lionel gave me her number, but it seems to have vanished."

"I'm the last person in London you should ask for Flora's contact details," declared Nathan, sounding amused. "I've never known them, and never will."

"I thought the police might have given you her number."

"Why on earth would they do that?"

"Someone had to break the news about — break the news to her."

"I never broke anything to the grieving widow. Sorry, Hannah, but I've really got to ring off. After all, our *Love Child* comes first."

Nathan was laughing as the call ended, but Hannah could not even pretend to join in. She put the phone down, and looked at Romney without speaking.

"Nathan told you that he never had Flora's number," stated Romney, but he was taken aback to learn that his theory might not be a joke after all. "Now what do we do?"

"Nothing," said Lionel. "If Flora had an affair with Nathan, it doesn't matter now. His father's dead."

"Exactly. That's the problem. Owen Wyatt was murdered. We'd be withholding information."

"Then we go on withholding it. Dad, you're the one who said that the police's favourite pastime was manufacturing evidence. We'd be handing them Nathan as a human sacrifice."

"And I thought I was the family tragedian," commented Romney. "Hannah, are you certain that Flora's mobile number came out of Nathan's wallet?"

"A hundred per cent certain."

"One phone number proves nothing," declared Lionel. "Why put Hannah through the ordeal of having some shifty lawyer accuse her of lying?"

It was Joel who might have to face the ordeal, and the thought of him being grilled on a witness stand was horrific, especially as all possible information on his background would have been gathered to discredit what he said. "The police might think I'd concocted the whole thing as revenge on Nathan and Flora."

"Hannah, the police will be a lot more imaginative than that," said Romney. "They'd probably assume that I persuaded you to cover up for my son."

"Then let's keep quiet," said Lionel. "Besides, what do we actually know? That Nathan forgot the police gave him a phone number, and that he spun a tale of being allergic to dogs because he couldn't face a night away from London." Nathan had also lied about the smell of paint in a flat, but that would be Hannah's word against his, and he was a self-possessed and gifted liar.

"Perhaps I should ring the police, and leave an anonymous message saying that he and Flora have had an affair," Romney suggested. "It'd take the heat off you, Lionel."

"I'm not even warm, and you've got the least anonymous voice in London."

"I'm an actor. I can do Uriah Heap or King Lear, and all stations between," declared Romney. "If Nathan had anything whatsoever to do with his father's death, he deserves to be caught, and it's doubtless my civic duty to shop him, but I feel like the sneak of the fifth form even thinking about it."

Hannah knew what Romney meant, but it was worse for her because betraying Nathan might also have unpleasant consequences for Joel, especially if his past got into the tabloids. "We couldn't prove anything," said Hannah, glad of an excuse to keep quiet. "The police would probably think I'm jealous of Flora."

"Nathan would simply go in for stout denial, and claim that I'm paranoid because Flora dumped me," said Lionel. "A phone number isn't enough to convict anyone."

However, it had been enough to convict both Nathan and Flora in the minds of the three people who continued to stare at the scrap of paper. Erith had said that the slightest detail could be an indicator, and Flora's mobile number in Nathan's wallet revealed a discrepancy: one of the discrepancies that pointed, with the clarity of a signpost, the direction the inquiry should take. Whatever the link between Nathan and Flora, the slender chance of *The Love Child* film was probably gone. Hannah could not grieve for the loss of a lover, but to let go of a dream left an emptiness that ached.

"These decisions separate the men from the boys," declared Romney.

"There isn't a decision," said Lionel. "The police aren't interested in amateur suspicions. It's up to them to discover anything that needs to be discovered."

Cowards Anonymous could recruit three fully paid-up members any time they liked, thought Hannah.

"We'll have a think, and talk about this later," decided Romney. "Back to work, everyone. We've got a TV series to get commissioned, as well as locating a mesmeric screenplay to make Farrenton Films the toast of Cannes. Lionel, grab a few scripts and start reading."

"OK." Lionel apparently thought that life had returned to normal, and he looked cheerful again as he took half the scripts that were piled up on Hannah's desk. "One day we'll find a winner, and that day could be today."

"Well, it wasn't yesterday," commented Romney. "Hannah, did you do that research into disaster-linked melodrama?"

"Yes. I'm afraid that Abraham Lincoln was actually at a comedy when he got assassinated: *Our American Cousin* by somebody called Tom Taylor. But there's quite a selection for you from Chicago, and the one at the Adelphi sounds as if it might be promising. *Secret Service* by —"

"I'll get my notebook."

"I printed you a copy of the details." Hannah waved the list she had prepared for Romney, but he ignored her and followed Lionel into the office, to return seconds later, closing the door behind him.

"I've got all the titles and playwrights here."

"Thanks." Romney took the sheet of paper from Hannah, but did not even glance at it. "Would you forgive me if I went to the police about Nathan and Flora?"

"You're going to do it, whatever I think," replied Hannah, although her spirits sank abruptly. "I know Lionel comes first."

"You won't clam up when Quayle checks with you?"

"You've got a pretty low opinion of my integrity," said Hannah, trying to smile. "Of course I'll explain how I found the mobile number." Hannah pictured herself going back into the flat after returning Nathan's wallet. She saw a scrap of paper on the floor, picked it up, and realized that it must have fallen out of Nathan's wallet. She put the telephone number into her shoulder bag, and then simply forgot about it. If Hannah told herself the story often enough, she might even start to believe that Joel's only involvement had been to shake his head when she asked him did he recognize the number.

"If Nathan and Flora are a team, Lionel could be their patsy," said Romney. "I want it stopped now. And, yes, I know I'm overacting."

"Not if there really is a plot, and if there isn't, a piece of paper isn't enough to convict anyone, as Lionel said."

"You're not going to break your heart over this, Hannah?"

"Wrong interpretation of my character."

"Nathan wouldn't think twice about planting something of Lionel's at the crime scene," continued Romney, not to be cheated out of any torment he could force into the dilemma that was no dilemma to him. "If Nathan's a killer, he's capable of anything, and if there's the slightest chance of him and Flora destroying Lionel, I have to prevent it."

"You're right." Hannah would not do Romney the injustice of thinking that he revelled in the part of anguished father desperate to protect his son, but an imaginary spotlight certainly shone on him. However, for all his exaggeration, Romney had probably made the correct decision, and Hannah was uncomfortable with her own instinct to keep quiet. She rummaged inside her shoulder bag, and handed Romney the page torn from Erith's notebook.

"Another phone number?" queried Romney in surprise.

"Erith's. He told me to ring, quote the case reference, and ask for him, if I thought of a detail that might help the investigation." And a link between Nathan and Flora would more than help because it offered a contingency that could be checked on CCTV footage: the use of Flora's car by Nathan to get from Hannah's flat to Candace's house.

It was a point of no return, and even Romney could not act his way out of the possible consequences for Nathan. "I won't phone from here. Don't tell Lionel anything. I'm out at a meeting, if he misses me."

Hannah nodded, the street door closed behind Romney, and she wished that doing the right thing did not feel so wrong. The phone buzzed, making her heart pound, and she grabbed the receiver as though the noise might warn Lionel of his father's decision.

"Hannah, he's interested! Portham's really interested!" Nathan sounded triumphant: a voice from another time, another world. "Of course he's more interested in Flora than *The Love Child*, but he's asked to see a script. Can you cobble something together by tomorrow evening?"

By tomorrow evening, Nathan would have been questioned about a mobile phone number, his sporadic allergy to dogs, and the name of the decorator who was supposed to have repainted his flat: minor details that, when added together, meant any interest Colin Portham might or might not show in *The Love Child* was probably irrelevant. It was horrible, knowing of Nathan's approaching crisis, and even more horrible to be part of his likely downfall. "I can't do a whole script by tomorrow, but I could expand the treatment with a few scenes," said Hannah, sure that her stilted voice would make Nathan guess something had gone wrong. She was never going to be able to work on a script for *The Love Child* because the story would always remind her of that moment: the ringer turned traitor.

"Have to dash. I want to pick up some Arts Council and BFI guff for Portham. I think I've convinced him that there might be a knighthood in all this."

"Terrific." Hannah was no Romney, and her delivery fell flat, but Nathan was too wound-up to notice.

"Everything's working out exactly as planned."

"Yes," said Hannah. But Romney's plan was the active one, not Nathan's. Erith would have his detail, Colin Portham would save some money, and whatever Nathan had or had not done, Hannah was the person who felt guilty.
